I0677465

Tales
and
More Tails
of
Beyonder

Volume 4 of
"Stories and Tunes"
a Four-Part Trilogy

Upper Granville (Before Flatlanders)

Tales
and
More Tails
of
Beyonder

Stephen Morris

The Public Press

Randolph   Caspar

© 2005-2009 by Stephen Morris

All rights reserved. No part of this publication may be reproduced or transmitted in any form or by any means, electronic, mechanical, or time travel, including but not limited to, photocopying, recording, scanning, or by any information storage and retrieval system, without permission in writing from the copyright holder.

Requests for permission to make copies of any part of this book should be mailed to

Permissions Department
The Public Press
100 Gilead Brook Road
Randolph, Vermont 05060.

Library of Congress Cataloging-in-Publication Data
Morris, Stephen
Tales and More Tails of Beyonder.
I. Title.
ISBN 0-9764520-5-7

Map by Barbara W. Carter

Book design by Michael Potts
for The Public Press

second printing

What is a "Four-Part Trilogy?"
It is a "Totally Beyondered" concept.

Life has a way of interfering with art. *Beyond Yonder, The King of Vermont,* and *Darwin and the Tunnel of Love* were always intended by the author as a single work, telling the epic story of the daily lives and times of the inhabitants of the tiny hamlet of Upper Granville, Vermont.

But life intervenes. It happens! Day jobs take priority. Parents grow old. Little publishers sell to big publishers. Editors move on to different jobs. Opportunities knock. Kids leave home. It happens! It happens! And it happens!

As a result, the epic novel came out in fits and spurts. First, *Beyond Yonder.* That's when the publisher got sold. Then, *King of Vermont,* that's when the editor quit. In spring 2006, *Darwin and the Tunnel of Love.*

Meanwhile, a real-life equivalent to Upper Granville began appearing on the pages of the *Vermont Sunday Magazine,* Livin': The Vermont Way, *The* Real Goods *News, Vermont* Magazine, and elsewhere. Now, the region had a name, Beyonder, to describe that part of Vermont that is next to nothing, but not far away from anywhere.

Tales and More Tails of Beyonder is an anthology of essays by Stephen Morris. It is the real-life counterpart to the world of Upper Granville depicted in his works of fiction.

This is Beyonder at the peak of foliage, at the depth of Mud Season despair, in the procreational frenzy of the vernal kaboom, and in the enveloping eternity of an August night watching the meteor showers in a part of the world where you can actually still see them.

Contents

Introduction: The Holy Days of Vermont

You know what I like about Vermont?...the holidays. Oh, not the Hallmark holidays (Mother's Day, Father's Day), not the religious holy days (Easter, Christmas), not the buy-something holidays (Valentine's, President's Day), not the stuff-yourself-silly holidays (Thanksgiving, Halloween), and not the military commemorations (Memorial, Veterans, 4th of July). Vermont has its own set of special days that don't require you to buy stuff you give away, send sappy cards, eat like a pig, or make things explode. Here's a quick tour through the annual calendar.

$\mathcal{V}$ermont holidays carry an extra drama, because you're not sure when they will occur. The Thaw, for instance, can happen anytime in the month of January. The setting: The world is frozen solid. The woodstove glows cherry red. Just as you accept the fact that you'll never see green grass again, a low-pressure system sneaks up from the South, and it's raining! Your stone steps freeze on contact, and you take a header going out for the mail.

This is a holiday? It is if you are smart enough to say, "I ain't goin' nowhere today," and settle in to watch daytime TV. It's even more of a holiday if you do this before you take the header.

Sometimes the January Thaw coincides with another local milestone, Glimmer Day, which is the first day in January when you actually notice that the days are getting longer, and there's a glimmer of hope that winter will actually end.

Ground Hog Day is not a Vermont holiday. We don't need no fat, stinkin' rodent from Pennsylvania to tell us, on February 2, that it's going to be cold for six more weeks.

The next important annual event is Mud-Season-as-a-Metaphor-for-Life Day, which happens somewhere between mid-February and late April. Here's how it goes. The day starts off bright and sunny. Your spirits soar. By midday the dirt roads are oily, but your good feelings are buoyed by the plink-plink-plink of maple sap hitting the bucket.

In the afternoon, however, things take a turn for the worse. You return home only to find that the last hill before your house has turned into a sea of gelatinous ooze. Thinking you can bull your way through the ruts, you floor it. With the engine whining at 8000 rpm, wheels spinning like a NASCAR pro, ten feet from the crest, your car starts moving sideways, inch by inch, toward the ditch. Slowly, almost poetically, the world becomes cocked at a 45-degree angle, and you realize that not just your car, but your entire life is now in a ditch. You are utterly, totally beyondered.

Next comes Town Meeting Day, sometimes called Blame-the-New-Guy Day, a high holy day throughout the state.

Springtime arrives. Fishing season opens with ponds still frozen. Baseball season starts with nary a blade of grass in sight. Your relatives from the Flatlands report that the daffodils are up and the dogwoods are in bloom. You can't go out to play in the snow, because it is gray, granular, and wattled, nature's version of cellulite. Unidentifiable frozen stuff starts pelting down, and you realize that even a trip to the quick-stop will be life threatening. Then, with a guttural scream that originates just south of your sternum, you proclaim it THIS PLACE SUCKS!! Day.

Not long afterwards comes the first of the spring holidays, The-Day-You-Plant-Peas. No matter that you freeze your fingers and the seeds rot in the ground before sprouting, at least you have the earth in your hands. The second spring holiday is The Spring Fling. After a grueling winter, 60 degrees makes Vermont seem like the Amazon. Euphoric Vermonters don tank tops, shorts, and sandals while gulping beer and throwing frisbies. Things inevitably get out of hand. Just remember the phrase, "It seemed like a good idea at the time."

Next comes The-Day-the-Creemee-Stand-Opens. If your local serves fried food, this is a chance to get onion rings before the grease makes everything taste like a tired clam.

The Solstice begins the High Holy Days when the days are long and the summer endless. These are the days of "damn poor sleddin'." The end of summer begins abruptly on July 4th, when you notice how few weekends are left until Labor Day.

The Vermont Holiday roster does not include Bennington Battle Day, or "DMV Day," which always occurs on the day you've arranged to take off work to go to the Department of Motor Vehicles for that long-postponed photo ID. Alas, the state employees are at home this day, solemnly remembering Vermont's nanosecond of wartime glory.

Summer reaches its zenith on The-Day-the-Sweet-Corn-Ripens. You know when this is, because it's the day after the corn has been devoured by raccoons. (This is known as "Vermont humor.")

First-Day-of-School used to be a major holiday, but now that it happens in August, it has lost its holiday status. Whoever came up with the idea to start school before Labor Day should be spit-balled to death. Its place has been filled by The-Last-Day-of-Racing-at-Thunder-Road. (The-Red-Sox-Figure-Out-Yet-Another-Way-to-Break-Our-Hearts-Day often occurs around this same time, but that's really a national holiday. Also, it happens as early as May.)

Leaf peepers pour into the state in late September. We keep our eyes on the hills and say that it's not a good year for color, because (pick one) a) The summer was too wet, b) The summer was too dry, c) Acid rain, d) The damn government doesn't know what it's doing. But then, just as we despair, we experience The Peak, a brief spasm of color, a death scream for the hardwoods. It brings a gasp, and we all agree, the foliage has never been more beautiful.

The year accelerates to a close. The leaves fall; the temperature drops; the tourists go home. There is a peaceful, but increasingly chilly period between when the greenery disappears and the snow cover arrives. Take a last look at the unadorned rocks and ground of the state, because we are about to enter the Autumnal Holy Days, otherwise known as—Deer Season. Unlike the other holidays, this divides the state neatly into its Chuck and Flatlander halves. The Chucks take gleeful command of the forests. The Flatlanders hunker down, put away jogging shoes, and research travel deals on Travelocity.

You can tell we're getting toward the end of the year, because we start repeating holidays. THIS PLACE SUCKS!! Day—Part II occurs on a day when you absolutely, positively have to take the Interstate, and a light drizzle has turned it into an iceball. The road crews can't keep up, and you creep along, amusing yourself by counting the cars off the road. The only solace comes from noting how many of the helpless victims are SUVs with out-of-state plates.

The final holiday coincides with the Winter Solstice. It doesn't have a name, but it is a festival of light. While the rest of the world storms WalMart and Circuit City in search of DVD players for $19.99, you opt instead for the woodstove, a candle, and conversation. The next few weeks will be grim, to be sure, but if you can hang tough, it's only a few weeks until Glimmer Day.

Part I—The Fall

Don't get me started. Someone screwed up big time. The New Year, in Vermont as elsewhere, used to begin very distinctly the day after Labor Day. Summer mode would end; you'd trade your bathing suit for a book bag; there was order and logic to the world. Then "someone," I don't know who to blame, decided that the school year would start before Labor Day and life hasn't been the same since. Not that it matters, because everyone just snoozes through those August days in the classroom.

The real back-to-school day still takes place when it always did, right after Labor Day. Humans are no different than the migrating geese or the swallows of Capistrano. You can't fool us just because it is more convenient for the teacher's union or whomever to start school in August.

Tunbridge Fair kicks off the official heating season. If your wood is not stacked and dry, you will be playing catch-up all winter long. It won't be long until the local Creemee stand closes. Thunder Road always goes out in a blaze of glory as the Milk Bowl features roaring engines, screaming leaves, and politicians trying desperately to humanize themselves by throwing dried cow poop.

The leaves turn and become fragile. Everyone has an explanation as to why the foliage is not as good this year as in years past. Then, when you think it's all over, it gets better. People say this is the best year ever, but before you can even get your camera, the peak has passed. The wind picks up and the air is filled with fluttering schools of leaves that fall, inevitably, to the ground.

The Amnesty Minute

Don't let anyone tell you differently. When you really lose control of your kids is when you give them over to the school bus.

School bus time is upon us. This is when our children, dressed in neons and expensive sneakers, carrying Ninja Turtle lunchboxes in Batman II backpacks, go down to the school bus stop to share with fellow students the new smutty knowledge gained over the summer. It is the end of innocence. Within a week the smut has been cross-pollinated, and a new generation of Vermont children—including YOUR INNOCENT KINDER-GARTNER—has been corrupted.

This is very discouraging for parents. After all, we uphold the most rigorous moral standards ourselves. We teetotal. We smoke only when the children are out of sight. We never throw trash out the car window, but most importantly, we never use foul language.

So where do the children learn it? Yes, they learn it on the school bus from their peers, but of course their peers come from upstanding, virtuous families like ours. Some of the smarm and smut comes from rented videos, but don't we always caution the children not to pay attention to the dirty language?

If your children are like mine, they are adept at hiding the depth of their foul-language capabilities. I became suspicious when our 11 year old, in relating the saga of a woebegone heroine, summarized the woman's plight by saying: "Her life was a living heck."

I sensed the sandbags being piled around me, so I devised a simple test, a lightning rod to the recesses of the preadolescent mind. I declared an Amnesty Minute. For 60 seconds—I even set the timer on my watch—the children were free to say anything they wanted with a guarantee of no parental influence or punishment. They could scream, blaspheme, cuss, swear...and at the end of 60 seconds, all would be forgiven. Life as we know it would

13

resume, except I would now have a detailed knowledge of where my children place on the scale of verbal corruption.

Here's what happened.

I pushed the timer on my watch. My nine-year-old son looked momentarily disoriented. Finally, his lip curled slightly and he snarled, "You butt-head! You stoo-pudd butt-head! You stoo-pudd butt-head! You ugly, stoo-pudd butt-head!"

You get the idea. It was one minute of increasingly embellished uses of the term "butt-head."

The 11-year-old child was a different story. The time started, and before the beep from the digital watch had faded, he had commenced a stream of staccato invective that continued until he paused for breath at the 30-second mark. I could count six references to male genitalia, four to female genitalia, and 14 allusions to the combination thereof. Some of the suggestions were physically impossible (not that I am about to try).

There was abundant use of the "s" word, and, of course, that old favorite, the "f" word. If I am any observer of social trends, the "a" word is becoming more fashionable. He did not repeat himself until the 58-second mark. All in all, it was a remarkable performance, a veritable compendium of contemporary, scatological colloquialisms (in other words, it was a display of foulness that would have made any drill sergeant proud). Mercifully, the beeper on my watch sounded. Quiet reigned. I stared in disbelief at this child who still sleeps with stuffed animals. His visage had returned to one of All-American innocence. Was it possible that only moments before, the same mouth now smiling so sweetly had been advocating acts of such perversion that I considered padlocking his lips?

The Amnesty Minute ended with me 60 seconds older but light years wiser. The school bus had claimed another victim. As you prepare to bundle your children off to be transported to our institutions of learning, be aware that you are waving good-bye to the last of their innocence as well. And if your children surprise you with a newfound vocabulary, well, you can blame it on my son.

Enlightening Thunder Road

Summer is over, but for a few weeks you've still got Thunder Road. I'm not a Thunder Road kinda guy, but I desperately want to be. Don't forget to come out for The Milk Bowl, the grand finale of the racing season.

I can imagine the archeologists in the year 10,000. At the excavation site at Beyonder Gorge they will uncover the cement bleachers that tier the hillside at Thunder Road. "These are the walls of the Great Pyramid of Barre," they will say, stroking their erudite chins. "These are the holy grounds where primitive Vermonters worshipped their deities."

They got that part right.

For those of you who don't know, Thunder Road is where the average Vermonter can reach deep into the part of the soul that craves action. It is the site of weekly auto racing where one pays homage to the internal combustion engine in a relaxed setting featuring a hundred-decibel roar, the nonstop patter of a hyperactive announcer, and fumes that make the air ignitable. The best part is, you don't have to reach deep into your pocket to enjoy the spectacle. A family of four can come with ten bucks and have some left over for Al's French Frys. With the exception of a Lake Champlain sunset, Thunder Road is probably the best entertainment value in the state.

Be forewarned, however. It's not exactly a Yuppie crowd. You can learn your lesson the hard way, or you can learn from my experience.

I arrived in a Plymouth Voyager (also known as a Yupmobile). I was early, so I picked out a nice spot on the hillside overlooking the banked oval. I tuned my boom box to Public Radio and listened to a nice Bach Cantata before "All Things Considered" came on. As the crowd filed in, I passed the time by reading *The Wall St. Journal*. People stopped to gawk. I assume they had seen a man reading a newspaper before; maybe it was my Gore-Tex™ jogging suit.

There was plenty of time until the races began. Luckily, I had on my Nike Air's, and went for a little run. The Thunder Road crowd is enthusiastic in its attitude toward joggers; I could tell from the way they pelted me with garbage and flashed half the peace sign at me as I approached the final straightaway. Most had apparently sighted joggers only through windows of pickup trucks, and then through the scopes of rifles.

Most of the crowd carried coolers packed with refreshments, and I was no exception. But while other coolers contained beer, soda, and junk food (the repast of the gods), I put forth a spread of salmon paté, softened French cheese, English water crackers, a veggie pita with tofu, and carrot cake, all washed down by a sparkling water from an obscure spring in Czechoslovakia. It was totally enjoyable, aside from the fans, who persisted in pointing and laughing. I don't know what was more amusing, my checked tablecloth or my crystal stemware.

"I could go for a crisp chablis," I said to my wife.

"Or a Peace Pop," she returned.

We went down to the concession area, and decided to indulge ourselves in some French fries, although we know they are bad for our cholesterol count. "Are these cooked in polyunsaturated vegetable oil?" we asked the girl behind the counter. She burst into laughter and repeated our remark to everyone else in the kitchen.

"They're cooked in motor oil," said the man behind me.

"That's why the taste so good," added the woman with him. They appeared authoritative, tipping the scales at a collective quarter ton.

"They change it every year," he added.

"That's why they taste so good," she chortled.

The first half of racing featured the "Crunch Bunch," plus flame outs, spin offs, and assorted motorized mayhem. Perhaps we did not understand the nuances of race strategies and tactics, but the excitement was contagious.

At intermission we were treated to a special feature, the Joey Chitwood Chevy Thunder Revue. After the genuine thrills of the street stocks, this seemed like white bread. Some of the daring stunts actually sent the crowd into gales of laughter. There was the "Slide for Life," in which a much-ballyhooed daredevil jumps off a car and slides on his butt for a few feet. Later, in the "Leap for Life," the same guy stands on a stepladder while another driver bombs under him, obliterating the ladder, at seventy miles per hour.

Yawn. The highlight of the Chevy Thunder Show was a pickup truck with a jet engine mounted on the back, which should have been named "The Environmentalist's Worst Nightmare." This machine can spew and roar, and fill the air with gratuitous heat and fumes, while accomplishing absolutely nothing. The announcer told us proudly that the truck burned 32 gallons of aviation fuel per minute. It didn't fly; it didn't go fast; its major accomplishment was going in reverse for twenty feet.

"Huh?" said the crowd.

But the Joey Chitwood silliness was over soon enough and the real thing returned to the track. By now a roaring rhythm had overtaken the crowd, dramatically punctuated by lightning in the Western sky. Was the thunder from the sky or from the track? It was impossible to tell, nor did it matter. For a few hours Vermont's cultural lines had been crossed by citizens paying homage to the gods of mobility. That's the significance of Thunder Road. The archeologists of the future will never understand.

Brilliant Ideas

Why am I not a millionaire?

"Where do you get the great ideas for your column?"

Boy, if I had a dollar for every time I've been asked that question, I'd be able to buy myself a six-pack (granted, Old Milwaukee, on sale, in 1993). The truth is, for every brilliant idea that graces this page there are many that are flushed right down the toilet. Just so you can have an impression of what makes the difference between good and bad, here is a sampling of great thoughts that were considered unworthy of inclusion in this volume. Hmm-m-m. Then, why are they here?

The Iditarod Barbie. I tip my hat to my wife for coming up with this one. What a concept—the symbol of our plastic culture, the curvaceous Barbie, dressed in the furs and leathers of the most grueling race on the North American continent. The idea is fraught with rich layers of meaning. Unfortunately, most of them evaporate when one reaches the point of applying pen to paper. I never got beyond the title of this stillborn classic.

My Friend the Stump. My neighbors in Upper Granville have observed me banging on the stump of a dead elm for the past few weeks. Sure, they snicker. Sure, they think I'm a little dull witted. What they don't know is that after a few weeks of banging on the thing with my Monster Maul, I've settled into a Zenlike rhythm that has brought me inner peace. In fact, the reason that I've decided not to do a column on my stump is that I'm going to make it the subject of a full-length book (and movie, too, starring Robert Redford as the contemplative stump banger).

Great Names for Rock and Roll Bands. How about General Chaos? Pandemonium? Run For Your Coats? Gary and the Gang Green? Oh, Never Mind (that's my favorite).

The Decade of Disease. This is an idea that has been fermenting in my brain since I turned forty. I went for the obligatory physical and my doctor said, "Welcome to the Decade of Disease." Now, there's a column idea, I told myself.

Unfortunately, every time I go to write it I find the subject so depressing that I spend the evening watching mindless sitcoms instead.

The Million-Dollar Tooth. This one is a sure-fire winner; it's about a dentist who keeps working on one single tooth in a patient's head until the poor sucker (the patient) has invested a million bucks in a single tooth. Meanwhile the dentist puts an addition on his house, buys a string of racehorses, and spends his weekends at the craps tables of Monte Carlo, all with the proceeds from this one tooth! Here, at last, was an idea teeming with poignancy and relevancy. Also, since it is based on experience, I could write about the subject with a degree of authority. In fact, I actually wrote the column; it's a riot.

Unfortunately, the thought occurred to me, "Where will you go the next time you have a toothache?" I can hear his fiendish laugh as he inserts the rusty pliers into my mouth. "You won't need Novocaine for this, big guy. By the way, I loved your column on the tooth. Hahahahahahahah." This idea, along with my own sense of oral hygiene, was buried for posterity.

The Economics of Town Meeting. Here is a real Beyonder subject. The last time I attended town meeting, a group of 150 adults spent a half hour debating the merits of a $35 expenditure. If each of us had coughed up forty-six cents we could have saved seventy-five man hours! Or we could have spent the same time stuffing envelopes for minimum wage and made a few hundred dollars profit. What stopped me from writing this exposé was the thought of those nasty letters I would receive about the sanctity of town meeting. This is turf upon which only idiots tread. (Take it from an idiot. It took about four trods for me to learn my lesson, but now I know. Town meeting is better than a religious experience. Or a date with Julia Roberts. Or the Red Sox winning the World Series. Or all three on the same night!)

You will be happy to know that I record all of my bad ideas in a notebook that is now about three inches thick. If the creative well runs dry, I have enough to keep *The View From Beyonder* going into the twenty-first century. How about a three-part series on "Weird Noises My Kid Can Make With His Saxophone?"

Less Is Less

This was inspired by the cuisine at the Tunbridge Fair. Ever eat one of those "onion blossoms"? If the world is shrinking, why do I keep expanding?

This is the world's first "lite" column. It contains the same number of words as previous essays, but has one-third fewer original ideas as well as dramatically reduced meaningful content. It's full flavored, peppered in fact with meaningful content without any chuckle, chortles, guffaws, or sniggers to contort your face and cause your voice box to emit ungracious sounds. This column is guaranteed to be 97 percent laugh-free.

America has gone "lite" crazy, a fact of limitless delight to the nation's food producers who make one-third more profit by giving us one-third less product, and, in the process, act as if they are doing us a big favor.

What's gone the way of "lite"? We all know about "lite" beer, but now the epidemic has spread to tacos, Doritos, Hostess Cupcakes, Coffee-Mate, Kraft Salad Dressing, Ruffles Potato Chips, Aunt Jemima Pancakes (and Log Cabin Maple Syrup, of course), and Alpo Dog Food.

Well, thank God we're up here in Vermont, where we're not about to fall for marketing hype. After all, this is one of the last bastions of regional pride where native producers embody the ethics of hardscrabble farmers, where full measure and honest value are considered intrinsic human rights. This is the state that gave you the Defiant Wood Stove and Ben & Jerry's Double Creme Kahlua Magic Chocolate Cherry Obscure Rock Star Fudge Almond Ripple Nut Crunch.

Wrong.

Ben & Jerry's now makes a "lite." And the same Vermont

Distillers who give us chest-beating Tamarack Liqueur flavored with native roots, bark, and berries now give us "lite" gin. "Lite" gin? It's a fact. What's happening to life's small, sinful pleasures? Is nothing sacred? Will we go to the Rutland Fair this fall and find the vendors selling "lite" fried dough?

Hey, it's fun up here on the soapbox. While I wallow in self-righteous indignation, let me descry our increasing facelessness, the decline in regionality, and the hypocrisy of a culture where one cannot be too rich or too thin.

What else can I be irritated about? Oh, I know, the corporate green movement. Not that I am stupid enough to come out against clean air and pure water, but it does anger me to see consumer product companies (that care as much for the environment as my nine year old does about opera) falling all over each other to tell us how ecologically sensitive they are. OK class, let's have a show of hands. How many of you believe that McDonald's is paying more than lip service to this fragile planet? If they love this planet so much, why have they blanketed it with enough hamburgers to cover all known land masses to a depth of three feet?

Or Dow Chemical. Now, there's a company that knows how to love a planet. I don't care how mellow the voice of their spokesperson is, or whether he wears a flannel shirt, or even if they show him canoeing down a pristine river. This is a company whose business strategy revolves around creating petrochemical goobers that kill potato beetles or make your living room carpet so stain resistant that you forget that you are living on what amounts to a fuzzy sheet of plastic.

Do I believe that Dow cares about my world? About as much as I believe that Agel-Corman Furniture, up in Burlington, has really gone out of business for the last time.

Do these companies think we are stupid? Obviously. And we prove it every time we drink a beer that tastes great, but is less filling. In reality we know that "lite" anything tastes not-so-great, and it is less filling by virtue of the fact that there is less of it. It is worth the price premium for the psychological relief of knowing that we are doing the right things for our bodies, our children, our countries, and our planets. And thank God for Big Macs, jumbo fries, and thick shakes. Maybe if we eat enough,

MacDonald's will make tons of money and save the spotted owls.

Attaboy, Rocky. Go get'em, Tiger. I think I'll get off this soap-box before someone pushes me. Maybe I'll go down to the Golden Arches and save the environment. Maybe they have come out with a Big Mac "Lite."

Plenty O' Nuthin'

This is my "day job." People actually pay me money to tell them this stuff. I will also do psychiatric evaluations, marriage counseling, and give investment advice. I also clean crawl spaces and basements.

People always ask me what I do for a living. They say, "You obviously don't earn a living with your writing, and you can't do much of anything else, so how do you get by?" The answer is, I make my living by doing nothing. I'm in Marketing, where the ability to do nothing is considered a terrific asset.

Being a professional do-nothing is not as easy as it sounds. My son, who can now sleep through entire weeks, thinks he is good at doing nothing. Wrong. He's sleeping. He's dreaming. He is a fountain of productivity compared to the modern-day Marketing Expert.

My other son, who sits motionless in front of reruns of "This Week in Baseball from 1989," fancies himself good at doing nothing, but he's a rank amateur. To be a professional Marketeer requires years of education, countless footpads on the sidewalk of life, and an advanced degree from the School of Hard Knocks.

This is not a profession for the run-of-the-mill vegetable. This is a battleground for the warrior who has devoted the best years of life to the pursuit of the unfathomable.

What is important these days is not what virtues a product has; it's what it doesn't have. And here's a secret—almost every-thing doesn't have something.

Take the doughnut.

Now the doughnut is, by universal consensus, about the most useless thing that you can put into your mouth. It contains not a scrap of nutritional value. It makes you fat, it rots your teeth. A glazed doughnut can sit in your stomach unfazed by digestive juices for periods up to a year.

Occasionally, however, there is an oral/intestinal urge that can be filled by a doughnut and nothing else. With full knowledge that you are destroying your insides, you fire down a couple of glazed chocolate beauties or jelly sticks.

But the people advertising doughnuts these days, do they publicize their fare as one of life's forgivable pleasures? No. After conducting millions of dollars of research they conclude one should eat doughnuts because they CONTAIN NO CHOLES-TEROL. These concentrated pellets of grease, fat, salt, sugar, preservatives, and petrochemical additives, should be consumed because they're clean on cholesterol.

Their ads don't mention it, but they contain no caffeine (another substance on the banned list), either. Isn't it perfect that they are typically washed down with hot java and followed by a cigarette? I don't even smoke, but I'm tempted to start whenever I have a glazed doughnut and coffee.

And what do doughnuts have in the middle? NOTHING! So what does the modern Marketing Guru do? He sells the chunks of nothing as doughnut holes. Catching on?

Perhaps my favorite nonfood is Nabisco Shredded Wheat. It's got no nothing. No sugar. No salt. No taste. But load a biscuit with strawberries and a spoonful of sugar, and voila!

I bought some Pringles Potato Chips recently. They contained at least ten polysyllabic ingredients, none of which were preservatives, as the package blazingly pointed out. What they neglected to mention is that Pringles do not need preservatives, because they contain nothing of nutritional value on which mold and bacteria can feed. Archeologists will be able to snack on these things when they unearth the Grand Union in the 23rd century.

In recent weeks I have pigged out on Chinese food that contained no MSG (tasted terrible), beer that had no alcohol (ditto), and fruit cocktail with no calories. All of these were terrible products, but represented marketing masterstrokes.

Now is the complex world of modern-day marketing beginning to make sense?

Perhaps the pinnacle of marketing achievement is Perrier, the
original designer water. Here's a product that contains no salt, no
calories, no preservatives, no cholesterol, no fat, and no canola oil.
It is nonsexist and protective of animal rights. It is also WATER
that is transported halfway around the globe so that we can buy it
for a buck a pop.

One might think that Perrier is the epitome of nothingness,
but the modern-day Marketing Genius (and yes, I consider myself
one. Don't we all?) can always come up with the improved
mousetrap. We'll call this one Beyonder Water and in addition to
all the other nothings, this bottle will leave out the water, because
research costing millions has identified a consumer malady even
worse than ring around the collar-"fluid bloat."

Think of the savings in transportation and manufacturing
costs. Half can go into our pockets, the rest into advertising pro-
claiming "No Bloating Fluids." Of course, we will have to charge
a slight premium for the completeness of this void, but the consumer knows (as does Bo, who could be our spokesperson) that
nothing doesn't come cheap.

So remember, if you are casting about aimlessly, wondering
what to do with your life, and someone tells you that you're "good
fer nuthin", you can look forward to a brilliant career in marketing.

Chuck 'N Jive

*I am proud to say that I made the "woodchuck"
part of the Vermont vernacular, meaning that it used to
be impolite to call someone a "Chuck." Now, it's
almost a badge of honor. The Fall is a busy time of
year for woodchucks. They're very busy raiding roadside trash pickups in Massachusetts and Connecticut,
so they can stage yard sales up here once the leaf peepers from Massachusetts and Connecticut arrive ... you
get the idea.*

In the old days, before 1980, it took generations to become a
real Vermonter. You needed to live in Vermont for 76 generations
to qualify as a native. In today's compressed world of computers,
cable TV, and televised lotteries, however, none of us has this
much time to devote to anything, let alone claiming residency in a
state that might be annexed by New York or Massachusetts any
day now. To help the neophyte accelerate through the learning
curve, I offer this handy guide to talkin' Vermont—talkin' Chuck.

In native Chuckese the number "nine" is pronounced
"noyne" to rhyme with "loyve," as in "loyve bait." Here are a few
terms and definitions so you will not be out of place at Thunder
Road or the beer hall at the Tunbridge World's Fair. -"Some."
This all-purpose word is perhaps the most important in all
Chuckdom, as it extends any other descriptive adjective. Hard to
explain, but easy to demonstrate. "Some cold today." "That dress
was some expensive."

"Don't you know?" (sounds like, "Dontchuno?"). A phrase
without meaning used gratuitously in conversation. Appropriate
at the end of any sentence or fragment thereof. Often used in con-
junction with "some." Example: "Some cold today, dontchuno?"

Master these two expressions alone and you will be able to
convince anyone that your pedigree is as pure as a snowdrift in

Buell's Gore. But don't stop now. Expand your vocabulary:

Mother. One's wife, girlfriend, sister (oh, I hope not), or significant other (now, there is a Flatlander term!). As in, "Mother gets some peeved when I drink too many beers, dontchuno?"

Boi Jeezum, or "boi the jumpin' jeezum," or in the Northeast Kingdom "boi the jumped-up jeezum." A North Country epithet with religious implications. Just stay out of the way of
anyone who gets to the "jumpin' jeezum" stage, especially if he is either drunk or has a gun.

Camp. A rustic house of worship where the native Vermonter practices semimystical rituals. Usually a simple structure deep in the woods, its period of greatest use is during the high holy days called "deer season."

Cree-mee (local variations "creamie," "cremee," or "creamy"). A soft ice-milk confection dispensed at roadside stands and quick-stops in the North. Served in several flavors, but any flavor beyond vanilla is superfluous. Ben & Jerry's with their White Russian Double Cheesecake Chocolate Cherry Chunk will never reach this audience.

Upstreet. A term of no geographical reference used in towns small enough so that specific location is superfluous. "Cross street," "downstreet," and "overstreet" are synonyms. Nuances in meaning have been lost over the generations.

Cord. A measure of firewood that fits exactly into a truck, whether the vehicle in question is a two-ton dumpster or a half-ton Toyota. This contrasts with the Flatlander definition of "cord" as a precise measure of stacked wood 4 x4 x8.

Dubblewoid. A trailer, or prefabricated home, double the normal sixteen-foot width, for many the fulfillment of a life-long dream. Spelled "doublewide." Often seen on Interstate 89, with accompanying signage "WOID LOAD."

Noice spread. Either an array of food including cheese cubes (Velveeta), Ritz crackers, decorated

Spam, and quart bottles of Genesee beer or, alternatively, a dubblewoid with lots of decorative lawn ornaments.

Quite a rigging (pronounced "*Kwoyt a riggin'*). Anything exceptional. Often used by males of the species to describe well-endowed females. A bad phrase to use in the presence of "Mother."

Doodlebug. An off-road vehicle, specifically for hauling wood from woodlot to landing, often a testament to mechanical genius. Once the forward gears are stripped, one turns the seat around, and reverse becomes forward.

Quick-stop. A convenience store, the best source for beer after hours and on Sunday. Must accept food stamps for bona fide quick-stop status. Often a source of Cree-mees.

Hopefully, this little dictionary will help would-be Vermonters, although some would argue that the effort is futile. The concept of Talkin' Chuck, they would say, is a contradiction in terms. Vermonters are notoriously toyt-lipped, dontchuno.

Still Don't Get It

Life is about cool. Even after all these years, I must admit that I've still got what it takes to qualify as cool. Let's not ask for second opinions.

As a white male and father of two wise-guy, know-it-all sons, I am quite accustomed to being told that I "don't get it." Perhaps it will help to have precise and scientific definitions of "it," "get," and "not," using specific examples culled from annals of real life. Here are some things I get, and some things I not … it … get:

I get rap music. A summer day, I'm pounding down the dirt roads of Beyonder, my Honda Accord throbbing as I listen to my homey talkin' trash about guns 'n hoes at 102 decibels. (Not the garden kind, you know what I'm saying?) I arrive at the farmer's market, hormones coursing through my body like the White River during the snowmelt. "Yo," I say to the dude known as J-Sun. "You be holdin' any Swiss chard?" "No," the dude say, "But I be packing tomatoes—big booty fruits, ready to bust out, like Martha Stewart."

See, rap is pure attitude. It doesn't matter that my hair is gray and that I could lose a few pounds. You got the right attitude, you take it to the bank. It's a no-brainer, like playing the lottery.

Speaking of which, I don't get the lottery. I get the idea of winning millions just for going to the quick-stop and reciting five numbers to the cashier, but this is the biggest sucker ploy since "weapons of mass destruction." See the ads that caution us to "play responsibly" as we partake in "good, clean fun" that benefits the education of our young ones? They don't mention the odds are fixed, and not in your favor. The lottery is just a tax on the dreams of people who want an easier life. Ever seen a state legislator, doctor, or executive standing at the register scratching away at his "Oodles of Cash" or "Barrels of Money" tickets?

I get professional wrestling. It's our contemporary equivalent to Shakespearean drama. It may be fixed, but you don't know if it's fixed for the good guy or the personification of evil. All you know is that the path from beginning to end will touch on every emotion within the human spectrum. For instance, there's the situation where the beloved old wrestler comes out of retirement to avenge his friend's humiliating defeat. Usually the old hero kicks butt, but every so often his butt gets kicked, and he limps back to his Barca-Lounger.

Think of rasslin' as sport, and you'll be contemptuous. Think of it as theater, with its colorful costumes, characters, and pageantry, and you will understand why The Rock has progressed to the best-seller lists and the silver screen.

I don't get the Jerry Springer Show, even though it appears to have the same script writers as professional wrestling. As opposed to heroes and villains, the characters come from places all too familiar. (You might have seen them at the quick-stop, scratching lottery tickets.) I don't want to know their dirty secrets; I don't want to see their bare bottoms; and I don't want to see their humiliation in front of an obnoxious, jeering crowd.

Maybe, you think, I do get "big exploitation" but not "small exploitation." How, then, would you explain that I do get Thunder Road, but not NASCAR racing. The Milk Bowl was held on an October day when the foliage seemed to be preening for the sunlight. The hills were aglow, while the grass was still green. The air was charged with the roar of internal combustion engines, and the unique aroma that is part fried dough, part gasoline fumes. Presiding over it all was Ken Squire, Vermont's Donald Trump, who had convinced Vermont's most prominent politicians to participate in a contest to see who could throw a piece of dried cow poop the farthest. How did you "doo" that, Ken? Thunder Road is an oasis of chaos within the serene island of Vermont, and, as with so many things in this state, the scale is perfect.

I don't get NASCAR, now the most popular spectator sport in the country. I say this with humble, profound respect, as I don't want to irritate the portion of the population with the highest percentage ownership of pickup trucks and shotguns. NASCAR looks like my definition of hell—an eternal bumper-to-bumper traffic jam, on amphetamines, chasing its own tail. My NASCAR friends have explained about the technology, the party atmosphere, the racing community, and the adrenaline rush of impending calamity. I dunno. I'm missing the NASCAR gene.

I don't get women, but we won't go there.

Red Sox, do get. Downhill skiing, don't get. Cross-country skiing, do get. Fishing, sometimes get. Hunting, don't do, but do get. Jewelry, should get, but don't get. Computers, try to get. Palm Pilots, don't get. Caribbean vacations, wanna get.

I don't get classical music. I enjoy it (especially that Beethoven dude), but don't get it. You can be the fifth-best bassoonist in the world and be working a job where the key qualification is the ability to say, "And would you like fries with that?" Be the fifth-best field goal kicker or utility infielder and you're making millions.

Classical music needs to steal a page from professional wrestling. What if the musicians dressed in wild costumes and gave themselves provocative nicknames like Killer Klarinet or The Vio-linz? What if the women orchestra members tart themselves up a little and start clawing each other at the smallest provocation? What if the conductor, now renamed The Beast, waves, instead of his little baton, a light saber that emits lasers that can blow a flautist five feet into the air? What if he shows us his butt?

Now we're cooking. I can see the people streaming into the concert hall.

Let's add a sound track with a throbbing bass line and lots of scratchy noises, then, our coup de grace, arrange the musicians on a rotating banked oval. The musicians advance their positions during the symphony by pushing others out of the way, roller derby-style. The one in front at the final crescendo gets a million bucks, endorsement deals from Pepsi and Ford, and a date with Sheryl Crow.

Musicians are allowed hit each other with folding chairs or instruments, so long as they remember to play responsibly. It's just good, clean fun.

The Writer's Conference

As the season turns punky, the frost comes more frequently, and the sole vestige of edibility in the garden is a stalk of Brussels sprouts that has already fed a generation of slugs. If you are desperate enough, and dedicated enough, you will eat them anyway (the sprouts, not the slugs!). It's a good time to realize that Nature is getting ready to hibernate, and if you know what's good for you, you will buff up your professional credentials.

Bad idea, guys.

I mean, it was a good idea, and certainly their hearts were in the right places, but it just didn't... you know, work.

Recently someone paid for me to attend a seminar for us writer-types to make us, uh, more like effective communicators. This piece kinda puts the principles we learned into practice. Y'know, it's amazing how just a few tips from a pro will make a piece of writing, howshallisay, "sing."

The most important part of a story is the "lead." The "lead" is an intriguing or provocative statement that draws the reader into the story and gives an enticing glimpse into what the story is all about.

The perfect lead does for a reader what a worm ball does for a catfish. Like the wind from the subway, it lifts the skirt of the pretty girl, giving us...oh, never mind.

Here are a few notes I made to myself at the writer's conference. "All stories begin with freedom and end with restraint." "Good writing does not draw attention to itself." And finally, "Follow the rules, except when you break them."

To which I reply, "Good point," "Oh yeah?," and "Hm-m-m."

Writing, according to our instructor, is quite the simple process. One gathers material, then organizes it into themes which are built upon blocks of supporting arguments. Start with a "lead" and end with a "bang." What could be simpler?

I sprang to the word processor, visions of a Pulitzer Prize in my head, and stared into its black abyss for the better part of an hour. Then I took a nap to recharge my creative batteries, and followed that with three cups of coffee to get the creative juices flowing. Instead, I gave myself diarrhea, and not the verbal kind.

I tried a different tack, taking out the old standby yellow legal pad and two pencils with points so sharp they could have been used for optical surgery. I put relaxing classical music on in the background, loud enough to be inspiring, but not so loud as to distract. I fine-tuned the temperature of the room so that it practically caressed my skin.

By this time I was hungry.

Well, to make a long story short (avoid clichés!), I had now produced less than the Carter Administration. I did not even have wadded-up sheets of legal pad to show for my efforts. I went back to the word processor.

I stared into the screen, its eternal blackness as bottomless as the northern sky at night (avoid overwriting!), its shimmering, onyx depths (avoid adjectives!) a reflection of a life devoid of meaning.

"Eureka," I cried. "This is it! I am experiencing a flash of creative inspiration." I went and found my twelve-year-old son who was listening to Vanilla Ice at 98 decibels on his Walkman.

"Don't you see?," I said, shaking him by the shoulders, "The blankness of the screen is a symbol of the void in my mind, which mirrors the utter lack of meaning in Life."

My son nodded to the beat. "I DID MY HOMEWORK," he shouted.

I attacked the keyboard with a fury unseen since Operation Shock and Awe. Within an hour I produced thousands of words about the meaning of nothingness. "The significance of my revelation," I wrote (and I quote) "is that a thought cannot die. True, with a single stroke on the keyboard I can make the words disappear, but the idea is immortal."

I reviewed my notes from the seminar and came across one that read, "Beware the Imitative Fallacy. You can't write an interesting article on boredom by being boring."

Oh.

I hit the "Delete" key, and found myself face to face with the blank screen, again. "Story of my life," I muttered. "There goes the Pulitzer Prize."

All that remains now is for me to figure out how to get out of this with both a bang and restraint. I'll try this: bang.

The Wonder Of Bread

One of my specialties is Vermont's "economic underground." By that I mean, "How the heck do you earn a living in a state that doesn't have a market?" There are fewer people in Vermont today than there were in the 1820s. There have been some creative solutions. This is one.

Our story begins at the Nantana Mill in Northfield. This red-brick complex alongside the Dog River is a testament to another era when manufacturing drove both the local and national economies. With a bit of research I could tell you what was made at the Nantana Mill, but the editors of this book have a strict rule against me doing anything that could be construed as "research." This saves them from ever having to "fact check."

In its heyday the Nantana Mill harnessed the power of the mighty Dog to run its bobbins or looms. The water still runs over the spillway, but the power for the complex now comes from Yankee Nuclear. (Well, probably. Remember the "no research" rule?)

The Mill now houses a variety of entrepreneurial enterprises of the types that flourish in Vermont. Yes, there is a chocolatier, but no salsa maker. I am visiting the Nantana Mill because I have heard a rumor that a company there is actually making something that is not a gourmet food. While technically not illegal, this kind of manufacturing is discouraged in America because it might damage the Chinese economy. Apparently, no one has delivered this message to Wall/Goldfinger, Designers and Builders of Fine Corporate Furniture since 1971.

By "fine corporate furniture" I don't mean things like chairs, and it's a good thing, because when company president, John Wall, invites me to have a seat, he warns me that the chair in front of his desk is prone to falling over. The chair, a prototype, once won a design competition in which functionality was not a criterion. I sit down gingerly, holding on to both arms.

Wall/Goldfinger makes exquisite, fantasy furniture that winds up in New York skyscrapers, corporate headquarters, and James Bond movies. Recently, a photo of one of their tables showing seated dignitaries including Rudolph Giuliani was pictured in the New York Times. Just one of their conference tables can cost as much as a nice house (or expressed differently, about a third of what is earned by a utility infielder for the Red Sox).The company started as Union Woodworks in Waitsfield, but within a few years had graduated from kitchen cabinets to one-of-a-kind masterpieces that combine elegant design, quality materials, and human craftsmanship to make a visual statement of corporate solidity. "We're still in business," says Wall, "because Vermont is accessible to Manhattan, Washington DC, Boston, and Philadelphia. We can speak the language of designers and architects, and we can translate the client's vision to the woodworkers or stonecutters who work the materials."

The products of Wall/Goldfinger feature fine veneer work and sensuous hand-rubbed finishes, using materials ranging from exotic hardwoods to Barre granite. Increasingly they are constructed with concealed wiring and communications electronics so that boardroom executives can play video games and surf the 'Net during dull meetings. There are only a handful of places that can make the type of furniture that comes out of the Wall/Goldfinger facility in the Nantana Mill, and no one can do it better.But what does this have to do with bread?

If Wall/Goldfinger has an equivalent in dough, it might be La Panciata, a bakery in the Nantana Mill run by Glenn Loati, coincidentally an ex-Wall/Goldfinger employee. He makes breads made with locally grown, stone-ground, organic flour. The company's products can be found throughout Vermont at food co-ops and other purveyors of all things delicious.

A business like this could not have existed a dozen years ago, because there was no source of locally grown, organic, stone-ground flour, not only in Vermont, but anywhere. We had become a nation enslaved to Wonder Bread.

(An aside on Wonder Bread. If you ever want to win a bet, bet someone that they cannot eat a single slice of Wonder Bread, without an accompanying drink, in less than one minute. I've won a lot of money on this one. Although Wonder Bread claims to build our bodies in twelve ways, it does so in a total absence of taste, freshness, and nutrition. It proudly boasts of being made with "enriched" flour, which is so called because they have artificially added back a small portion of the nutrients that they removed in the quest for whiteness, uniformity, and a long shelf life.)

Did you know that at the time of the Civil War Vermont was known as the "breadbasket of New England?" Back then there was no shortage of locally grown, organic, stone-ground grain. In fact, that's all there was. But that changed as people discovered what is now known as "the Midwest," with six feet of topsoil that could be plowed into furrows as long as the entire state of Iowa. The long-story-short is that grain growing migrated to the Midwest, much as "making things" has migrated to China. Before long, Vermont had only farms that can coexist with rocky soil and subzero temperatures. (That's why we farm primarily ice cream and cheese in Vermont.)

I learn all this from Richard "Jez" Harrington, a project manager at Wall/Goldfinger whose job it is to coordinate ten million details so that the fifty-foot conference table that costs more than a yacht arrives on the 77th floor of the skyscraper without a scratch. He is also, in his spare time, one of the proprietors of Green Mountain Mills, a producer of organic, stone-ground flours that sells its products to none other than La Panciata. His company evolved to fill the void in the wake of Wonder Bread's success.

Green Mountain Mills and La Panciata will never export their products to China, nor will they ever face competition from the

Third World. Their artisinal products, so dependent on local pro-
duction, can exist only within a relatively short distance of their
origin. While the finished loaves are not one-of-a-kind, they are as
distinct from Wonder Bread as a Wall/Goldfinger conference
table is from a folding picnic table from Wal-Mart.

The worlds of these three Vermont survivors fully intertwine
on the Wall/Goldfinger loading dock. Green Mountain Mills
ships thousand-pound pallet-loads of flour to La Panciata which,
unfortunately, has neither loading dock nor forklift.

Enter Chet Brown, who manages the loading dock at
Wall/Goldfinger. Chet is one of those pragmatic guys you find in
Vermont who can always get a car started when it's forty below.
Chet offers to off-load the pallets and break down the shipment
so that the bakery can deal with the grain bags by hand. He even
comes up with the appropriate compensation—finished loaves of
bread.

Thus, the company that makes mind-boggling corporate furniture in a country that doesn't make things any more is able to give
its employees delicious, nutritious bread made from locally grown,
organic, stone-ground flour. The baker that couldn't have existed
a decade ago doesn't have to buy a forklift, and concentrates on
baking and delivering the staff of life within its local market terri-
tory. The Vermonter who, not too long ago, could choose between
white bread and white bread, can now choose among dozens of
specialty breads, none of which are named "Wonder."

That's how it works here in Vermont.

Are Wood Guys Good Guys?

Tunbridge Fair's over. About the only thing left to look forward to is the Milk Bowl at Thunder Road. If your wood is not stacked and poised for the stove now, you are in deep shit.

I'm totally confused.

The subject is wood, a material I have used to heat my home for the past fifteen years. I know it's more work to burn wood, but I like the exercise. It makes more sense to burn calories splitting and hauling hardwood than running in front of a television set on a treadmill at the health spa. I enjoy the fresh air; I even enjoy bugging the kids to get them to help stack. Once they get past the whining about the disruption to their electronic entertainment, it is surprising how quickly they become human beings again. Lots of people in Beyonder burn wood.

I like the warmth. I like the flicker and glow of embers, I like the freedom from the whir of an electric motor from a furnace that blows hot air up at my face, complete with all sort and manner of dust, mites, and hairballs.

Sometimes when I am stacking wood so that a summer's worth of sunshine can make it a cleaner, hotter fuel, I think of those supertankers carrying immense cargos of black gold from the ancient forests of the Middle East. I think of the wells that Saddam set afire, and the noxious roar of the jet engines of the warplanes we used to assure our access to cheap oil.

My wood comes from hills that I can see. It's delivered by a guy named Paul who cuts it with his chainsaw, then loads it in his one-ton pickup. We always have a few good-natured words about the types of wood delivered, its burning characteristics, conditions in the woods, and whether or not I've received a big cord, a little cord, or a medium cord.

Can you imagine a conversation like this with your oil delivery person. ("This here's Venezuelan oil, boi jeezum. Been some dry down there, dontchuno?")

Of the different ways that I direct my life to Power Down, burning wood is the one with the greatest impact. Unfortunately, and this is where I begin to get confused, there is another side to the wood-burning issue.

My eco-Yuppie friends (all right, I admit, the term applies to me, too) say that my stove pollutes their fresh air. Moreover, my partner says that the unavoidable clutter of wood chips and ashes pollutes her kitchen, and certainly the kids' complaints about filling the wood box pollute my ears. Then, there is the horrifying dread every time I'm at work and the town fire alarm sounds, and the sheer joy of trying to climb an icy roof when it's ten below to clean a chimney.

I burn my wood in a "clean" stove. Theoretically, I should be able to feel good about wood, but life is never that simple. Now, along comes evidence that the emissions from airtight stoves contain insidious carcinogens, and further indications that a home's internal environment can be more adversely affected by burning wood than by hosting cigarette smokers.

My environmentally active friends say that the only good smoke is no smoke, and that even my supposedly high-tech stove is smogging up their skies. But then comes the information that wood burning, in combination with responsible reforestation, actually helps the environment by reversing the greenhouse effect.

What's a fella to do?

Obviously, no solutions will be forthcoming in the final few words of this essay. The point here is that powering down is not always as easy in practice as in theory. Even the process of taking a step back to supposedly simpler times does not necessarily solve problems or provide the right answers. The many factors involved in something as simple as burning a stick of wood can touch on so many diverse and complex issues that coming to a clear, uncomplicated answer can be next to impossible.

The wood burner, perhaps more than anyone, appreciates what powerfully concentrated stuff oil is. I know the impact of one summer of sunlight on my woodpile. Think of the immense quantity of natural energy that goes into making such a powerful fuel. Oil literally is, at least to my simplistic mind, Black Magic

In the meantime, I have to keep warm, so I have to decide

something. I know it's not for everyone, but I'm choosing to burn wood. In my never-ending quest to power down, I can't escape the conclusion that humans have been burning oil for slightly more than a hundred years and wood for fifty million. I know this is simplistic, but it seems that most of our problems from the planetary perspective have come during the Age of Oil. Perhaps we must learn to better control this "Black Magic" before we use it all up.

Part II–The Bleak

Summer keeps turning up for guest appearances, but they are shorter and shorter. On warm days cluster flies gather on the south-facing windows, making you look forward to the ground actually freezing. The official change from Fall to Bleak occurs on All Hallows Eve. This is a night that works best in the country. In the towns it becomes a sugar-crazed greedathon, just like everywhere else.

The earth is naked, stripped of foliage and not yet blanketed with snow. If you like the gradations of brown and gray, it's quite lovely in a sad, lonely way. The road crew comes by and puts in sticks before the ground freezes, so that they will know their boundaries when they are working behind the plows.

While some folks settle into the nuances of family dynamics, others think it a good time to get the hell out of Dodge for at least a little while. The elections do or don't engage us. It's not as exciting as a pennant race, but you have to do something to fill the time. Then it's time for the High Holy Days, beginning with deer season, then continuing through to Thanksgiving.

The weather in the early part of December always includes some of the worst of winter driving. To make matters worse, you haven't put your snow tires on, and the rest of the world has forgotten how to drive in snow. It's a good time to get pissed off at everything. Then, in short burst, come the Solstice, Christmas, and New Year's. The family gathers, if we are so lucky, and we remember those who are no longer with us.

It may look bleak outside, but the world within is rich and full.

As the Cluster Flies

Is there a more insidious villain in the North Country?

Do you remember the old Warner Brothers cartoon where Elmer Fudd gets so annoyed at a mosquito that he goes after it with a double-barreled shotgun? Before long, he has blasted away the entire house and the mosquito is still buzzing. Poor Elmer was driven to violence and self-destruction by a bug.

I feel this way about cluster flies. Lying quietly in bed, reading a book, minding my own business, suddenly my world is violated by a buzzing fly that lurches like a drunk into the bedside lamp, pinging randomly into the lampshade, and eventually landing on my head. After a few minutes of this routine I would happily employ any weapon of mass destruction against this nemesis.

Horror stories about cluster flies abound in the North Country. I have a neighbor who claims to remove them by the bushel basket from his summer camp. A carpenter friend reports finding walls in old houses so packed with fly carcasses that they were actually providing pretty good insulation.

I'd rather freeze.

Pushed beyond my ethical boundary by this fulsome critter, I broke a long-standing personal rule and actually did some research for this article. The cluster fly is 1/4¼to 3/8 inch in length, somewhat larger and slower than a common housefly. It is distinguished by the presence of golden yellow hairs on the front and top of its thorax. Its wing tips overlap while resting.

That's when you should smack it.

Female cluster flies lay their eggs in cracks in the soil. After three days the larvae emerge and seek out their food source, the earthworm. (I should stop right here.) The larvae burrow into the worms where they enjoy a lovely parasitic relationship. (I'll wait until you get back from the bathroom.)

An effective way to combat cluster flies, therefore, is to remove the topsoil for a hundred yards in any direction from your house and replace it with a non-organic substance. Alternatively, you can create a moat, but that might result in a mosquito problem. Or, move to Nevada.

After feasting on worms the emerging flies seek a protected over-wintering site, which means your house. Any crack or crevice in your siding or foundation will be a welcome gate for cluster flies. From what I can tell, the only way to stop them from getting in is to wrap your house in a giant plastic bag. They get in through miniscule openings in window frames, door frames, soffits, and eaves, through pulley holes, under shingles. You can plug all the cracks, but you won't stop them. You can spray with the most toxic insecticides known to mankind, BUT YOU CAN'T STOP THEM!

You can, however, kill them.

Once inside the house, the cluster fly does something that only a creature as dumb as a cluster fly would try to do—they try to get out. Specifically, they gather at the warmest, sunniest window and knock themselves silly banging against the glass. They often choose sunny, winter days when the radiant solar energy causes your heart to soar, until you hear the pinging drone of a thousand flies bopping against the windowpane. This disgusts normal people, especially visitors from the Flatlands, but not me.

I live for this.

My killing methods have evolved over the years. Cluster flies are slow enough and stupid enough that they do not offer much in the way of sport, except through their sheer numbers. Initially, I used a rolled-up newspaper. That provided a rewarding visceral thud, but left me to deal with the little fly carcasses, which were often smeared on the wall. Also, ceiling kills were quite difficult.

The wire-shafted fly swatter came next. I became quite adept at this and was able to deliver a lethal blow from either hand, forehand, backhand, or my favorite, the overhead smash. I was the Andre Agassi of the fly swatter. There was still the carcass problem, as well as the revolting task of cleaning the swatter.

I went through a vacuum cleaner phase, which was momentarily effective, but the vacuum cleaner is always on the other side of the house when you need it. Also, I couldn't be sure that sucking up the flies into the dust bag actually killed them. Maybe they even enjoyed it! If they can penetrate the house, escaping from a vacuum cleaner might not present a problem.

Trying a different tack, I ordered something called the "Cluster Buster 1000," which attaches to the window with suction cups, then traps the flies in finely powdered eggshells and suffocates them, insuring a slow, agonizing death. The theory sounds fine, and would be even better if you could hear the little critters screaming like so many doomed passengers on the Titanic. The reality was that I couldn't get the "Cluster Buster 1000" to stick to the window. Instead of coming back to a container bursting with fly carcasses, I came back to a white mess on the floor and the gleeful buzz of window pelting.

Then I found my ultimate weapon. These should be standard issue for every Vermont home. I found mine in a mail-order catalog, but, alas, the catalog no longer carries the item.

I call it The Wand. It's a plastic tube, about the size of a paper towel tube, attached to a handle that contains a battery-powered fan. The tube has a removable cap that you lift off, aim, press the magic button, and watch with infinite pleasure as that cluster fly realizes that man really does have dominion.

You can suck up fifteen or twenty flies at a time. I used to have a concern about how to dispose of the captured flies. You don't want to let them go outside, lest they live to buzz another day. I tried flushing them down the toilet, but a few inevitably escaped. But then I hit on the perfect solution.

I freeze them. Just put The Wand and its buzzing load of flies in the freezer. Within minutes they are either dead or dormant. In any case, if they wake up, it will be the septic tank from which they will need to escape.

If I can ever find where The Wand is made (please help Dear Reader), I'm going to buy them by the container load and sell them at every general store and quick-stop in the North Country. Not only will I make my fortune, but also I will take great solace in what I am contributing to collective mental health of Vermonters.

Kidzstuf

One of my deeply held spiritual beliefs is that somehow, somewhere, all time exists at once. And so it is with this book. My kids exist as little nubbers, gawky teens, and fully realized human beings, all within a few pages. More fun than a family album!

I pose to you, dear reader, one of life's eternal questions, a simple query, the correct answer to which will enlighten the path of human existence, while the incorrect response will leave us all in the eternal quandary of Mud Season, stuck in a ditch with no means of escape. Here's the question (drum roll, please): Is it
    a. "Super Teenage Mutant Ninja Turtles?"
    b. "Teenage Mutant Super Ninja Turtles?"
    c. "Ninja Mutant Super Teenage Turtles?" or..
    d. none of the above.

If you know the correct answer to the above question you are either between the ages of 17 and 12 (most likely male), a toy company executive, or socially maladjusted and in need of confinement.

Here are some other eternal questions, all having to do with Kids.

Do children inherit a sense of humor? I think so. The other night I found my nine year old fooling around on his electric piano. "Whatchu doin'?" I asked. "Writing a song," he told me. "What's it called?" I asked. "Local Cheese," he answered. Why would a kid write a song called "Local cheese?" For a while I tried to make sense of it. Maybe this was a song about Vermont. Maybe it was really "Lo-Cal Cheese," which would take us to an entirely different level of meaning. Maybe, I decided, the little twerp just inherited my sense of humor.

Why is washing hair the greatest torture of all time? Adults find the process gratifying. Women pay big bucks to have their scalps caressed and anointed. Why do kids cling to matted and stringy locks as tenaciously as Texans held the Alamo? Our son once pleaded with us to beat him rather than subject him to the dreaded soap and water on the noggin.

When is the last time a male of the species ever picked up his own underwear? I'm breaking ranks here, but why would anyone ever pick up gross, disgusting underwear if someone else will do it, and I am referring to Moms. Until Moms brace for a long, bitter, and very smelly strike, they will continue to pick up the u-trow just because we guys know if we leave them on the floor long enough, they will find their way to the washing machine.

What is the world record for the most consecutive nights sleeping in the same pajamas? Seriously, I think my son is making a run at it. At last count he was at 130 nights and going strong. As you know, a streak of this magnitude is the result of training and dedication. A few nights ago, when my wife discovered his pajamas still in the washing machine at bedtime, our son refused to go to bed until we promised to deliver them clean and dry. We had to stay up until one a. m. (which, as you know, has been done only four times in the history of Vermont). The real question remaining is whether or not he will outgrow his sleepwear before he breaks the record.

What is the "spiked bra" and why is it such a forbidden subject? Go ahead. You're so smart. Try to worm something out of a ten year old about the significance of a spiked bra. You'll never break their code of silence unless you stow away on the school bus and eavesdrop.

Why do my children speak a foreign language? The "why" is easy—so that we can't understand them. Here are just a few examples of kidspeak to help you break through the verbal maze. The glossary is by no means complete, but sprinkling six or seven of these words into a sentence will guarantee a one-way ticket to preadolescence:

    "Ossss"—short form of "ossum."

    "Ossum"—mega, mega, mega, mega-good

    "Mega"—very

    "Mega-ly"—adjective form of "mega," literally "very, very"

    "Minorly"—not very, the opposite of mega-ly

    "Wicked"—mega-ly ossum

"Dude"—all-purpose name reference

"Dudical"—shorthand for "Radical, Dude"

"Dweeb"—A Dude who is genetically defective

"Stooo-pudddd"—alternative name for "father"

You are now prepared to communicate with your twelve year old. Start off like this:

"Yo, Dude, the mega-Dweeb (that's you) finds it wicked irritating that you are being minorly uncooperative on the subject of cleaning up your room."

Your child, amazed at your new-found verbal acuity, will stare at you with a crooked face and invent a new language faster than you can say Weird Al Yankovic.

Well, here I go again. Not long ago I attempted to record the verbal idiosyncracies of native Vermonters, thereby violating an unwritten law that local social observations must be airbrushed to resemble the center spread of Vermont Life, and here I am, taking on the youth of America.

The portrayal of Vermont speech patterns (no one found it inaccurate, just unflattering) resulted in several invitations to go back to where I came from, as if that will change the way people talk. Now that the subject of lampoonment is kids, it is inevitable that some indignant preteen will likewise tell me to go back to where I came from.

I could live with that. Yo, Dudes, here comes Stooo-pudddd.

Teenspeak

Look, they aged a few years in just a few minutes!

What a difference a few years make. My ten year old asks nightly when I am going to do a column on the unusual noises he can make with his saxophone. His brother, three years older, says that if I ever, ever write anything that one of his friends can identify with him, he will sue me for everything I'm worth, run away from home, start smoking cigarettes, buy a motorcycle, report me to local authorities for child abuse, and never speak to me again.

He also says he'll stab me in my sleep, but I think he's kidding. He's got quite a sense of humor.

Nonetheless, I am taking the ultimate risk by writing about the forbidden subject—Junior High. Call me crazy, call me daring, call me the Salman Rushdie of the North, but I have nothing to lose. If my son never speaks to me again I won't be missing much. You see, his vocabulary is now down to about six words.

The State of Vermont, in its infinite wisdom, requires that children in the seventh grade take a course called "Living Arts." In this academic pursuit the young tykes learn the fine points of home economics, which is, of course, what the course was called until someone decided that the term was inappropriate in today's sexually neutered environment.

In this course my thirteen-year-old son spent six weeks making a pillow. Don't get me wrong. I have nothing against pillows. Pillow making might turn out to be an indispensable skill for my son. Call me old-fashioned, but I would have preferred the time to be spent in a more classical academic pursuit, such as speaking the English language.

Because, at the moment, he don't talk too good.

His verbal parsimony is directly attributable to adolescence, a time of dramatic physical growth. I'm not a doctor, but the growth seems to be fueled by his vocabulary. For every inch he grows, he loses about a thousand words.

My son's verbal world now consists of six words. These

words, with minor regional variations, are cross-cultural, enabling him to communicate fluently with any other male, female, nerd, geek, and wuss of the teenage subspecies.

The heart of his language is the word "no," a word so versatile in Teenspeak that it can sustain a forty-five-minute phone conversation and requires more than a hundred words to translate into other languages. It is the basis of the word "not," which can be shouted (as it is in the Budweiser commercial about the guitar-playing granny) at the end of any statement to reverse the meaning. That makes sense NOT!

A similarly rich verbal utterance is the simple sound "u," pronounced "u." Combined with the aforementioned "no" the key Teenspeak phrase of "u-no" is created. This phrase precedes and often follows every, you know, declarative statement, prepositional phrase, or word.

"Like" is another pillar of Teenspeak, often preceded by the guttural "ummm." It's used, ummm, like, where you like want it to go. It's like, versatile.

You have now mastered the key phrases of the language, but if you want to achieve advanced linguistic status (like, you know, to be a poet or write rock songs or something), here are a few embellishments.

"Die!" is an especially useful syllable if one has a younger sibling upon whom one periodically reigns noogies, Indian rope burns, pink bellies, and other physical tortures. Its utterance is usually followed by animated expressions of intense pain.

The word that serves all communications purposes with parents is "duh." This concisely brilliant word, as amazing in its versatility as it is in its thudding musicality, can answer any inquiry.

"Do you want some dinner?" DUH.

"Did you do your homework?" DUH.

"Did you know that tiger pits must be exactly twenty-one feet deep because tigers can jump out of twenty-foot pits and falls of twenty-two feet will kill the tiger?" DUH.

"Are you still going out with the red-headed girl?" DIE!!!

Of course, if you want to achieve total fluency in this language, you will have to practice the mannerisms that accompany the words. The curled lip is essential for "duh." Practice in front of a full-length mirror so you can work on your slouch at the same time.

I really like, ummm, shouldn't be like so, you know, critical. I was like, you know, the same way when, ummm, I was his age. It's like not his, you know, fault that his hormones are like interfering with ummm, like the brain connections between like his tongue and his, you know, brain and making his moustache turn black and all that stuff.

Despite it all, he's really a normal kid.

NOT!

And In This Corner

Generally, I've tried to remove topical references from this text, reasoning that the book is immortal and will be on the shelves at deer camps and lakeside cabins for the next century. References to the ephemera such as the politicians in this essay will be, at best, quaintly nostalgic. More likely, completely obscure. Quick, who was secretary of state under Warren Harding?

John Edwards visited New Hampshire recently in what reporters called "the kick-off of the 2008 Presidential election campaign." Of the many things I have been called in life, "astute political observer" is not one, so I won't comment on how idiotic this is. My idea of good political theater is when Gary Hart tells the throng of reporters, "If you think I'm fooling around, then catch me," and then the next day the front page shows Gary and his bimbo on the fantail of a yacht named "Monkey Business."

And for many small-minded Americans like me, the theater can be as important as who actually wins elections. My favorite politicians are the Jesse Venturas, Arnold Schwartzeneggers ("girly men"), Wilbur Mills, and the Bill Clintons of the world. What scriptwriter could come up with a line like "I did not have sexual relations with that woman?"

But John Edwards stumping in New Hampshire reminds me that another Presidential Sweepstakes will soon be upon us, so it's not too early to consider what will make the most entertaining match-up. On the Democratic side, there's no question that Hillary Clinton should be the nominee. This would carry the huge fringe benefit of bringing Bill Clinton back to the edge of the limelight. Even slowed by the passage of time and his quadruple by-pass, Bill is sure to have some entertaining moments in him. If nothing else, he can play his instrument. The man is a sax machine.

The Hill-Billy duo will be trumpeted by the Democratic party's new bantam rooster, Vermont's own Howard Dean. It took a while but Howard finally has a suitable stage for his best asset, his vocal chords.

How can the Dems lose? With 16 years combined White House experience, Hillary's standing with women, Bill's charisma, and Howard's ability to scream ... maybe the Republicans shouldn't even contest the race.

Not so fast. Before the Democrats chortle too loudly about dominating the voting blocs of women, liberals, Hispanics, and blacks ... what if the Republicans nominate Condoleeza Rice? Suddenly, women and blacks would have a more textured political landscape to consider. Condoleeza equals Hillary in political experience, and she currently stands on a highly visible, international stage. She gets a sound bite a night on the evening news. Plus, she's a better dresser than Hillary, who can't seem to break the black pants suit and pink blouse habit.

On the positive side of the ledger for the Democrats, Hillary has already completed her extreme makeover phase. This is when middle-aged women become blond-beyond-their-years and start to look disturbingly like a painted-up version of Katie Couric. (Have you noticed how Jane Pauley, Diane Sawyer, Paula Zahn, Meredith Viera, and even Barbara Wawa now look like the same person?)

But what about personal lives? I know nothing about Condoleeza's, but assume she is available. She will need an escort. And who better than an obscure humor columnist in central Vermont to do the matchmaking for the secretary of state. My criteria for a perfect mate for Condoleeza are clear—I'm looking for what will get the cheapest laugh from my audience. Remember, we're going for high theater, not responsible governance.

Considered and rejected as potential Rice-mates: Brad Pitt (too pretty and looking for a woman who wants to have his baby), Ellen Degeneres (too politically correct), Dr. Phil (married).

Hm-m-m-m. Is Karl Rove married? How about Michael Moore? I know! What if Bill Clinton, already known for extra-marital womanizing, took up with Condoleeza? That will level the playing field.

For running mate, the Democrats , again, have a clear advantage. The perfect vice presidential candidate will complement, not compete, with Hillary. This suggests young, male, multicultural, and Midwestern, someone with the perfect combination of a Democratic pedigree and a life story that will make a great made-for-TV movie.

Enter Barack Obama. "Hello, Central Casting? Could you send over a vice presidential candidate who's too good to be true. African American is fine. Harvard Law? Great. Make sure he's happily married and a churchgoer. He's spent his entire professional life championing the poor and underprivileged? Does he wear blue tights with a red cape and an 'S' on his chest?"

The poor Republicans. They are caught between a Ba-rack and a hard place. What can they possibly do to make a respectable showing for themselves? There's no two-term limit on serving as vice president, so Condoleeza could stay with Dick Cheney, who will secure the voting bloc of sour, old, white guys, and war mongers. Curt Schilling would be a good choice, but only if they let him keep his turn in the Red Sox pitching rotation.

But I am choosing, since this is my article, a relative unknown as Condoleeza's running mate, a dark horse from the Green Mountains of Vermont, someone who will earn the respect of men and women, alike, someone who understands the rigors of hard-scrabble life and why Americans are willing to fight, even to die, to protect it—Major General Martha Rainville of the Vermont National Guard.

Think it through. She's a woman, but a woman who has succeeded admirably in a man's world. She's a general and therefore a reliable leader and administrator. Standing by Condoleeza's side, she will earn the respect of curmudgeons, the military, the blue staters, and the red staters.

We have already had plenty of generals as president—from Washington to Eisenhower. Just over a year ago, even little-known Wesley Clark was running for president.

So from this point it is easy to connect the dots to the Rice/Rainville ticket. And how could anyone resist the slogan "Vote twice for Rainville and Rice." It's better than "Condoleeza, just wanna squeezah!"

Man Versus Mouse

*As it turns colder, we experience the annual infes-
tation of the vermin. The mice are allowed to live in
the house, but they are not allowed to be visible during
daylight hours. Oh, and they should clean after themselves, too.*

It's man versus mouse in this cold, hard world.

I don't think I had seen more than four or five live mice
before I moved to Vermont. I see that many in a night now. Up
here we live close to the land. Because mice live directly on the
land, we, therefore, live close to the mice.

An uneasy truce exists between rodents and other inhabitants
of old farmhouses. There is a sense that we both belong, that it is
as much their house as ours. After all, they have been here for
generations. Can we make that claim?

The mice have their own nooks and crannies in the plaster
walls. They can squeeze under the dishwasher where we see no
gap. They leave cigar-shaped calling cards on booby-trapped
kitchen counters after all-night eating orgies. They show us no
respect.

We counter with heavy artillery. When we hear scratching
inside the wall, we bang the plaster, as if they were rowdy upstairs
tenants, and yell "Hey! Shaddup!!" Mice have perfect comic timing. After we bang, they remain silent for just a second, just long
enough for us to say, "There, that took care of them." That's their
cue to recommence frenzied scratching, accompanied by staccato,
high-pitched mouse laughter—hee-hee-hee-hee. We endure, feeling very large—and very stupid.

The human arsenal also contains the Stealth Bomber, otherwise known as the house cat. This defensive weapon is intended
to scare mice into underground bunkers. Meanwhile, the cat costs
a small fortune in shots, gender-altering operations, food, kitty litter, and broken knickknacks.

There is also the domestic equivalent of the Patriot missile—
the spring-loaded, standard mousetrap. These masterworks of bal-
listic design provide family entertainment, much as did the

Evening News during the Gulf War.

You bait the trap (peanut butter works best), you set the trap (always against a wall—mice can't be caught in the open), and you place the trap (behind the toaster works great). It becomes a battle of wits and technology.

Our family once spent a week stalking, planning, and trying to outguess a foe so wily and brazen that we nicknamed him "Gorgon." The hunt was more fun than a week at Disneyland. Cheaper, too. Then, finally we caught him, all fuzzy, two ounces of him. There was a nanosecond of exhilaration, followed by an overwhelming sense of guilt as we saw his lifeless body grotesquely twisted by the trap. Neither the kids nor the wife would touch the thing, leaving me, the grim reaper, to bear the guilt.

"Murderer," hissed my youngest.

"Hey," I protested, "Man has Dominion. It says so in the Bible."

"The Bible also tells how David slew Goliath, so you better watch out," he countered. Gorgon's blood was on my hands.

But technology has now come to the rescue. I found an outfit in California (wouldn't you know?) that sells a "Humane Mouse Kit." The trap, oops, "Kit," is made by Earth Friendly Products. The package even contains a heartwarming dramatization of a conversation between child and parent:

"Mommy, must we kill the mouse?"

"No, Honey. The world is big enough for all of us."

Here's the idea. The mouse enters this ecologically green plastic box. He passes over a spring-loaded trap door. Boom! He's caught (this is the good part). You then transport the little fella a safe distance to a pleasant meadow. By lifting a false door, the mouse has direct contact with the cracker used to lure him. He commences eating until he discovers freedom on the other side of the cracker. New Age music swells up in the background, the mouse goes free to propagate and reinfest your house, and the kids have learned a sensitive lesson about the Meaning of Life.

And if it works on something as smart as a mouse, why couldn't the same technique be used on Saddam Hussein? We could airlift a giant green plastic box to the outskirts of Baghdad. Inside would be a humongous cracker, with peanut butter on it.

The only thing I can't figure out is where we would release him so that he wouldn't get back into the house.

Bringing Back the Beard

You can tell that deer-hunting season is getting close. Even if I don't own a gun, the animal in me is starting to emerge. I grow grizzled. I smell bad. I talk tough. "If y'r lookin' fer trubble ..."

One of the joys of having your own column is the occasional opportunity to abuse the power of the press. In my case I do this by subjecting the denizens of Beyonder to protracted descriptions of personal minutiae—in this case the hair that grows out of my face.

Tell the world—THE BEARD IS BACK! As to why this might be of interest to the general reader, I haven't the foggiest. But I can tell you why it is of great interest to me. Every time I pass a mirror, I see one of the ugliest people I've ever seen, and he looks a lot like me!

I am currently in the "serial killer" phase of my growth—mottled gray/black, prickly nubs sticking out of my head as if I had swallowed a porcupine. Let's put it this way, I'm your worst nightmare. My son calls it the wino look and suggested that I attend business meetings with a beer bottle hidden in a paper bag. He even offered to help me find a cardboard box to sleep in and a shopping cart for my belongings.

"Look, you insensitive little scuzzbucket," I retorted, careful not to slur my words, "When this thing grows out, I will look distinguished, even professorial. Maybe I'll start smoking a pipe, just because it looks good with my beard. This is just the stubble phase, a necessary evil. It's quite fashionable at the moment to have a stubble; they call it the 'Don Johnson Look'"

"I call it the 'Gabby Hayes Look,'" chimed in my wife, thinking herself quite the wit. She forgets that I'm the humor columnist in this family.

Everyone seems to be having fun at my expense these days. There is something about a grown man (supposedly a responsible member of society) looking like a bum that brings out the wit in everyone.

"Break your razor?" I've heard that one a few times. Very

funny. How about "Mid-life crisis time?" Chuckle, chuckle. There are some very funny people in Vermont. The most common comment I get, and by far my favorite, is "What are you doing? Growing a beard?"

Try to come up with a civil response. The best I can do is to borrow our teenager's response to any statement of fact, "No, duh!" Couldn't these people just point and laugh? And for all you people out there wondering, don't ask. The answer is, "Yes, it itches."

My wife has a point with her Gabby Hayes observation. The last beard I had was a nice chestnut brown. I shaved it off when it showed the occasional fleck of gray, because I didn't want a visual reminder that I was getting old. Now, I'm growing it back, in part, out of curiosity to see how the intervening half-decade has affected my hormones and pigment cells.

It is not pretty. OK, it's disgusting. The man in the mirror is an old guy! I mean really old. Really, really old.

But let's focus on the positive (like I'm always telling my children). Think of the money I am saving on razor blades and shaving cream. I can use that money for electrolysis. And think of the energy I am conserving from not using hot water to shave. That's the kind of simple thing that saves the planet, right?

And what if I get hungry? There are always a few scraps left somewhere in the beard to suck on. And where would all that hair be if it wasn't hanging off my face? That's right—inside my head. Think of the clutter with all that gray hair inside! No wonder I can't think clearly. Maybe this column will get funnier. Then more people will buy the paper to read my column, and the paper will pay me more money.

I'm rich, I'm rich! Well, almost. Won't be long now.

More reasons for a beard. Your pimples don't show. You can't have telltale lipstick marks on your cheek. Men think you're rugged, and women think you're sexy....

They do?

So what if there are a few thoughtless comments to be endured? I'm a Beyonder kinda guy. I can take it. Besides, I notice that most of the comments come from hairless guys whose faces are as smooth as babies' bottoms. Eat your hearts out.

So, I will keep this thing, at least through the winter. We Beyonder guys are supposed to be rugged and hairy, close to nature. I will get used to that homeless guy in the mirror.

Buck Fever

*All year long I am a model of political correctitude
just so that for a few weeks in the fall I can give full
expression to my slovenly male essence. Excuse me,
but I've just got to kill something.*

I apologize in advance for inflicting this on you. I try to focus
on subjects of unique interest to denizens of the north, weighty
subjects like cluster flies, swimming holes, and demolition derbies.
But I have been pushed over the brink by being told I still "don't
get it." It's a familiar conversation stopper to tell the male of the
species that he is crude, insensitive, exploitive, moronic, adolescent, unthinking, hypocritical, and criminally insane and that the
cause of this behavior is inexpressible.

I used to take offense, but now I find I can explain my clue-
lessness with two words:

Buck fever.

I once asked someone who shall remain nameless (because
he's a respected community member who would prefer not being
dragged into the mire of a war between the sexes), why he was so
passionate about turkey hunting. This man, this anonymous man
who is a professional educator, a native Vermonter, a sensitive
Beyonder kinda guy, answered by saying, "It's like having Buck
Fever, but for hours, not seconds."

I asked him to describe Buck Fever. "It's like being in love,"
he answered without hesitation. I'm not a hunter, but I instantly
understood.

The reader might need to make a conceptual leap. You might
imagine a young man "in love" as dapperly dressed, the bouquet
of flowers held behind his back, as he stands at the front door
awaiting the sight of his sweetie. She's wearing a white dress, and
of course, they are going to live happily ever after.

Now this other guy, the anonymous one, who's an educator
(he even won an award as educator of the year not long ago), a
native Vermonter, has an image of being in love that involves a
three-day stubble, a wool shirt that has not been washed in almost
twelve years, baked beans heated up in the can over a camp stove,
and remaining motionless for hours at a time making mating nois-

es like a turkey, uh, where was I? His definition of being in love is totally out to lunch, and yet, I, by all acknowledgment a sensitive, non-hunting type of guy, understood him perfectly.

Herein lies the crux of the problem. "Not getting it" implies that men are Neanderthals, incapable of changing the imprint of thousands of generations. You're right. The spears may be out of our hands, but we still act like tribal animals trying to corral wooly mammoths over cliffs. But we act like we do because we don't know any better. But the truth is, we're diseased—unfortunate victims of Buck Fever.

Buck Fever is not limited to a few isolated shacks in rural Vermont, but affects the entire species. This includes unshaven, beer-swilling, gun-toting yahoos, and clean-shaven, natty, public officials, most of them apparently graduates of (lower your voice and put on the echo chamber) The Yale Law School. How can we think clearly when our brains are addled?

And why would we elect, of our own free will, fever-afflicted men to public office? It mystifies me why anyone would vote for a man for anything beyond dogcatcher, one of the few public offices where Buck Fever is an asset.

Don't you see? Men are animals—poor, dumb beasts acting consistently with fifty million years of genetic programming. You can dress us in coats and ties, but we've still got Buck Fever. And any doctor will tell you (particularly if he hunts), Buck Fever impairs judgment.

The real question is, can we men be held responsible for our behavior, or should we just be judged criminally insane? And what should be the penalty? You might try swatting us with a rolled-up newspaper, but I'm afraid we will still act like dogs.

I say lock us up (preferably in isolated, rustic structures), and throw away the keys (and our razors while you're at it). Just make sure we have lots of baked beans, and society will finally be rid of the menace of the male of the species. As with all essays from Beyonder, this one is using silliness and sarcasm to obscure its piercing social commentary. Turkey and deer may be defenseless, but most men just enjoy romping around the woods (smelling bad) trying to shoot one. Despite the slaughterous instincts of the hunters, the populations of turkeys and deer are healthier than ever.

Meanwhile, it's open season on males. I think that the people who think we "don't get it" should at least pay a license fee and take some responsibility for managing the herd.

The Local News

At deer camp there is always a stack of newspapers from a few years ago. Who needs new ones; there's just as much good reading in going through the papers of yesteryear. I steal some of my best material from the local news.

Occasionally, the creative well runs dry, leaving me with a blank sheet of paper and a deadline. For inspiration I turn to an unfailing fountain of stimulation, the local newspaper.

Some nameless columnists exist by pilfering material from stories readers send about exploding cows and monkeys who can sing "The Star Spangled Banner."

I cannot, however, because my readers are different. They're Vermonters, and Vermonters don't laugh...well, not out loud. Their idea of a good yuk is seeing a Flatlander's BMW burrowed in a ditch (ok, I admit, it's funny), but in general this is not a funny place. And Vermonters work hard enough at their own jobs that they don't think they need to help me by sending funny news clips.

They can't stop me from reading the local paper, though. Here's a sprinkling of what is passing for hard news in Beyonder:

Hm-m-m-m. Here's a little piece under the headline "Tomato Surprises Local Woman." Seems that local resident Vendla Cushman (a wonderful name—I'll have to steal that for my next book) cut into a tomato and found what appeared to be a "family of worms waving their tails." In reality she had discovered a rare miniature audition for the spokesmodel segment of Star Search. Had she used a microscope, she might have discovered a little bitty Ed McMahon.

The local news is always laden with little pearls, especially if you get into the nitty gritty of visiting relatives. It was here that I learned about the folks from Massachusetts who had to take their son to the emergency room because he stuck a bean up his nose. The reporting was sketchy so I never found out whether it was a string bean, lima bean, or baked bean, but I did conclude they sure eat funny down there!

I always check out the weddings, in case someone has done something in shockingly bad taste. "The bride wore a lavender bowling shirt and carried a bouquet of nondescript shrubbery. The cake, a Twinkie the size of a large watermelon, weighed almost 50 pounds and was put on display afterwards in Floral Hall at the Tunbridge World's Fair."

But I'm being silly. Back to the hard news stories: "Pig Found Swimming in Lake Fairlee." No, this wasn't about the bride in the bowling shirt. This was about a 40-pound piglet from Post Mills that managed to elude the game warden and a vigilante posse from Thetford for the better part of two days. Ya gotta love a little porker with that kind of spunk.

An item out of Vershire a while back was carried in the local rag under the headline "Landowner Threatens Town With Blacks." The gist of the story is that a dispute about a stone wall became so heated that the owner of the wall threatened to donate his land to the NAACP for use as a summer camp. This was a classic Beyonder fracas, with a matter of small significance being exaggerated onto a larger stage. (And, in this case, getting ugly in the process. Moving right along)

How about, "He-Man Woman Haters Club disbands?" This was from the little town of Burlington where some love-scarred UVM students brought the wrath of the entire student body, the administration, and the American Civil Liberties Union down upon their pointy little heads by declaring their independence from the opposite sex. It does not matter that activities like this form the dramatic nexus of most Shakespearean plays; you don't do this in the enlightened twentieth century where man and woman exist equal and entwined, like vanilla and chocolate cree-mee swirl.

That's what I like about the local news. It makes you think. What started out as a goofball prank by some bozos at the pinna-cle of bozodom ends up as a lesson in the finer points of the First Amendment.

Then, there was the case of Ken Royer, reported in the Barton Chronicle in the article "Royer Sentenced for Jacking Fake Deer."

This is a complex case with overtones of Peewee Herman.

Mr. Royer was nabbed for plugging a fake deer, set out by the game warden. He then led enforcement officials on a merry chase that ended when his car swerved off the road. Knowing that he was caught, Mr. Royer went over to the game warden and shook his hand, congratulating him for catching red-handed such a clever deer jacker as himself. Then, in a speech that seems crafted by a member of the screenwriter's guild, he said, "My father was a deer jacker, I jack deer, and my boy will probably jack deer. It's in my blood. I just cannot help it. Jacking deer is in my blood."

With the right press agent, I think Mr. Royer could become a surprise celebrity guest on the MTV award show.

Makes you think, doesn't it?

Listen, all ye faithful out there in Beyonder. You don't have to send me clippings. My mother does that, and has since I went off to college. Just keep doing what you're doing, and don't forget to call your local reporter.

The Airlines Revenge Kit

Thanksgiving arrives and we become crazed to connect with family. We don't go "over the river and through the woods," however. We go "over the by-pass and into the parking garage, then onto the shuttle, then through the metal detector, then onto the jammed plane, then out to the tarmac, then sit on the tarmac, then back to the terminal ..."

'Tis almost the season to be jolly, but not if your loved ones are coming by plane. Holiday travel, especially via air, is (how can I put this delicately?) a pain in the butt.

I was at O'Hare Airport, the navel of civilization—or do I have it 180 degrees off?—trying to return to Burlington International in time for Thanksgiving. (And, why do they call it "Burlington International" when no international flights originate or terminate there?)

In return for safe transport, I paid the airline several hundred dollars along with a fuel surcharge, even though most others on the flight were traveling free, thanks to complicated mileage plans that everyone but me understands.

I'm reasonable. I understand that airlines, especially since deregulation, are so complex that they charge an individual according to what the reservation clerk thinks of your suit. Two people eating the same swillacious food, paying vastly different fares. What's unfair about that?

So there I am, being reasonable, wanting to get home, minding my own business, wondering why airline terminals are the modern-day equivalent of Greek temples, when we are informed that our flight is delayed for a half hour. We can live with this. Why, we wonder innocently, is the flight delayed?

"You've got nerve," says the person at the ticket counter, his face a mask of disdain. "Don't you know we're trying to run an airline here? We've got to get the planes from here to there, then back again, blah, blah, blah. You're lucky we let you come along for the ride."

Suitably chastened, we apologize. What business is it of ours that the flight is delayed?

We are then strip searched for our own protection, and, an hour later, loaded onto a plane, where we wait another hour. By now everyone's intelligence has been totally insulted. The weather is fine, air traffic is moving smoothly, there is nothing wrong with the goddamn plane, and the last flight for Burlington on a competitive airline has just left.

"Let's turn into an unruly mob," I suggest to the lady on my right. "OK," she responds, "By the way, you might be interested in knowing that it is costing me two hundred dollars less than it is costing you to be subject to this abuse."

Along with six or seven fellow berserk passengers we corner our helpful air host who, believing our threats of dismemberment, confesses that the real cause for lateness is that the flight time to Burlington will take the pilots over the twelve-hours-per-week limit that their union allows them to fly, and that the airline has loaded us onto a crowded, polluted plane to keep us from switching to alternative carriers.

The mob turns ugly, like a scene from the first days of the French Revolution. We ransack O'Hare, binding airline employees with baggage tape, emptying cash registers and distributing the money to the zealots carrying placards that claim the Kennedy assassination was masterminded by Jane Fonda. Not really. (Never take me seriously.)

But I did, while waiting on the O'Hare tarmac, come up with a million-dollar idea—the Airlines Revenge Kit! What a perfect Christmas present. Not a frequent flyer in America would be without one. (And at $19.95, I hasten to add, it will not be long until I am a very rich man.) Here is what you get for a double sawbuck:

1. A button saying, "I know it's not your fault, but I'm going to abuse you anyway." This would enable you to be petty and obnoxious toward a stewardess, ticket clerk, or even a baggage handler without guilt. You've already apologized in advance.

2. A bumper sticker saying, "At Least In My Car I Get Treated Like A Human being."

3. A booklet containing the home address for every executive in the airlines business along with a list of suggested pranks (soap on the windows, toilet paper in the trees—immature, but totally, satisfying, adolescent fare).

4. A T-Shirt reading, "I Love Flying (P.S. I Also Like Burning Myself With Cigarettes)."

5. A plastic grenade, for when you want to take matters into your own hands.

You get the point. Let's hope the airlines do, too, and get our loved ones here in time for the holidays.

Pieces of Wood

West Brookfield was the real-life model for the Upper Granville of Beyonder.

West Brookfield is the classic Vermont hamlet—dirt crossroads, a church, a one-room schoolhouse, and a half dozen farmhouses. Stella Maloney, who taught at the schoolhouse until it closed in 1968, lives in one of the homes. The Wakefield family who has operated Meadowbrook Farm since 1852 owns several others. The farming success of the Wakefields has kept the town looking much as it did fifty years ago, a hundred years ago, and a hundred and fifty years ago. As one after another of the hillside farms "gave up," Meadowbrook Farm expanded to fill.

Another village home, a modest cape built around the time the Wakefields started farming, was for sale when we moved to Vermont in 1979. There is an illustration of the house on the cover of West Brookfield and Thereabouts, a town history written by Alice Webster Wakefield. The image, taken from an advent calendar made by a village resident, portrays a Vermont of our mind's eye, without junk cars, mud, and houses wrapped in plastic. In the foreground is a house—our house!—that spills its radiant light out onto the immaculate snow. Presiding over all, majestic even without summer plumage, is a towering sugar maple whose branches spread a protective canopy over house and town. Inside the book are a half dozen other photos of the house and tree. The constant is that the horizon, even a hundred years ago, is dominated by the massive maple in our front yard.

We were charmed by the tree, the house, and the village of West Brookfield. We proudly made it our home. The tree even had a thick first limb that would be perfect for the tire swing that our sons, one just born, one not yet contemplated, would forever associate with their childhood.

Not long after moving in we were approached by a neighbor, Gregory Schipa, founder of Weather Hill Company, a firm that specializes in historic preservation and restoration. Schipa seemed determined to keep West Brookfield in the 1850s.

"Those trees, especially the maples, are getting on. You should think about replacing them." Part of me thanked him for his advice, but another part—the speaking part—said, "Those trees are good for another fifty years."

"I know," Schipa replied, "That's why you should be thinking now about replacing them."

Schipa proved a man of his convictions, and helped me plant a line of maples over the next two years. The saplings looked slightly ridiculous dwarfed by the behemoth, but he assured me I would thank him some day. For the next few years the saplings grew much as did our young family. We were shaded by the big trees in the summer as we watched the kids take countless rides on their tire swing. In the autumn I raked leaves into playful piles. The favorite game was "Leafman," in which one person buries another in leaves, then lures an unsuspecting third person to the pile. Upon the pronouncement of "Leafman" the pile stirs and a roaring, snarling leaf monster emerges. Works every time.

After the leaves were pulverized by the glee of kid power, they became winter mulch for the perennials, as purposeful on the ground at thirty below as they had been on the branches providing summer shade. The first official act of spring was removing the leaves to give the crocuses a better look at the sun. Afterwards we took the leaves to the vegetable garden, tilling their remaining organic matter into the rocky soil.

Just as Gregory Schipa had been our partner in planting young trees, Bruce Cameron became our partner in keeping the maturing trees healthy. (Our signature maple was flanked by a lanky Dutch elm and a second maple that would have been impressive anywhere else but alongside its larger cousin.) Cameron, Central Vermont's resident tree expert, is an ex-Shakespearean actor with a soft voice that still manages to articulate each syllable so that you can hear clearly from the cheap seats. Cameron explained to us about the lifecycle of maples, how they start breaking apart in chunks when they reach a certain age. How they die from the center out. And ours had reached that age, give or take a few decades. Through proper maintenance and strategic cabling, the maples should last our lifetimes, said Cameron. The Dutch elm, however, even though it looked healthy, was living on borrowed time.

Mere months later it was gone, a victim of the disease that bears its name. I spent a frustrating summer trying to split elm with my maul, using the stump as my base. When I was done dealing with the sinewy wood, I kept right on banging on the stump to reduce it to ground level. For all the aggravation it caused in splitting, the elm kept us warm that winter.

The next summer disaster struck the lesser of our maples. I got the call at work, one of those traumatic moments frozen in time. At least it hadn't fallen on the house. I had another stump to keep me busy for the summer. And another warm home that winter. The saplings now had six or seven years' growth and were sturdy young trees whose vitality took some of the sting away from our loss. Schipa had been right, and if I didn't thank him properly then, I do now.

With two of the three down, we redoubled our efforts to keep the remaining maple standing. Cameron ordered specific care and maintenance, which included me climbing into the tree's central cavity and removing all accumulated soft material with a post-hole digger. This unique chore yielded exquisite compost for the garden, as well as an assortment of golf balls, Star Wars figures, MatchBox cars, Whiffle Balls, and Transformers. This unexpected "trip to the toy store" so delighted my two sons that they wanted me to perform this maintenance on a weekly basis.

The maple held up well for the next dozen years. A chunk or two fell off, but the basic canopy remained intact. The trees I had planted with Greg Schipa were now in an adolescent growth spurt, just like my boys. Each year Bruce Cameron would stop by, tighten the cables, and give us a progress report. He's the kind of guy who will do this whether you ask him or not and whether you pay him or not. With Bruce, the tree comes first. The maple, he reported, was holding it's own.

But meanwhile, life around the maple changed. Flash-forward what seems like an instant but was in reality a decade. The family has spent a "year abroad" in California and returned. They've moved in town to be nearer the school and all things teen-aged. The boys are poised on the brink of the nest. Strangers pay rent to live in the house and to enjoy the maple's shade.

Eventually the strain of being absentee landlords took its toll,

and we put the house up for sale. Prospective buyers were interviewed as much for their willingness to keep alive ancient maples
as for their ability to meet the asking price. Eventually, a deal was
struck. The new owners, a young couple from California, brought
new energy and vitality to the homestead, as well as a reverence
for the intact Vermontness of West Brookfield. They put a new tin
roof on the house. Soon a baby was on the way, and within a year
the big tree was down, practicality overruling sentiment.

I stumbled, unprepared, upon the scene with my younger son,
now a young man. We turned the corner into the village to see a
massive stump surrounded by dismembered eighteen-inch sections. It was overwhelmingly sad. The new owners were in the
front yard. They, too, are saddened by the loss, but felt they had
no choice, citing Bruce Cameron, the patron saint of venerable
trees, as advising them that it was time to put it down. My son
asks if they found any toys in the cavity. Turns out, they did.

(Months later, I see Bruce at the local bank, and he mumbles
condolences about the tree, as if he had somehow failed. Nothing
could be further from the truth. I'm glad he was the one to bring
it down. I'm sure he did it with love.)

A hidden blessing is the sudden prominence of the line of
sturdy, young maples, now some twenty-five feet tall and producing their own sap, shade, and foliage. We request, and are given,
some lengths of the fallen maple.

My wife bursts into tears at the news. It is months before she
is able to go back to West Brookfield. I harbor thoughts, maybe
delusions, that I am going to transform the chunks of maple into
hand-sculpted keepsakes of our years beneath her canopy. I tell
the family that this will be my Christmas gift for the next year. I
contact a friend who had a similarly sentimental maple taken
down in her front yard. She contracted with a local artisan to
work with her downed wood. After many hours struggling with
old, punky wood he produced a disappointingly small number of
artifacts for a disappointingly high price. I can tell from her
cocked eyebrow that I am setting myself up for the same fall.

But my plan is different. I will work the wood myself, freeing
bowls and spoons and toys and tops and trinkets from the heavy
blocks. I have visions of myself, Gepetto-like, working by firelight.

I see my sons, unwrapping their Christmas packages, and the look of awe as they recognize the simple treasures that have been created by my hours of loving labor.

By the following December, with Christmas season in full swing, my forward progress consists of buying a book on wood-working and staring forlornly at maple chunks that look much as they did when thrown into the back of my pick-up. It has taken a year, but I now recognize that I lack the skill, tools, knowledge, time, and will for this plan. Having created the expectation of Christmas gifts from the maple, I resort to Plan B. I go to the local dollar store and find some wooden spoons stamped "Spain." I leave on the 99-cent price tags, wrap them in dollar-store paper, and write a sentimental story about the mighty maple. On Christmas Eve the family convenes over coffee—we're all adults now—and I make the presentation. There's a moment of silence between reading the story and unwrapping the presents. The silence is repeated as they see the simple spoons, read the price tag, and see "Spain" stamped on the back.

One son says, "This is so lame."

The other says "This is so you."

Then we laugh. Together. The maple has delighted us once again.

The story has an epilogue, and a new hero. Later that same day I am at a seasonal craft show staged for the holidays at Chandler Gallery in Randolph. A handsome wooden pen catches my eye, and the signage tells me it comes from Fat Rooster Farm in nearby Royalton. I know the farm as a local CSA (Community Supported Agriculture). As have many of today's practitioners of sustainable farming, the folks of Fat Rooster have broadened their definition of "farming" by offering diversity in an increasingly commodified world. Although only six years into its existence, Fat Rooster has already been immortalized in a handsome coffee-table book Harvest: A Year in the Life of an Organic Farm (The Lyons Press, 2004).

A few days later my mind links these pieces of wood, now resting atop my stacked woodpile, with the pens. Then, things happen fast. I wonder if Fat Rooster has a website? Click. Do they say anything about their wooden pens? Click, click. Hm-m-m. They will work with your wood or theirs. Light bulb. Click, click.

Contact us. Click, tap, tap, tap, click.

That evening there is a return email in my inbox from Kyle Jones of Fat Rooster Farm. The next day I deliver five lengths of maple, formerly of West Brookfield, to Fat Rooster Farm. Two friendly dogs (one with one blue and one brown eye) and a pair of intimidating "watch" geese herald my arrival. I am about to leave when Kyle emerges from the barn and calls after us. Along with Gregory Schipa and Bruce Cameron, Kyle becomes the third hero of this story.

Kyle tours us through his shop, examines the pieces of wood, and tells us how he happens to be turning out hardwood pens from a remote vantage overlooking the second branch of the White River. An ecologist by profession, he works two days a week with the National Park Service in Woodstock. The rest of the time he tries to make ends meet at Fat Rooster Farm. He is a native of Ohio who married a Vermonter. He's not a woodworker by trade, but he has developed a woodworking sideline as a way to generate some revenue during the cold weather. He's an easy guy to like.

He walks us through the process. The wood is chain sawed into rectangular slabs measuring roughly six inches thick. On a band saw in the shop the wood is sliced again and again into sticks ¾" x ¾" [dimensions missing]. The wood is dried for about a year before being worked. Pieces are then cut to length, drilled, and the internal fixtures glued in place. He then takes upwards of an hour turning each pen on a lathe, feeling the grain, giving each a unique look and curve, and applying the finish. If all goes well, pens can be ready for Christmas.

He looks at my wood, says it appears to be good, but he won't know for certain until he looks inside, i.e. rough cuts it with a chain saw. The next day I receive an email titled "Grand Opening" that says "I was very impressed by the wood in your logs. Lots of color, a little spalting and crotch grain. I reply back that I hope "spalting" and "crotch grain" are good, and he responds "Trust me, they are." So I am trusting Kyle to take this special wood and to give new life as pens, and maybe even bowls. In the process he can redeem me for trying to preserve with a lame joke the memory of a tree that gave us buds in the spring, shade in the summer, piles of joyful leaves in the fall.

Next Christmas Eve we'll convene over coffee. I will let them unwrap their pens, and then tell them that these came from our majestic sugar maple in West Brookfield. Use the pens, I will say, to write poems, love letters, or to sign autographs. They will look for price tags or telltale stamps of origin, but won't find them. Not this time.

My Career in Show Biz *(Hi, Jim!)*

Every so often life imitates art in a delightful way that is impossible to anticipate.

I watch the evening news, not for the latest on world events, but for the pharmaceutical commercials. Specifically, I look for commercials about that little purple pill called Nexium. When it comes on, I wave at the television and say, "Hi, Jim!"

The Nexium ad is the one where they keep referring to "that little purple pill" while they show a humongous purple cylinder (must be a propane tank) that could choke a sperm whale. I can't tell you what "Nexium" means, what it does, who makes it, or what scourge it cures. I do know that the little purple pills make you "better." I know this because the spokesperson, right at the end, leaning on the purple propane tank, looks directly into the camera and says, "And better is better!"

The spokesperson for Nexium is James Naughton ("Jim" to me, "James" to the rest of you), and he's a great actor. You can tell the by the way he makes eye contact with the camera, furrows his brow in a way that exudes credibility, and says "And better is better!" without cracking up. Not even a little smirk. That, Dear Reader, is the mark of a great one.

Jim and I started our show biz careers together back in college. I was the head of a small undergraduate theater group. Jim was a graduate student in the drama school. Because there was an overall shortage of acting and directing venues, drama school students were desperate to pad their resumes with anything that smacked of experience. This actually put me in a position of some power. Here's how powerful I was: I once turned down Henry Winkler, who went on to become a household word as Fonzie from Happy Days, for a directing position. Instead, I hired a guy named, to protect the innocent let's call him Zocorâ, who proved so inept that to do something idiotic in our theater group became known as "to do a Zocorâ."

Back to Jim. I had the good sense to cast him in a lead role in a play that became a big hit on campus. He had it all—good looks, could sing and dance, fun to be around, always came prepared. You could tell he was headed for great things. Graduation came and went, and we went our separate ways—Jim to Broadway and Hollywood and me to Haverhill, Massachusetts, where I took a job selling ads for a second-rate boating magazine.

The rest is history.

Jim comes into my living room every few years in a new and unexpected way. He's almost always a good guy, never a thug. Sometimes he's a guest star on a series. He drew rave notices on Broadway for Chicago. He's had several TV series of his own, none of them very memorable. For a while he was Ally McBeal's father. He's done a bunch of commercials. I think he was one of the guys who said "I'm not a doctor, but I play one on TV." Jim exudes credibility.

His name is not a household word, but I bet you would recognize his face. He does some cool things on the Nexium commercial. In addition to furrowing his brow, at one point he materializes out of thin air. Try doing that at home. For a few seconds he just stands, looking bemused (but credibly bemused) while his voice-over continues. His lips don't even move. You don't often see such dazzling special effects in a drug commercial.

I'm sure that Jim is constantly wondering what has happened in my life. Our paths haven't crossed, but they almost did … once. This was a dozen or so years ago. Jim was on some TV show or commercial that brought him into our living room with some frequency. At each appearance I would start the obligatory shouting "Wife! Kids! Hurry!"

Thinking an emergency, at least a heart attack, was in progress, they would come scrambling in, sometimes in time to actually see Jim on screen. I would then treat (subject?) them to the story of how Jim and I started in show biz together. Usually the story provoked only yawns and rolled eyebrows, but once my youngest son said "Oh yeah? Well, why doesn't he have any gray hair?"

Hm-m-m. He raised a good point. While I had gone the way of all flesh, Jim looked just as he had when I knew him in college. I began not to like Jim. I began to resent Jim. I began to hate Jim's guts. Now, when he appeared on screen, and one of the kids said, "Hey, isn't that your friend?" I would just mumble and turn away.

As fate would have it, we made a trip a few months later that took us through Williamstown, Massachusetts. We passed by their summer theater and I noticed "James Naughton" on the marquee. Minutes later we were driving through Williamstown's downtown, and one of the kids said:

"Hey, isn't that your friend?"

It was Jim. There was no mistaking that erect posture, those fine features, the strong chin, and that thick shock of completely gray hair! Instantly, Jim was my friend again. I considered making a u-turn and stalking him, but decided not to inflict myself. Just as well, too. Of the various outcomes that could have transpired in a face-to-face meeting, most of them would have been deflating, especially in front of my kids. Stephen who? This way we could just move on with our travels, with me blustering that if I dyed my hair, I would look like I was still in college, too.

So, Jim, if you're out there and wondering what happened to me, I'm ok. I'm living here in Beyonder, writing my articles and stoking the woodstove. So far, knock on wood, I don't need those little purple pills, but you keep right on taking them. "And better is better," dontchuno? I hope they paid you a small fortune to recite that line. Good to see ya.

(Postscript: On Christmas night I get a call from backstage at the Brooks-Atkinson Theater in New York City where they are preparing to go on with the show "Democracy." The voice is deep, rich, and familiar. It's Jim! Someone sent him the article. Hope he doesn't sue.)

Last Flight

My friend Don Lariviere of Northfield Falls was killed in a car crash several years ago. He was a pilot with "the right stuff." He was 45 years old.

I had not seen Don for several years, but he led one of the most "beyondered" lives of anyone I have ever known.

"Beyondered" describes a unique style of contemporary rural life. Rather than defining it for you, I will just tell you about Don.

Don was a pilot, and in my judgment a damn good one. In the early eighties the two of us logged tens of thousands of miles in a corporate jet as we crisscrossed the United States and Canada looking for people to sell our wood stoves. Within our company his name became synonymous with air travel to the extent that we referred to the company plane as "Air Don."

We always flew single pilot, so I would sit in the co-pilot's seat, bewildered by dials and the right stuff dialogue overheard through the headsets. The plane was a mystery to me, and I was glad to leave its intricacies to Don. That suited him, because if there was anything he hated it was an overly inquisitive passenger who disrupted his concentration.

You cannot sit with someone in a small metal tube, hurtling through the heavens at 22,000 feet on a coal-black night with the Northern Lights on your left and Wilkes-Barre, Pennsylvania, on your right, without baring some soul.

Don's soul was on his farm. He lived on a farm with his wife Cassy and beloved Belgian workhorses. His life was entirely "Off the Grid," the power grid, that is. There was no indoor toilet, and the indoor plumbing was dependent on a gravity-fed spring that was prone to going "GLU-R-R-P-P-P" on frigid nights, leaving them without water until the next thaw.

Each morning he tended the animals, shaved without hot water (no wonder he preferred a beard), walked almost a mile to the paved road, drove to the airport, and hopped in the jet. A typical day for us might involve stops in Connecticut, New Jersey, and Pennsylvania, then home for dinner. He always tried to buzz the Northfield farm before landing so that Cassy would know

73

when to expect him. From the high-tech, high-expense world of corporate travel he returned home to a silent trek up an unplowable drive and a subsistence lifestyle forgotten by most Vermonters since the turn of the century.

The same guy who thought nothing of flipping out the Gold American Express to pay for a $650 fill-up of jet fuel, wore a pilot's uniform of down vest, flannel shirt, jeans, and Sorels.

Don talked a lot about his horses, and about poultry. He majored in poultry sciences in college and filled me with more than I ever cared to know about the nuances of exotic fowl. He was as meticulous about his poultry house as he was about his aircraft, which testifies only to the immaculate living conditions of his chickens.

We had our share of adventures, too. There was a cargo door that opened during flight over Williamsburg, Virginia, and an autopilot that put us into a nosedive over Cleveland, and ice on the wings while crossing over the Continental Divide.

Whenever the unexpected happened Don's voice would become calm and modulated, explaining each emergency procedure in detail, knowing that the unknown is what causes fear. I never considered that anything bad could ever happen to anyone on Air Don.

The last time I saw Don was at a pre-Christmas party. A small crowd was gathered around, as people do with pilots, pumping him for stories of aviation derring-do.

"Hey Don," said one of the partygoers, "What's the closest you ever came to buying the farm? Was there ever a time when you thought, 'I'm just not going to walk away from this one?"

"Just once," he said in a soft voice that everyone strained slightly to hear. "We were climbing to 20,000 feet over the Continental Divide when we began accumulating ice on the wings."

"But, but, I was on that flight," I sputtered. "I never, you never...."

He just laughed. You can always laugh when you walk away.

On Friday, April 12, the pilot who mastered complex jets and huge Belgian workhorses was killed when the car in which he was a passenger went off the road. He wasn't even wearing a seatbelt. Air Don will fly no more, but there won't be a time when I hear the drone of an airplane over Beyonder and don't think of him.

Lamson's Bus

*The yellow school bus is as much a part of the
rural landscape as the red barn or the hay silo.
Sometimes we forget about the precious cargo.*

I've never met Lamson. I don't even know his first name (or is
"Lamson" his first name?), but for the past eight years I have
entrusted him, twice a day, with the safety of my children. Lamson
is the bus driver who has the route that extends to the far reaches
of our hamlet. Although less than ten miles between here and the
school, it is a forty-five minute bus route that takes place almost
entirely on unpaved, hilly back roads. The route passes dairy
farms, rushing brooks, sugar bushes—the best of Beyonder. But to
experience it, one must brave the nether side of Vermont's scenic
roads—mud, washboard, and ice.

Lamson spends little time sightseeing. The challenge of
maneuvering a yellow steel box jammed with kids from five to
thirteen does not permit the luxury of leaf peeping. Although I've
never met him, he's like one of the family. He takes care of nose-
bleeds and other unexpected emergencies. The children tease
him, and he gives it right back. At Christmas he provides candy,
and on the last day of school, sodas.

I hear about it at the dinner table. It is the highest form of
compliment when I say that Lamson is a Beyonder kind of guy.

Last year, on the Friday just before Christmas, a drizzle, so
fine as to be almost imperceptible, began around noon. I realized
there was a problem when I fishtailed on the Interstate. It was one
of those situations that the veteran Beyonderite recognizes as
Trouble—moisture meets frigid pavement, resulting in ice.
Conditions get even worse on the back roads.

The mist became a light rain. In offices around the state, holiday revelry was curtailed in favor of driving home while there was
still daylight. Even with last-minute shopping and errands, these
were conditions to grind Vermont to a standstill, with residents
content to make it to the comfort of the hearth, and no further.

The real extent of this particular Trouble became evident when I saw seven cars awaiting the sand truck at the bottom of the hill leading to Upper Granville.

"The hill's an ice ball," said one of the stranded seven, a native Beyonder, and no foreigner to Trouble.

"Any word on the school bus?"

"It's late, but that's all I know."

The school bus is late. These four words bring many elements of life in Vermont into sharper focus. This is a world where the elements must not be taken for granted. A small slip, an error in timing, an unseeable patch of ice, and our entire lives can instantly be inverted in a ditch.

Because I am not too bright (and because I felt emboldened by my four-wheel-drive vehicle), I charged up the hill, taking with me two neighbors who balanced my chances of making it positively against the time it would take for the sand truck to reach our neck of the woods. Piece of cake (well, maybe not for the ordinary guy, but for someone with my driving abilities, no problem, ma'am).

There was tension apparent in the village, settling in as visibly as the fog and the darkness. The reports were grim. Yes, the bus was stuck, caught between two hills too steep and icy to climb. The sand trucks (both of them) were shuttling back and forth to help, but the rate of icing was too great for them to keep up.

Maybe we should have voted for that third truck at town meeting. It had not seemed necessary at the time, but the kids— our children—had not been stuck in the cold, dark, middle of nowhere then, with no one to comfort them and keep them safe.

Except Lamson. That's when we all began appreciating the guy. We gathered in the kitchen, warmed by the stove and cups of coffee, and the mood lightened as the ice worsened. "Poor kids," we thought, then, upon reflection, "Poor Lamson!"

The phone network kept us informed. After the obligatory Christmas parties at school, the kids had been put on the bus early, where Lamson provided them with even more candy. Now the guy was captive in his steel box with forty-five sugar-juiced, hyper-banshees looking forward to Santa. The man was probably tied to his seat, the wheel commandeered by a ten year old.

It was pitch black, nearly three hours late, when we heard the sand truck grinding up the hill. The school bus was inches behind. The kids poured out, bubbling tales of adventure, none the worse except for one common woe-——everyone had to pee. As the children ran to bathrooms, Lamson barely had time for a wave, let alone the formal acceptance of accolades. Like another man who delivers precious gifts at Christmas, he had more promises to keep. All was well once again in the land of Beyonder, and I swear, as Lamson and his yellow sleigh clattered down the hill, the chains on his tires sounded like jingle bells.

Part III–The Endless

It sneaks up on you. You're still in the post-holiday funk, wondering how you are going to lose that extra weight when it's too frigid outside to exercise. Spring, even Mud Season, seems too far away to even contemplate. Maybe you should have taken that offer that came in unsolicited over the fax machine promising four days and three nights in Disney World, if you don't mind having the salesmen for the timeshare holding onto your leg the entire time.

This is a good time for contemplating, and thinking big thoughts, and being silly. Anything to laugh, anything to pass the time.

You get out of work—another bad day—and, it's not as dark. You can actually see a sliver of sky and it's almost five o'clock. The days, imperceptibly, have gotten a little longer. It's Glimmer Day. You can't see the end of the rainbow, but you can see the tip.

You limp to Ground Hog Day, hardly a Vermont holiday, but it should be. How we got aced out by Punxatawney Phil is beyond me. It should have been Hardwick Harry. Farmer's Night at the State House is a lovely affair when a special cultural performance is put on for the farmers before they get busy again. It's open to all Vermonters, and it's free. It makes it clear why Vermont is The Chosen State.

Sap could start running any day now.

Town Meeting, sometimes called, "Blame the Newcomer Day," is the first Tuesday in March. It's a religious experience for some. Personally, I like getting the town report so I can see who's delinquent in their taxes.

Thawed Thoughts

There are days when the thought of global warming is as comforting as the first bite of Thanksgiving dinner.

The call came at 7:30 a.m., the earliest polite time to call in Beyonder, even if you know people are up. It had the sound of trouble. The thermometer had dipped to forty below the night before, the temperature at which pipes freeze, engines won't start, and oil tanks run dry.

It was Hadley, the young woman who rents a house from me. My instincts were right. The pipes had frozen.

My initial reaction was anger. Hadn't she remembered all the tips I gave her when she rented the house—leave the cabinet doors open under the kitchen sink, let a little water drip, run the hot water before going to bed? But I stifled it, knowing full well that the frozen pipe was not the result of negligence, but rather what happens when a long run of pipe goes through an uninsulated crawl space on a night when Vermont is unsuitable for creatures without fur.

"I'll be right there," I said, already wearing my game face. I took a last sip of hot coffee and went upstairs to dress. There would be no fashion statement today. I put on long johns, then sweatpants, then jeans, then my woolies from Johnson Woolen Mills. For once, I didn't care if I looked 40 pounds overweight. I topped off the outfit with a coat that would not be ruined by rolling around in the dirt, because I had already ruined it by rolling around in the dirt.

I waddled down cellar to gather my tools—propane torch, lighter, and a little board that I've improvised for holding the torch at odd angles. I know the drill.

Outside the sun was bright, but ineffective against the chill of the blue norther that had swept down from Hudson's Bay. Each step in the snow produced a loud, dry crunch. I pulled myself clumsily into the cab of my truck, said a prayer to the god of

DieHards, and turned the ignition. My engine moaned like teenager being roused from a warm bed. I cranked it again and got it to scream "It hurts! It hurts! It hurts!" I tried swearing at the engine, and threatening to stomp on the gas pedal. The engine responded by sputtering a metallic "okmaybemaybemaybe." I gave it thirty seconds to think the situation over, then another crank. Fearful of my wrath, it started.

By the time I reached the house my forehead was beaded with sweat from the eighteen layers of clothing. Hadley was a little sheepish, but I said "no big deal" because I had transformed from landlord mode to most-competent-male-of-the-species mode. There was no mountain too high, no valley too deep, no pipe too frozen that I couldn't conquer it.

Underneath the kitchen ell, in the crawlspace, I lit the propane torch, then tried to guess which pipe was frozen and the best place to apply the heat. With the outside temperature hovering at minus twenty-five, the problem was getting worse by the minute.

To make a long story short, for the next six hours, I lay on my back and watched the little blue flame lick the copper pipes. I stopped only to pee and to change cylinders. (Thank goodness I brought extras.) The readers of *Livin'* might wonder what goes through one's mind during such an ordeal. To share the experience, I suggest you read the next few paragraphs aloud for six hours straight while lying on your back ... outside ... during January.

C'mon, Baby. C'mon, Baby. Come to Papa. You can do it, Baby. Just relax and feel the soothing heat of the propane. Oh, feels good, doesn't it? Makes you want to release that frigid water and let it flow. C'mon, Baby. Hey, batterbatterbatter.

I cannot believe I am doing this. I mean, I'm a grown-up. I have gray hair. I'm clean and very polite. I'm nice to animals, so why am I lying on my back in a cramped, dusty crawl space beneath an old farmhouse? What did I do wrong? OK, that, but what else?

Are the Patriots playing tomorrow? Is today Saturday? Where are the Patriots in the standings? Have the playoffs started yet? What are the teams in the Eastern Division? What was the lineup for the 1975 Red Sox?

*C'mon you miserable piece of copper, friggin' scumbag pipe.
Gimme a gurgle, just a little gurgle so I know something's going on
in there. Are you freezing up on me as fast as I thaw you? You
wouldn't do that, would you? No you wouldn't, because that would
make me very angry, and I will start banging on you with a crescent
wrench just to cause you pain.*

*So why didn't I hire a plumber who knows what he is doing?
Why? Because I am stupid, because I am stubborn, because I am
cheap, and because I am a guy, and guys are supposed to be competent in matters of the house. What kind of man can't thaw the pipes
in his own house?*

*Please let me hear a gurgle. Just a little one. C'mon, one little
gurgle for Papa. Please?*

*Let's be rational. If I can't get the pipes thawed, they will burst.
My stupidity and stubbornness will cost me ten times what it costs
to do things right. I am so stupid. I am so stupid. I'm stupid to be
living in this stupid state where stupid water freezes in stupid pipes.*

The sweetest sound in the world is, at first, imperceptible, a
baby's burp. It is followed by a sucking sound, then a gasp for air.
Then slurping, sweet slurping. Upstairs, the first spurts of rusty
water are coming out of the tap. Water. The essence of life.
Restored to the home. We are saved. Hallelujah!

I yell to open all the faucets. I crawl triumphantly (if that's
possible) out into the sunlight. Inside, the taps are gushing—the
kitchen sink, the bathtub, the shower, the bathroom sink. There's
a symphony of flowing water. The theme music from *Rocky* wells
in the background.

It was, I say with the right stuff, a little harder than anticipat-
ed. I turn off my torch with a ceremonial puff, tip my hat, and
head back to the truck, each step producing a loud scrunch.
There's a noticeable swagger to my waddle. I showed those damn
pipes who was boss.

The Erotic Car Wash

One of the great things about Beyonder is its proximity to Quebec, and the great thing about proximity is that you can make fun of them with impunity. Say something derogatory about an Iraqi, an Eskimo, a Chinese, and you will be resoundingly chastised as a racist bigot. Say something about someone from New York, however, and people will be slapping you on the back.

January, by the way, is a great time to get your car washed.

So maybe I'm getting older and wiser. In my brash, youthful days I thought nothing of insulting a whole nationality in print. Now, however, before committing character assassination, I always try to butter up the group to be offended by extravagantly praising them in advance. Let's take, for instance, our neighbors to the immediate north—the Quebecois, or in the harsh tones of Yankee dialect, "kebbekkerz."

Can anyone deny that the women of Quebec are beautiful? Or that the food can be marvelous?

The relationship of Vermonters and the Quebecois is enigmatic, not unlike the slogan that appears on the provincial license plate, "Je Me Souviens." Everyone agrees that the slogan is hauntingly evocative, but no one can agree what it means or how it is properly translated into English.

Having now praised the Quebecois, let's point out a few of their humorous foibles so that we can all share a cross-cultural chuckle.

Montreal is a cultural center, right? And the people are all fashion conscious. Why is it now considered fashionable for men to wear loud, hideous sweaters, with meaningless English slogans on the front? I had a business lunch with two Montreal gentlemen recently. One had a sweater that proclaimed "Point Zero Trend," while the other proudly stated "Le Authentic Garment."

OK, check "clothes" off the insult list. Now, food. We have already established that one can eat pretty well north of the border. There is one notable exception, called "poutine," that will make your arteries harden just by reading about it. Poutine is the national luncheon dish, favored by truck drivers and working sorts, and a staple at the roadside canteens that are French equivalents of diners. Poutine is no more than a Mont Blanc-sized mound of french fries, swimming in a gravy, over a nice bed of cheese curds. Cheese curds! Nutritional balance is obviously not the point of this dish.

What I like most about Quebec, however, is that one can be driving along (usually at 120 kilometers per hour), through pleasant rural countryside, and suddenly find a joint offering nude dancing. This is not my imagination; I've looked up "danseuses nue" three times in the dictionary to make sure that my interpretation is correct (as if the signs are not graphic enough).

Even more insight to the Quebec psyche is provided by a small incident that took place recently in Granby, Quebec, when town fathers, in a staunch display of Puritan ethics, decided to ban erotic car washes.

The erotic car wash, or L'Auto Lavage Erotique, is a concept that threatens our way of life in the Northland. Think it through. Everyone knows that keeping a car free from road salt is essential to maintaining a vehicle past the payment period, but that washing one's vehicle is a task of such monumental unpleasantness that it makes going to the dentist or watching reruns of the ETV auction look recreational by comparison.

Now, some Quebecois came up with the idea of having your car washed by a nubile nymphette "san vetements," as they would say. And if what is good for the goose is good for the gander, the Quebecois might have L'Auto Lavage Erotiques with pieces of beefcake wearing little more than bow ties to revive mother's interest in vehicular hygiene.

Think of it. People washing their cars twice a week. Cars would last for ten years, mufflers would not need replacing every year. To put it succinctly, it would be an economic disaster; precisely what the town fathers of Granby foresaw.

The chances of an erotic car wash opening in Vermont, are, therefore, roughly equivalent to the chance of anyone in the state growing a watermelon larger than a hardball this summer. Besides wreaking economic holocaust, the erotic car wash would violate the local character-building ethics that holds that winters should be hard, the ground should be rocky, and washing one's car should not be fun.

Most of us agree. We are, after all, Vermonters. We don't want to go around having fun and hardening our arteries like those crazy Quebecois. Still, the car is a little dirty, and it's only a couple of hours drive to Granby. Maybe that ban on erotic car washes has not yet gone into effect.

Man Versus Machine

But what do you do to keep yourself amused during those long Vermont winters? Well, I like to spend long, frustrated hours dealing with technological issues that I don't understand, then destroying the very products that are supposed to make my life easier.

If Man has Dominion, how come there are at least a dozen machines in my house that are smarter than I am? I can understand my computer being smarter than I am. A computer is supposed to be smart. The purpose of this machine is to be smart; that's why you buy it. Therefore, when it keeps flashing nonsensical messages like, "I/O Error" or "Bad Command," you take it in stride. Sure, you feel incredibly STOO-PUDD, but since you paid several thousand bucks for a machine smarter than you, full value is received only if it occasionally makes you feel like a stub-fingered weenie. The home computer is the 1990's version of the English butler. Your television set is a different matter. This particular machine is supposed to entertain, not intimidate you. Such a machine needs an on/off switch and a channel selector. Ideally, the controls should be on the side—a toggle switch or button for the on/off and a spin dial for channel selection.

Life used to be so simple. You didn't need a channel selector because Channel 3 was the only show in town. Now, if you get one of those little dishes, you'll get every channel except Channel 3, which costs extra even though it's free.

The controls for the modern TV are packed into a small, rectangular device called a "remote control" that is designed to fit neatly in-between the cushions of the couch. The buttons on the remote are small, hard to use, and if you're over 9 years old, incomprehensible. (It is with some perverse pleasure that I am now observing my teenager becoming incompetent with machines. This is a sure sign of maturity.)

Nothing differentiates between the front and back of the remote, so one spends a lot of time standing in front of the tube, making thrusting motions with the remote while sending little electronic impulses into one's own stomach. It would be very helpful if the designers of this masterpiece of modern convenience either painted on a big, white directional arrow, or at the very least, could have a "turn it the other way, STOO-PUDD!" message appear on the screen.

They tell me the remote will operate the VCR, too. Imagine that. I wonder how I'll handle videotapes when my kids leave home?

You've heard about these insidious computer viruses? Would it surprise you to find out that there is a TV virus, designed to incapacitate your machine at some point so that you have to buy another? Do you really think the TV manufacturers would build a machine that could last forever?

On my wrist I wear a small machine called a watch, whose purpose is to constantly remind me of my inadequacy. The watch is adjusted by buttons much too small for fat, adult fingers. I know the watch is smart, because its alarm feature self-ignites only when I am in a room of business associates. For about thirty seconds (actually, closer to an hour) the watch squeals a high-pitched "stoo-pudd-stoo-pudd-stoo-pudd" chant while I display oafishness to the assembled masses.

(One time I was on the West Coast and I needed to set my alarm for five a.m. But my watch—without telling me—decided to remain on the East Coast, and went off at two a.m. I dutifully showed up at my appointment three hours early, wondering why it was not yet light. I spent three hours in a parking lot feeling incredibly STOO-PUDD.)

The video camera is completely beyond me, as is the graphic equalizer in the car, and my clock radio in the bedroom. I have mastered the electric coffee maker, although I can't set the clock. And, so that you'll not think me a total klutz, I can make microwave popcorn.

In the garage, where I keep my machines of conveyance, are more devices of inadequacy. Remember the feeling of mastery and control you had when you gave your '57 Plymouth a tune-up? You can't tune up your own car any more. It's too smart, or you're too dumb, depending on your perspective. I'm not even smart enough for my bike. Refresh me on why a bicycle needs eighteen gears?

You will be able to read this poignant story only if my computer is virus-free, and if I can somehow convince the laser printer that it owes me a favor. C'mon, little darlin'. Do it for Big Daddy. Then finally, I have to plead with my ten year old to show me how to use the fax again.

Pity the poor male of the species. He can't master his women or children; he can't master his machines. He can't even kick the dog without getting into a heap o' trouble. (Most dogs are smart enough to have the local animal rights organization programmed on the auto-dial of the cordless phone.)

This ain't Dominion, this is Beyonder. And the poor puppy writing this story feels totally beyondered. *(Editor's note: And this was written before DVDs, cell phones, GISs, PDAs, digital cable, optical fiber, or any of those other innovations that I don't understand. Earlier this year I actually took a cell phone and wireless laptop to the sugarhouse. There ought to be a law.)*

Fifty Crummy Bands

Music is one of the sure-fire antidotes to winter.

I was offended.

At the recent Muckety-Muck Famous Author's Convention, someone thought it would be fun to get some well-known writers, including Stephen King and Dave Barry, to perform in an impromptu rock and roll band.

They never asked me.

Not only did they not ask me to be in the band, they didn't even ask me to attend the convention. Well I don't care. I'm just as happy being a cult figure among the cognoscenti (which, for all of you morons out there, means anyone who thinks I'm a good writer). I'll accept my lot as a beloved legend in my Beyonder homeland.

On the literary pecking order I may be strictly bush league, but that's no excuse to overlook my rock and roll credentials. As a rock and roller, I was awesome. Ask anyone who saw me, if you can find anyone, and if they are still functioning mentally.

Like most males of contemporary Beatle age (40-49), I was in a band. Our music was....simple, rude, loud, stupid—just the way rock and roll is supposed to be. I must have been in fifty crummy bands. If not fifty, then close to it. Well, at least ten (maybe).

The first band was named Iron Cross, because we thought the symbol was neat. We had no idea what it meant. We thought it had something to do with surfing. We changed the name to the Usurpers. Eh-h-h-h. Lacks something. So we became the Eunuchs, but people pronounced it the "yoo-nooches," so we changed it to the Uniks, then the Unix. When we found out the meaning of eunuch, we immediately changed the name.

Next was the Pop Tops, a cross between "top of the pops" and that which stands between you and a beer. Next we entered the "and the" phase of our careers. There was Randy and the Rangers, Randy and the Rainbows, Randy and the Dakotas.

No one in the group, by the way, was named "Randy." In fact, no one ever knew where these names came from or how they changed. We tried Billy Joe Steel and the Metallics for a while, just long enough to permanently exit the "and the" phase.

There was a certain ritual and etiquette to the selection of the name. Once selected, the first thing to do was to have it painted on the bass drum. The bass drum, thus, became the band's most important marketing vehicle, a matter of some delicacy whenever you found a better drummer. Often the decision boiled down to which was more important, keeping the name or keeping on beat.

My next band was the Van Goghs, "the artistic sound in rock and roll." You know how rock and rollers today have these fancy, dangling earrings? Our gimmick was that we cut off our left ears. (No, not really, check out my picture.)

We wore black and red simu-velveteen v-neck sweaters with white turtleneck dickies. We were, in one word, sharp. The Sixties progressed, however, and so did we. The Beatles expanded our collective consciousness, and we realized that the "Van Goghs" was too limiting for the expanded creative expression of which the band was now capable. (We had now purchased a fuzz-tone distortion device so that we could play the opening notes of "Satisfaction" just like the Rolling Stones.)

We had outgrown the "Van Goghs," and became the "Van Goes," which is a good reason to tell your kids never to smoke marijuana. Subsequently, following in the lemming tradition of the day, we named ourselves—for no apparent reason—after an obscure place with no association with the band, its members, or music—Wood River Junction.

Then we signed a record contract, only to discover to our horror that we were slated to become minor players in the musical movement known as "bubble gum." We were renamed something along the lines of "The Great Bubble Gum Conspiracy of 1829." I've repressed the specifics. And needless to say, there was no bubble gum conspiracy in 1829. We fully expected to be compensated for our humiliation with large piles of money. Never happened, however. We sold out but were paid with a rubber check.

When it became clear that our fortune in bubble gum was not imminent, we overreacted in the equal and opposite direction and tried to regain credibility by giving ourselves a name that combined psychedelic depravity with a recognition of our roots. We became Vinny Van Gogh and the Severed Ears. Within weeks we

were out of rock and roll and seeking our fortunes as paper salesmen, management trainees, and bookkeepers.

I, of course, set out to become a famous writer, never dreaming that I would someday become the voice of Beyonder.

The reason this has all come to mind is that my thirteen-year-
old son is now starting a band. They are trying to think of a name.
Naturally, I have lots of suggestions, but they would rather be
gummed to death by toothless frogs than to choose a name of my
suggestion. The last thing they need is an old guy preventing them
from making their own mistakes. Right now they are calling themselves "Phlegm Cake."

Maybe they could use my help.

Joining Other Odd Ducks

*Winter is a good time for the rubber chicken cir-
cuit, maybe even the virtual rubber chicken circuit.*

Maybe my mother dropped me on my head.

I'm not sure what went wrong, but while most men my age
join fraternal-type organizations, I never have. Oh, it's not that I
dislike rubber chicken, and I can sing silly songs and recite the
Pledge of Allegiance as well as the next guy, but the appeal of the
Lions, Kiwanis, Rotary, Grange, or Jaycees has always eluded me.
(The appeal of "me" has eluded them, as well. None of these
clubs has ever asked me to become a member.)

I have joined organizations, however, and a brief examination
of the roster will tell you a lot about what makes the man from
Beyonder tick [note to editor: please do not mis-typeset this as
"sick," "lick," or "thick"—no one would understand the mis-
take].

First there is the Del Shannon International Appreciation
Society, to which I pledged in 1971. Del, as most Beyonderites
know, was the greatest rock star who ever lived, even greater than
David Cassidy, churning out hit after hit (he had two) back in the
mid-sixties. Two years ago, in one of life's greatest injustices, Del
was denied entrance into that citadel of culture, the Rock and Roll

Hall of Fame. A man whose principles were as high as his falsetto, he promptly killed himself (although there are those diehard Del fans amongst us who maintain that he was killed by a rival faction of jealous rock and roll has-beens). In any case, future generations will continue to sing one of the truly great lines of rock and roll, "As I walk along, I wonder what went wrong...." (I promise to devote an entire column to Del this February, on the anniversary of his death.)

Hmm-m-m. Looking through the other membership cards in my wallet, here's one for the Beer Can Collectors of America. This organization is dedicated to the proper enshrinement of the beer can, which club members proudly tout as the greatest technological innovation since the bottle opener. (Think about it—how do they get the beer to stay in that conical shape while they wrap the can around it? Boggles the mind.)

True purists in the pursuit of the perfect can will never sully the object of their desire by buying or selling. They will only trade. Many of the most prized cans have been uncovered on expeditions to old dump sites. Wallowing around in an old dump on a crisp November morning while the rest of the world lounges in bed sipping coffee and reading the sports page is a can collector's dream. Yep, I'm a member of this organization. Nope, nothing wrong with me.

I'm also a card-carrying member of the American Society of Dowsers, whose headquarters is located right in Danville, Vermont, Beyonder, USA. Some people think dowsers are odd-balls who go around trying to find water with forked sticks. Au contraire, dowsers are very normal people who go around trying to find everything from water to dead bodies using everything from a nail suspended on a thread to rods shaped like miniature TV antennae.

I've yet to find water, mostly because all the water I've ever needed has already been found. My dowsing tools would just lead me to the nearest kitchen sink, toilet, or water fountain—no big thrill in that. Now that I think of it, I don't know why I became a card-carrying dowser.

You're probably asking yourself, "How does this guy have time and energy for all this, and still have enough left over to write this column?" But there's more, yes, there's more.

Like Ducks Unlimited. I joined up for the name alone. Imagine my disappointment when I found that this is an organization of serious environmentalists dedicated to preserving North America's wetlands so that there will always be ducks to blast with five-thousand-dollar, special-edition, engraved Remington shotguns. I expected a gaggle of kooks and yahoos, but found a bunch of pseudo-sportsmen who drive around in Jeeps with leather seats.

I did not last long in Ducks Unlimited, but the Hash House Harriers (running beer drinkers) count me as one. I'm also in The Author's Guild, the Catamount Trail Association (diehard cross-country skiers), and the American Homebrewer's Association (motto: "Relax, Don't Worry, Have a Homebrew"). I've heard of an organization called the Odd Fellows, but have not found a local chapter. I wonder what they're all about.

Yes, I wonder, I WAH-WAH-WAH-WAH WONDER.

A Tribute to Del

Yes, I am a little "touched in the head" about Del Shannon. And now that I'm older and entitled to be a little eccentric, I've decided that Del was one of the seminal thinkers of the Western World. Most of the wisdom of life is contained in the lyrics of his songs. "I wah-wah-wah-wah wonder."

Regular readers of "The View From Beyonder" (both of you) know that this column is not afraid to tackle THE BIG SUBJECTS. Life, Death, Art and the Cosmos, the Eternal Battle of the Sexes, the Eternal Battle of the Chuck and Flatlander—all have been forthrightly addressed on this page.

This is another Big Subject piece, when caution and petty regionality are put aside in favor of filling a gaping hole in the culture. As you have probably guessed, I'm talking about Del Shannon.

Ho, ho, ho, you say. This writer with his warped, petty sense of humor is going to wax eloquent about an obscure, dead rock-and-roll star in mock heroic terms the same way that he describes Spam as a gourmet delicacy.

No, I'm serious. And besides, I happen to really like Spam.

Most people, if they remember Del Shannon at all, remember a young singer who burst on the pop music scene in 1961 with a smash hit, "Runaway," who then deflated into deserved obscurity. Not me. I think of a talented, but tortured, artist who had the misfortune of scoring his biggest success on his initial recording session, then spent the next thirty years trying to climb again to the pinnacle of pop. Just when he was within reaching distance, he slipped back. (The exactsame thing happened to me the other day when I was trying to cross over Rochester Mountain.)

Del burst upon the American cultural scene in 1961, a time in American history now shrouded in the gauzy nostalgia of a dim memory. These were the Camelot years, when no achievement seemed impossible. Our president was young and handsome. He played touch football, even though he had a bad back from his war wound. He had a beautiful wife, cute kids, and he told us we were going to put a man on the moon. And we did it.

Roger Maris and Mickey Mantle spent a summer in assault of Babe Ruth's supposedly unattainable record of 60 home runs. And they did it, too (Roger did, anyway)! I defy anyone over forty to come up with anything but positive associations with 1961. It was the dawn of a new era, we thought, when we, individually, and America, collectively, would achieve the greatness for which we knew we were destined.

Now, with the benefit of thirty years of hindsight, we know that 1961 was the dawn of nuthin', but rather the final scene in a giant sham known as The American Dream. The fair-haired president was slumming around with starlets and gangster's molls; Roger Maris, after one Ruthian season, went back to being Roger Maris.

Del Shannon told us all of this, if we listened closely enough. Del wrote his own songs, and specialized in tales of unrequited love, the kind you experience when you're thirteen (as I was in 1961). The poor guy's girl always ran off with his best friend; he was continually teased by the little town flirt, and made to cry two kinds of teardrops while running from the stranger in town. Get the picture (yes, we see)? To judge from Del's music, the guy never had a pleasant day in his life. The connection between the real-life Shannon and the agonized persona of his songs was easy to make. Del was short, and, well, funny looking, the kind of guy who would take up the guitar to compensate for his shyness around girls. Somehow the emotional scars of the early teen years always crept through in his music, even the songs he wrote in his fifties (not in the Fifties, when he was in his fifties). Along the way, Del became a truly professional performer who plied his trade at clubs, nostalgia shows, and country fairs—wherever someone would pay a buck to hear the guy who did "Runaway" do "Runaway." (Del performed at the Rutland Fair just a few years ago. He gave the people what they wanted, capping the show with a "Runaway" fresh enough that one would not guess he had performed this tune every night since hitting the charts back in '61.)

In his final days, Del seemed to have achieved some sense of inner peace. He was, for the first time in his life, happily married and financially secure. His career even teetered on the brink of revival, as he was widely rumored to be the replacement for the deceased Roy Orbison in the popular group of rock and roll legends, The Travelling Wilburys.

Del? Onstage with Beatle George Harrison and the great Bob Dylan? The thought was overwhelming for lifelong Del fans like myself, who had remained faithful through his many lean years and failed comebacks.

The thought must have been too much for Del, too, as he took his own life before his Renaissance occurred. Del's suffering was over, but for those of us who lived his anguish and who became affectionately attached to it over the years, it lives on in scratchy records cherished by middle-aged guys who know now that seeing your two-timing girl holding hands with your best friend will generate the most intense feelings to be experienced in life. Not the deepest, mind you, but the most intense. It's all there in one line from "Runaway:"

> *I think of the things we've done,*
> *Together, while our hearts were young.*

It's not a bad legacy. Del Shannon, a Beyonder kinda guy if ever there was one.

Local Hopeful

This was the first in what was to become a regular feature honoring individuals in the North Country who in some small, twisted way have made this a better planet. Never happened. John O'Donnell holds the claim as the only "local hopeful" ever.

They called him a fool, but John O'Donnell persisted. They laughed in his face, made fun of his heritage, pitied his wife and children, and yet he trudged forward, oblivious to the ridicule, building his rink of dreams.

This is a side of John O'Donnell that his students at Vermont Technical College do not see, probably because he wisely keeps it hidden. After all, it's one thing to be regarded as a lunatic in the neighborhood, and a completely different matter to lose credibility on the job.

No one knows why John O'Donnell decided that our village of Upper Granville, Vermont, needed an ice skating rink. Maybe he's hearing voices ("build it, and SHE will come," meaning Katarina Witt, of course). Or maybe something has stoked the competitive fires that made him a top-notch scholastic goalie in his native Massachusetts. Or maybe he just took one too many pucks in the head. In any case, last November, when the leaves had fallen and a barren winter stretched before us, John O'Donnell decided the town needed an ice skating rink.

There's a rule in Upper Granville. Every half decade or so, each person is allowed to do something incredibly stupid. The others in the town will even assist the person in his folly, so long as he buys the beer.

Thus, it came to pass on a bleak day cold enough to numb fingers, that several of us helped our neighbor rip plywood into retaining walls and stake them to the ground. O'Donnell teaches physics, but could not seem to grasp some of the principles involved, such as the fact that water runs downhill. Ignoring our sage advice, he plunged forward.

Before long it rose before our eyes. Of course, it only rose about eighteen inches. It was a masterpiece of chain saw carpentry, done the pure way—without rules or levels. Then he laid the plastic, turning the one-time garden into what looked like our own little landfill.

Construction complete, the rest of us abandoned the project. "It's not going to work, John," we said, trying to spare him the inevitable humiliation.

"It'll work," he countered simply, the glint of ancient Celtic warriors in his eyes—the same glint that led thousands of them to their deaths on ancient crusades of folly.

The season plunged forward, and so did O'Donnell. Night after night one could drive by and see him standing there holding his hose (which ran across the street and through his kitchen window), grooming the fitful ice.

"How's it going, John?" we'd ask.

"I think I've stopped the leaks," he'd say.

"Keep up the good work," we'd say, muttering under our breath.

Then, just around Christmas, it all came together. The temperatures dropped, and stayed there. What had been a gloppy mess became a smooth, slippery plateau. Almost instantly a hockey net appeared, and ice skates which only weeks before had seemed as superfluous to local life as snorkeling gear became prized possessions.

The addition of gliding, sliding children brought the rink to life. Before long it had a name (The Smooth Spot), and a local tradition had been born. As we watched the children's delight, the strength of John O'Donnell's vision became clear, and for our doubts, we felt small and petty.

The story should end here, but it doesn't. Like all men of excess, O'Donnell did not know when to quit. Not content with having successfully created a rink for the kids, he is now trying to make The Smooth Spot into O'Donnell Square Garden. He hasn't booked the Ice Capades (yet), but he has announced the formation of the Upper Granville Curling Society. The rink is splotched with his attempts to create colored lines, and there are gallon milk containers, filled and frozen, that are meant to serve as curling stones. (Of course, no one in town has even the remotest idea of what curling is all about.)

O'Donnell, obviously, does not know when to quit, which, come to think of it, is what this story is all about. Had he quit when the rest of us supposedly sane people did, then there would be no sunny days when the snow is bright, the ice is hard, and the kids are laughing.

John O'Donnell...our first Local Hopeful.

Perfectly Normal

It's thirty below outside. There's nowhere to turn for help. You are on your own. I like how I give myself a daughter in this essay.

There was a strange noise upstairs.

"What was that?" I asked my wife.

"I don't know," she answered. "Sounds like water dripping. Better go check the kids."

I headed toward the steps, noticing a small trickle of fluid dripping off the final one. I muttered a grim "Omigod," and took the stairs three at a time. Within seconds the trickle grew to a small torrent. The source was unmistakable—my oldest son's room. I had just put him to bed moments earlier. Now there was an ankle-deep flood of liquid sweeping baseball cards and Ninja Turtles out of his room.

Frantically, I groped for the light. It was one of those moments that a parent dreads, when a lifetime flashes by in a second. Seems like only yesterday, although it was twelve years ago, when we carried our newborn son to his freshly decorated nursery. Now the room is a landfill of toy parts, discarded comic books, and junk food remnants. The walls, once covered with stars, planets, and The Little Prince, now feature the biceps of Jose Canseco and the,er,whatchimacallits of the girls on the Snap-On Tools calendar.

The light clicked on, and I beheld a vision from the dark

recesses of Stephen King's brain. My son lay there, deep in innocent sleep, while liquid spurted from every orifice of his head as if
a water main had burst within his skull. Luckily, a conference at
our local school had prepared me for this.

"What is it?" called my wife, the frantic edge of maternal concern in her voice, "What's happened to my baby?"

"Nothing to worry about," I said calmly, clicking off the light
and returning to the top of the stairs. "A small eruption of the
pituitary gland, causing an excess of hormones." I breathed a
sigh of relief, the sanctity of my home, my castle, now restored.
All that was remaining was the summary statement:

"It's perfectly normal."

The aforementioned conference I attended was entitled
"Adolescence, Normal Passage? or.... YECH-H-H-H, Gross!"
The point of the gathering, as I was best able to discern, was to
assure parents that abnormal behavior from children between the
ages of 12 and 15 is in fact "perfectly normal," and attributable to
the hormones coursing through their veins.

The doctors and educators at the conference put forth their
information with sober dignity. They wore jackets and ties, hand-
ed out indecipherable graphs and charts, and repeatedly assured
us that our experiences, far from unique, are common, mundane,
and totally unexceptional.

Having grasped the concept, I now consider myself an expert
on the subject and am prepared to answer questions:

Why don't my children talk to me any more? It's perfectly
normal. They don't talk to you because you are the biggest embarrassment on the face of the earth. Besides, you exaggerate. When
you ask them what happened at school, don't they say "Nuthin'"?

Why is it, when I talk to my child, he looks through me as if
I'm not there, then does exactly the opposite of what I said? It's
perfectly normal. Your child is at a point in life when the influence of his peers, who are sharing the experience of dramatic
body change, is more important than the approval of his parents.
This means that he or she will be listening more to those snot-
nosed, spotty-faced creeps in his or her class than to you.

My child's left arm is eight inches longer than his right arm.

His head is approximately twice normal size, but is attached to his body by a neck that looks strong enough to support a grape. He requires half of the household budget to be kept in footwear. He remains motionless for days at a time, followed by exhibitions of frantic activity that he describes as "hyper-spaz." What's going on? It's perfectly normal. To be specific, he is exploring expanded cognition in order to reestablish body image during a period when preoccupation with fantasy and idealism lead to a sense of omnipotence marked by periodic reversion to concrete emancipation to abstract thought.

Oh, never mind. Just take my word for it. It's perfectly normal.

When my daughter gets together with her friends, they giggle uncontrollably. What's so funny? A brief examination of the handout they gave us at the conference gives some clues as to why adolescence is such a hoot. Here's a quick scan at some of the words that appear in the handout: auto-eroticism, puberty, narcissism, menarche (pronounced "Men-Are-Key" heh-heh-heh), seminiferous, glans, engorged, papilla, and spurt. I have no idea what most of the words mean, but if they are as lurid as they sound, no wonder the girls are laughing. Their behavior is, in two words, perfectly normal.

My son stole our car and all our credit cars and drove to San Francisco with eight of his friends to attend an M. C. Hammer concert. Should we be concerned? Not to worry. This behavior is perfectly normal. What would be abnormal would be if any of the kids thought to bring a toothbrush or change of underwear.

My daughter has been in the bathroom since she was eleven. She's fourteen now. How can we get her out? This, too, is perfectly normal. Your daughter, like her peers, is fixated on her body (as will be most of the fourteen-year-old boys in your neighborhood, soon). To get her out, we suggest letting the telephone ring, unanswered, just outside the bathroom door.

So relax, parents. So your kid has four ears, pink hair, talks in ciphers, and smells like a beauty parlor. In the words of one of the conference leaders, "These are not aliens we are dealing with; these are our children."

That's Not Funny

Why do dogs lick themselves? How do you know if your roommate is gay? And how many feminists does it take to screw in a light bulb? Don't answer these questions unless you want animal rights activists, the Queer Nation, and every woman in the world descending upon you.

Remember the Imitative Fallacy (not to be confused another concept one learns about in high school, the Imitative Falsie)? The Imitative Fallacy is a rule or law or something that states that you can't write a story about being boring by just writing a boring story. You have to write an interesting story about being boring in order not to be found guilty of violating the Imitative Fallacy.

I think this also means you can't write a funny column about not being funny, and yet I persist. I find the national lack of humor one of the most humorous subjects around. Here's the funniest joke I've heard making the rounds of Beyonder lately:

How many animal rights activists does it take to screw in a light bulb? (scream)THAT'S NOT FUNNY! I suppose not, but you have to realize that good taste has never been my long suit. Let's try this:

How many environmentalists does it take to...THAT'S NOT FUNNY! OK, OK. How many feminists does it...THAT'S NOT FUNNY!

Let's change course. These two gay guys walk into a bar.... THAT'S NOT FUNNY! All right, what's the Polish definition of...THAT'S NOT FUNNY! A dyslexic Irish guy walks into a bra. That's kind of cute.

You can see how difficult it is to be a humorist in an age of special interest groups. This last summer I wrote a column that I thought was about Little League. Alas, I arrived at the next game to find out that I had authored an anti-feminist treatise.

"Your article was demeaning to women," one of the mothers told me. Howso? says I. "You said that the women sit in the stands discussing the strategic nuances of meal planning while the men pace nervously on the sideline."

"That's right,"I admitted, caught red-handed. "But that is what happens at the games. You, in fact, have been a regular participant in those discussions about eating logistics while I, even as we speak, am nervously pacing the sideline waiting to see if my ten year old remembers not to step in the bucket."

"True," she said, "but you can't say it, because it's demeaning to women." I mumbled something semi-conciliatory and slunk away, a branded sexist, knowing that I was doomed to make the same mistake again. (And I thought the article was about baseball.)

The animal rights people got on my case when I advocated that people buy local cheese, a notion that I thought might be considered popular in Vermont. I never heard from the pro-cheesers, but I did learn that cheese consumption encourages the slaughter of infant bulls, who can never produce the milk from which cheese is made. Get it?

The pinnacle of humorlessness was reached during this fall's favorite miniseries, The Clarence and Anita Show, when we were treated to the sight of real, live, freely elected public servants competing for the title of Self-Righteous Twit of the Century. At times it was hard to realize this was not a Monty Python sketch:

"I, the distinguished blubbedy-blah from the grand commonwealth of Mumbletypeg would like to say that I am surprised, perhaps chagrined, even shocked, or maybe horrified, indeed even shockingly dismayed with a small pinch of self-effacing disgust, to hear my esteemed colleague, a cum laude graduate from that venerable bastion of higher learning, the Yale Law School, not express moral indignation, even outrage, perhaps as much as...."

All I got out of the whole show is that more pompous, self-impressed, stuffed shirts have come out of the Yale Law School than anywhere else. Maybe I missed the point. What I did not miss throughout the process was that there were too few belly laughs.

That's what is missing everywhere. We're too busy saving furry little seals, preventing child abuse, demanding equal rights for overweight people, and saving the planet for future generations—worthy causes all. The ozone hole won't get much bigger, however, if you go into the bathroom, close the door, and make stupid faces in the mirror until you begin to laugh. Don't come out until it happens.

A Language Lament ...sorry, Lapeople t

Going on thirty days now. Haven't been outside, except to get more wood for the stove. Haven't changed clothes in weeks. Not sure what my skin feels like. Don't know how much longer I can keep hanging on.

I try to keep current on cultural changes. Just this week I tried sexual harassment, which I hear is rampant in the workplace. Unfortunately, I work in a one-man, oops, -person, office. I hung around the water cooler for hours, waiting for someone to harass. Finally, the UPS guy showed up. Now, UPS tells me I'll have to pick up my packages at the depot. Bummer.

So, I used the phone to call a female colleague, my editor at the Vermont Sunday Magazine, in fact.

"Ooo-o-o, Mama," I cooed into the phone. "I must say, you are looking foxy, today, if you catch my drift."

"See if you catch my drift," she responded, struggling to maintain professionalism in the face of the blatantly offensive onslaught. "Your column is late, and you keep writing the same thing over and over. Quit rehashing the same material and give us something original for a change."

I forgot about sexual harassment for a moment and defended myself. "I'm recycling words in order to walk lightly on the planet. I'm concerned about exhausting planetary resources. Now, as I was saying, ooo-o-o, my foxy lady, you are looking ..."

She responds in a clipped, professional tone that translates to THAT'S NOT FUNNY, but her actual words are, "There are some commodities in no danger of depletion. One is an organic substance that emerges from the southern end of the male cow. You seem to have an ample supply. And if by looking 'foxy' you mean that I have a furry face and a pointy snout, then your face is in serious danger of rearrangement."

Click.

Having failed to sexually harass my editoress, I went upstairs

101

to an office where I found an unsuspecting female. "Hey Babesy," I said, grinding my hips in a display of hideously graphic lewdness, "How 'bout a little of this action?"

She didn't even look up.

"Babesy," I pleaded, "Don't you recognize sexual harassment when you see it?"

She looked annoyed, as if an unwanted mosquito had to be swatted off her wrist. "Stephen," she said, "Sexual harassment happens when a male of the species tries to intimidate or inflict his will on a female. You are such an ineffectual joke that you would have difficulty inflicting your will on a garden slug. By demonstrating an arrested state of social development you prove yourself—and I'll be as kind as I can about this—an over-the-hill, middle-aged buffoon."

"You mean 'over-the-Anita Hill?'"

"I rest my case."

I made a feeble move to accost her, but she performed a flawless spin kick to my throat, then pinioned me against the wall. "Go ahead," she hissed, "Make my day. Now, slink back to your rock."

What started all this was yet another accusation of sexism (I average three or four a week), for using a cliché coined in a day when men were Neanderthals and women were too sedated from martinis and soap operas to care. I quoted the late Vince Lombardi, a renowned male chauvinist pig who could whip the Green Bay Packers into a frenzy by saying, "A tie is like kissing your sister."

A couple of questions. Isn't that incest? And, how did he know?

But a quarter century ago, we'd let a guy like Vince get away with it. Today, in the interests of sexual neutrality, I've developed some variations of this well-worn chestnut.

"A tie is like kissing the dusty top of a vending machine." Hm-m-m, doesn't have the same ring. How about, "A tie is like kissing your brother?" Besides the risk of misinterpretation by the Green Bay Packers, this version might be unacceptable to gays. I finally settled on, "A tie is like kissing a sibling of the opposite gender."

The forces of sexual equality might be appeased by this option, but I'll bet the language gods are really ticked off. It is a solution as satisfying as a...well, a....tie.

Our liberated lexicon is stripping us of colorful verbal imagery. Before long, people won't be "manhandled," they will be "people-handled." "Managers" will become "peoplagers." A Fu Manchu mustache will be called a "Fu Peoplechu." A man-eating tiger will be a "person-eating" tiger. Holes in the street will be covered by "people-hole covers," and the capital of the Philippines will be changed to "People-ila."

"There he goes again," comes the collective sigh from Beyonder's enlightened. "He still doesn't get it." To which I reply:

A mannequin can become a "peoplekin." Nelson Mandela can become "Nelson Peopledela." We can "personipulate" other slogans to make them sexually neutral. For instance, the bumper sticker saying "The Best Man For The Job.... Is a Woman" can become "The Best Person For The Job Is a Person."

Now, there's a slogan even the late, great Vince Lombardi could rally around.

Ootisms

Have lost all contact with reality. Send reinforcements or at least some sign of Spring!

"Ootisms" are sounds that resemble words. You can tell what they mean, but you can't find them in the dictionary.

As far as I know, the term "ootism" (which is itself an ootism) was made up in 1967 by a guy named Brian Heaney who lived in the same college dormitory as I did. He has never earned any royalties from his creation, and mention in this column is the closest he will come to fame and glory.

1967, you will remember, was when it was very cool to have long stringy hair and to wear shirts upon which someone had apparently vomited after a meal of Chinese food. Conversely, it was uncool to be large, cleancut, and clumsy. No word in the English language existed to describe such folk. "Jock" was close, but suggested too much physical prowess. So Brian took matters into his own hands and invented the first "ootism":

"Fadoofus."

The word fit perfectly. It sounded large, clumsy, and totally moronic. Suddenly, a whole group of classmates, previously amorphous, currently fadoofus, had a convenient label.

A similar challenge was faced with a different group of fellow students who were well dressed, privileged, and indisputably correct on every subject. So enamored were these students of themselves that, in the "ootistic" sense, they were said to suffer from "Bagdasarian's Disease," a rare tropical infection in which the rectal area becomes so inflamed that it encompasses the entire personality.

Whenever in the company of a pretentious bore, Brian could look over to me, and with the somber look of a doctor explaining a terminal illness, mouth the word "Bagdasarian's." Further words were superfluous.

Many, but by no means all, ootisms are invented to describe males of the species, usually between the ages of 10 and 21.

Society changes too quickly for language to keep up with the nuances of adolescence, thus creating the need for ootisms.

Consider ootistic evolution over the years. In the Fabulous Fifties we had jerks, nincompoops, and Palookas. The Sensational Sixties served up "spesses" (short for "specimen"), bozos, hippies, and yippies. Then, the Slumbering Seventies gave us geeks and numbnuts.

The Eighties produced nerds and dorks and clinks. There were also Yuppies and Limmies and Yurpies and ten thousand other ootilistically boring variations.

The Nineties are already the Decade of the Dweeb, a term that is distinguishing itself for verbal versatility. There are "Mega-Dweebs and mini-dweebs." A scholar of the phenomenon, who studies all things "dweebalacious," can be called a "dweebolo-gist." Everyday speech now includes "dweeby," "dweeboid," "dweebotomy," and "dweebalectomy."

Let us delve further into the world of contemporary linguistics. Barely a sentence is initiated from the proto-teens in our household that does not contain one of the following three words: "lame," "hyper-spaz," and "hissy fit."

Definitions:

Any activity or action by the dominant, alpha male of the household (a.k.a. the "Dad") is , by definition, "lame." A person exhibiting such behavior is a "lay-mo," and his practices described as "lamazoid."

A "hyper-spaz" is an uncoordinated activity that ends in humiliation for its perpetrator. Walking into a street sign or missing your mouth with a bite of food are acceptable examples, although the possibilities in the adolescent world are limitless. (Did you hear about the kid who went into "hyper-spaz" after drinking a Coke through a straw up his nose?)

"Hissy fits" are exactly what they sound like, mini temper tantrums with no justifiable cause that make their practitioners look petty and foolish. Teenagers are very prone to "hissy fits." Food that isn't arranged correctly on the plate, a hair out of place, a fledgling pimple, a phone call that does not arrive on time—all can launch world-class "hissy fits."

There are always new ootisms evolving on the linguistic horizon. The new term in Washington, for instance, for anyone who is obviously from the hinterlands of Vermont is a "Bernie." Only a Bernie, for instance, would deliver an impassioned harangue on the folly of Desert Storm to the empty chambers of Congress while the TV cameras were rolling. What a totally Bernie thing to do. Or is the correct word "Bernazoid?"

(I hope our congressman keeps his sense of humor and doesn't have a "hissy fit" when he reads this.)

Moments to Forget

It's mid-February. We're losing our grip on reality. Oh God, I don't think I can go forward. Self-humiliation is the only path left!

"You have no hesitancy," say my loyal readers, "to skewer, embarrass, or otherwise humiliate individuals, groups, and even entire societies. Why don't you give yourself a dose of your own medicine?"

OK. I will. Here are a few of the most humiliating moments in my life.

There was the time I put a can of STP in the radiator of my car. (At the risk of being too technical for the layperson, any jerk knows that STP is correctly poured into the oil hole.) I could not bear to tell the guy at the garage I had been so unmacho, so I explained (with a smirk) that my wife was the idiot who didn't know her carburetor from her radiator.

Yeah, right. She let me get away with it, and I did the ironing for a month. But, you know, the car ran better with the STP in the radiator.

Then there was the time in Little League when I smashed a mighty drive over the left fielder's head. I went into a world-class home run trot until the catcher intercepted me with the ball in his glove. That's not the humiliating part. Bursting into wails of hysteria was the humiliating part.

Then there was the stout woman with whom I was taking a CPR course. "When's the baby due?" I asked cheerfully. "I'm not pregnant," she hissed. To which I replied:

"Oh."

Then there have been the reviews of my books. I tell all my friends, "I don't care what they say, as long as they spell my name right." What's really going through my mind, however, as I see myself disemboweled in print is, OMIGOD! ! THIS SAYS MY BOOK IS THE MOST TASTELESS PIECE OF TRASH SINCE "THE BEST OF HUSTLER"!

I've been called a "bore," "sophomoric," and a "misogynist" (which I had to look up in the dictionary). A letter said I should be tied on a short length of string. Try explaining that one to your kids.

Other minor thrusts at fame have ended with similarly disastrous results. My big break came when I appeared on the nationwide public broadcasting show, "All Things Considered."

"This is it!" I told myself. "People from sea to shining sea will be hanging on my every word. By tomorrow I'll be a household word." I was interviewed by Noah Adams. Unfortunately, somehow this registered in my brain as "Noel Perrin," and I proceeded to call him by the wrong name throughout the interview. I became a household world all right—"Dummy."

Airports have been the site of several numbing humiliations. My wife and I once had a fabulous getaway weekend to a national park near Chesapeake Bay. When we arrived at the airport in Baltimore for the last flight back to Burlington, we discovered that Daylight Savings Time had happened without us. We forgot to "fall ahead, spring back." As a result the plane went home without us.

Even worse was the time the entire family arrived at O'Hare with two hours to kill before our connecting flight to Burlington. Anxious that the kids not be bored, I invented an elaborate game of hide and seek. What a riot! The time slipped right by. The wait was entirely painless, in fact, until we noticed the ticket agent closing down the desk.

"What's happened to flight 342!" I asked.

"It's gone," she said.

"What! You never even announced it!" I said with suitable indignation. "My family's been here the whole time."

"Oh, yes, we did," she said, wearing an expression that told me what an idiot I was, "You played your way through the entire boarding process."

That was another tough one to explain to the kids.

Oh, but there's more, there's lots more. There is every time I have tried to speak French in Montreal, and I am answered in English. Or how about the time I took a date to a fabulous Winter Carnival weekend in Montreal. It seemed very quiet, too quiet. Eventually we found out the reason for the lack of festivities. Carnival is held in Quebec City, not Montreal.

Another time my wife and I were driving through Austin, Texas. "Hey," I suggested, "since we're here, let's visit the Alamo and see where ol' Davy Crockett fended off the Mexicans by swinging his rifle butt." We must have asked ten people for directions and received nothing but blank stares.

"You'd think," I said to my wife, "that these people would have more of a sense of their state's heritage." The 11th person provided the overdue and humiliating directions: Take Interstate 35 south about a hundred miles to San Antonio, then get off the highway and ask directions to the Alamo.

Heh-heh. We knew that.

Now that I think of it, life has been a nonstop succession of humiliations. What a dumb idea for a column! In the immortal words of William Bendix in *The Life of Riley*:

"Wotta revoltin' development this turned out to be!"

Postscript. Humiliating Postscript. I went on a business trip from Beyonder to Santa Rosa, California. I was accompanied by my sales manager (manageress? peopleager?), a lovely person named Alice. We arrived around 9 p.m. (midnight, Beyonder time). Alice decided to go to bed, but I was hungry and set out for a beer and a burrito. A few hours later I was firmly lodged in slumberland when I had to get up to, you know, release what was left of the beer.

Not wanting to overly awake myself, I kept my eyes closed and

*felt my way over to the bathroom and let myself in. Only when I
realized that this was an awfully bright bathroom did I realize that I
had let myself into the hotel corridor. Uh-oh. And I had latched the
door behind me, meaning I was locked out of the room.*

I haven't mentioned that I sleep in the nude.

*2 a.m., naked, locked out of my room, 3,000 miles from
Beyonder. What's a lad to do?*

Part IV–The Mud

People get ugly just after town meeting. You still haven't lost the weight from the holiday. You still can't get out to exercise. The town report came out and listed YOU in the delinquent tax-payer column. And the road between your house and the paved road has turned slimy and sadistic.

The snow starts melting, and it's pretty ugly, too. As the snow melts the dogshit rises. It's a miracle! Who knew there were so many colors of dog food? It's as colorful as the foliage! And you are lying to yourself.

To amuse themselves people do frivolous things like bet on when the ice will go out at Joe's Pond. In my household it means betting when the last patch of snow melts in the backyard. Every year it comes right down to the wire, and every year requires some third-party intervention and marriage counseling, because SOME-ONE THINKS IT'S MORE IMPORTANT TO WIN THAN TO PLAY FAIR!

It's a desperate time. You're so desperate to reconnect with the earth that you plant peas, knowing the seeds will rot in the wet muck. You go on the last day of the downhill skiing season, convinced that you will be the one to make it across that little pond. And you don't. You go fishing on opening day convinced you will find a stretch of water not covered by ice. And you don't. In a perverted way, it's hilarious.

Small consolation that it's Spring in the rest of the world!

Grudgingly, the season evolves through Earth Day and Green-up Day. The snow has finally melted so you can see the trash. Then there's a robin, and then a crocus, and then a tuft of green, and finally a bluebird. You don't want to take off the snow tires yet, because you know what that means. Oh hell, you might as well leave them on all summer.

Sugarin'

*Has anyone done the math on sugaring? This
sacred rite of Vermont passage is so labor and energy
intensive I'm amazed that we haven't exported the
whole business to China.*

The Ol' Vermontah Goes a' Sugarin'.

After more than a quarter century and half of my life in
Vermont, I am, at last, participating in this annual rite of spring.
The best part—no, it's not the syrup, no it's not the easy cama-
raderie of the steamy sugar house—the best part is that people
will now have to ask me how the sugaring season is going, rather
than the other way around. Now I will be able to stroke my chin
thoughtfully before answering in my highly practiced, laconic,
Vermontah way:

"Ya never know."

This is a one-size-fits-all answer to life's eternal questions.
Why does the sap sometimes flow at night, other times not? Why
does it flow sometimes in the rain, sometimes not? What does the
moisture in the ground have to do with the color of the syrup?
Why do some seasons last a week and others a month?

"Ya never know," "ya never know," and "ya never know."

If you say it just right, people think you are the wisest man in
the world.

As I set out for the first day of sugarin' season, like with so
many other Vermonters, my mind is on China. The sun is bright,
and the wind is gusting. I put on my Sorels, bought on sale at
Lenny's, Vermont's Mecca of warmth. I remember my first pair of
Sorels when I first came to Vermont, bought at the Snowsville
General Store. "Made with Pride in Canada," they said. If there is
anything that Canadians should be better at than anyone else in
the world, it should be keeping feet warm and dry in the winter.

And these were pretty dang good boots, too, unless you let
mice build homes in them over the summer, which I did. But the
good thing about the Sorels of yore was the changeable lining.

The bad thing is that it became impossible to find replacements. Instead I went with those injection-molded foam moon boots that were absolutely terrific for the first half of the first season, but then they would rip. By the end of the year they were more duct tape than boot. For the last five years I've just worn old sneakers in the snow, like a teenager.

I forgot about Sorels until I saw them in Lenny's. These new Sorels are made in China. At $49 they cost less than my originals, and I think they are better—lighter, warmer, with better adjustments. So I'm better off, the Chinese people are better off. I do worry, however, about the Canadians who lost their boot-making jobs. Have they found new positions as software engineers and video game designers, or are they slumped in front of the TV, watching "Days of our Lives"?

I put on my Sorels, then my Tubbs snowshoes. Here we go again—made in China rather than Vermont. Made out of tubes and synthetic as opposed to wood and rawhide, and upsetting the balance of payments even more.

My sugarin' companion is Kent Batcheller ("Batch" to his friends), who owns a handsome piece of property along the Third Branch of the White River in Bethel. I pepper him with questions. How did the Abenaki boil sap without metal pots? What's the impact of acid rain on the maples? Has global warming affected the sugaring season? Kent considers each question thoughtfully, then answers:

"Ya never know."

We set out with a canvas bag full of drills, hammers, spigots and sugarin' paraphernalia. Kent knows I'm a rookie, so he demonstrates everything, before letting me try it myself. First he demonstrates how to get a drill bit stuck in a tree. Next, he shows me how to tap an ash tree. Then, when I've got that down, he shows me how to tap into a maple that's been dead for ten years. It's not rocket science. I think I'm what sugar makers call a "natural."

When I've mastered the basics, Kent shows me how to fall "ass-over-teakettle." Maples grow on hillsides. If the snow is deep enough you can manage on these steep slopes fairly well. As the snow level decreases to an icy skim coat over the frozen ground, however, the footing becomes impossible, even with Sorels and snowshoes. Kent shows me how to send all the tools flying when his footing gives way and the appropriate swear words to use as you are sitting there on your wet butt. He's a master.

We get all the lines cleared and the buckets mounted in a few days. Then it's just a matter of listening to the sap drip—thunk, thunk, thunk—and boiling it up in the arch. Oh, there's some cleaning and other stuff, but I don't want to get too technical for the consuming public. One good thing about sugarin' is that you don't have to be overly concerned about being sanitary. Everything gets boiled to bejesus, which kills everything, then you run the finished syrup through a filter which removes any remaining bug bodies.

Collecting the sap is relatively easy. The only trick is that instead of letting the tools go flying when you fall ass-over-teakettle, you let the plastic gathering bucket go flying. Kent tells me that some fellows use a different set of swear words for this, but he sticks with the same ones.

When sufficient sap is gathered the boiling begins. What is critical here is not the temperature or time, but rather the topics of conversation and the food. Traditionally, cider doughnuts and dill pickles are served. When I say "traditionally" what I really mean is "any sugarhouse open to tourists." Any real Vermonter knows that the fare of choice for real sugar makers is beer, and it don't make no difference what kind.

The conversation, however, is critical. Within the dark, steamy, womb of the sugarhouse rugged Vermonters exchange their innermost feelings. Words flow like sap—thunk, thunk, thunk—as we exchange thoughts on boots, the Chinese, acid rain, the Red Sox, and, most of all, the infinite mysteries of sugarin'. The thoughts boil to the surface on the open vats of our lives. And if you run out of thoughts, just shake your head slowly and say, "Ya never know."

The Zen of Mud

What can you say about Mud Season that has not been said? This subject has been scrutinized from more angles than Camel's Hump. But Mud Season isn't about a season, nor is it about mud. It's about the human condition and how grace is achieved through humility, the enlightened state. But, before you think I've gone squishy and New Age-y, listen to this:

The stretch of mud on the hill leading up to your house is bad, but testosterone overrules reason. Who does Mother Nature think she is, anyway? You are one with your vehicle. Your logical mind knows it doesn't help to gun the engine, but what is Mud Season, if not a time for stupidity? You turn the steering wheel to the right, your vehicle goes straight. You stomp harder on the accelerator, you go slower and sideways. The ditch moves closer, inch-by-inch.

The Mud Season neophyte screams obscenities and tries to pull the steering wheel off its shaft. The true Vermonter, as he nestles into the ditch, enters a calm state known as the Zen of Mud. You are not hurt. Your vehicle isn't even damaged. You don't have to call a tow truck, because when the temperature drops and the mud hardens, you can just drive out.

This is a time of great humility. Everyone in your neighborhood will drive by and know your predicament is directly attributable to your own stupidity. This is a time to reach deep, and understand that getting stuck during Mud Season is both a penance and a badge of honor. It rewards your male ego by showing that you pushed the envelope by venturing out when the rest of the world is cowering in front of daytime TV. Your soul, however, uses this time for serene contemplation. As you wave to your passing neighbors (none of whom seem to having the same difficulty making it up the hill), you experience true Christian humility, approaching Nirvana, because you realize how much worse things could be. Here is a litany of fates worse than Mud

Season endured by residents of Beyonder.

High on the list is getting stuck in snow because you were too lazy and or stupid (or both) to put on your snow tires by Labor Day. The embarrassment is worse if you are in a four-wheel-drive vehicle, or, shame on you, a truck. [Editor's note: In this part of the world SUVs are not considered trucks. A truck is something you can use to haul a deer carcass in or take garbage to the dump. A truck does not have leather seats or a CD player.]

Worse than getting stuck during Mud Season is when your personal check is posted by the cash register at the general store with "Deadbeat" scrawled across in angry red pen. "Do not take checks from this person!"

Worse than getting stuck during Mud Season is when get your town report and see your name on the delinquent tax list. You only missed the deadline by a few days, paid a hefty fine, and now this!

Or, you open the local paper and see your name listed in the County Court Round-up, along with the other area miscreants—the ne'er do wells, drunks, and scofflaws that give this part of the world an edge of personality. Or, even worse, you are scouring the classifieds and see one of those "I, wife of, refuse to be responsible for any debts or obligations incurred …" Yup, it has your name.

There are things to contemplate from your ditch-side vantage. Count your blessings. You have not been arrested for drunk driving, nor is your picture in the post office as a deadbeat Dad. You are not even listed on the sex offender website. Life is looking better by the moment.

Worse than getting stuck during Mud Season is being pulled over for speeding, especially in the middle of town. It's bad enough that the cop looks fourteen years old and was a classmate of your kid in junior high. But, why does everyone you've ever met have to pass by while you are sitting in front a flashing cruiser? They honk, you wave. It's like you are running for office. You'd much rather be relaxing here in the ditch.

Humiliation can be political. Ask Elizabeth Ready, whose resume misstatements became the focus of her opponent's entire campaign. Or, what about the candidate for selectboard whose opponent spray painted her name on a giant hog that he left downtown in the back of his pick-up. Ouch. That's hardball! Rather be in a ditch any day.

As a parent, is there anything more character building (read: "humiliating") than having your kid sent home for head lice? Well, maybe one thing. A few years ago some youngsters decided to display their Mud Season defiance by spray painting obscenities on the school busses. Unfortunately, they misspelled the obscenities, even the four-letter ones.

You are not even safe in your own home. You can, for instance, have a chimney fire that brings the fire trucks and all the neighbors. Mud Season is a particularly bad time for chimney fires, because you accumulate creosote during the warm daytime that ignites when you crank up the stove in the evening to ward off the plunging temperatures. Think this through from your ditch-side vantage. Not so bad here in the ditch.

Hi, howya doin'. No, I'll be ok. Just waitin' for the mud to firm up a little.

Another thing more humiliating than being in a ditch during Mud Season is to fall off the roof, ass-over-teakettle, while chopping ice dams. These are the ridges of ice that form along the dripline when melting water meets cold air. The dams cause a build-up of standing water that seeps under the shingles and drips into the walls and window casings. You remove ice dams by perching precariously on a ladder and hacking at them with an ax. Alternatively, you can chop from above, which is safer until the ice lets go, whence you find yourself buried headfirst. You stare, immobilized, into the ice-blue light, wondering if this is how you will die, and wishing you could be in a nice, soft, muddy ditch.

But, that's the Zen of Ice Dams, not mud.

So your life is in a ditch? Don't worry. Relax, enjoy it. You won't freeze to death (probably). Turn on the radio. You might even find a Red Sox game. And the Red Sox are, the last time we looked, World Champions. It will pass. Peas will get planted. Om-m-m-m-m.

Om-m-m-m-m.

Mud Season Romance

I wrote this song thinking it would make me a household word. Is "obscure" a household word? By means of explanation, Ashley's is a local watering hole in Randolph, Vermont. All people, places, and incidents are 100% true. I still think it's one of the greatest songs ever written, although my musical skill and performing abilities are so limited that one listener asked, "Does this song ever end?"

I was thinking about the meaning of life,
Seems you never get the things that you want.
Ah, such a depressing thought on depressing night
During Mud Season in Randolph, Vermont.

I was thinking about the Winter,
And how you never lose the chill from your bones.
I've been a slave to my stove since the Tunbridge Fair,
And I've felt to be always alone.

Only the liquor,
Only the highs,
During Mud Season,
Keep me alive.

I went down to drown my sorrows at Ashley's,
A bar where locals run amok for a buck.
I made the most of time during Happy Hour
And stayed on to try my Friday night luck.

She came in like a wind from Jamaica,
Filling Ashley's with her breath soft and sweet,
And I say unto you with my hand on my heart
This was not your average Friday night meat.

Only the liquor,
Only the highs,
During Mud Season,
Help me survive.

So, I sidled up to her with my Friday night grin
And asked if I could buy her a beer.
Oo-o-o-o she answered me with eyes soft and brown
About the color of a Mud Season deer.

Then I said, "You live in town?" She said, "For all of my life,"
And I said, "Why haven't I seen you around?"
"I guess our paths move in different ways;
let's be happy that a crossroad's been found."

> *And only the liquor,*
> *Only the booze.*
> *Don't forget this was Mud Season,*
> *I had nothing to lose.*

After fifty-two Budweisers at Ashley's
I asked her for a ride in my truck.
Couldn't help but smile as we pushed our way outward;
This was unbelievable Friday night luck.

So I took her on my favorite back roads.
You could almost hear the maple sap flow.
And I can't say she didn't warn me
what would happen if I didn't go slow.

Impaired by liquor (as I was)
I confronted a ditch.
Goddamn those muddy roads.
Son of a bitch.

I struggled to tell the cop who arrived,
"It's the girl whose condition I fear."
I couldn't think, I couldn't speak, and my heart stood still,
Then he said, "You're the only one here."

Then he said, "Listen up boy!" he said:
"Every year when the winter runs short, all you bucks try to
jump the high fence."
I see the same scenes on all the back roads,
I'll be happy when Mud Season ends.

Only the liquor,
Ok, I admit I smoked some grass.
I had to admit the words of that cop
Saved my ass.

And I still put in my hours at Ashley's
Though the buds have now appeared on the trees.
And I search the smoky dancehall horizons
For a romance that was never to be.

It was only a Mud Season Romance.
It never really happened at all.
And the lesson is, don't be fooled by the daylight
You'll be in a ditch by nightfall.

It was only a Mud Season Romance.
It happened between winter and spring,
and I still don't know the meaning of life,
but at least I've stopped wondering.

Ironing My Shirts

I iron my shirts in front of the television, usually watching something mindless, like March Madness. In this case I had an old "Sopranos" video, which turned me deeply introspective. This essay may be too profound for many readers.

Let me tell you about my shirts. And Ethan Allen. And Tony Soprano.

And me.

I came to Vermont more than thirty years ago. I moved to a small town in Central Vermont and discovered pitched warfare between the entrenched (the Chucks) and the invaders (the Flatlanders). It seemed like a perfect world to me. I am one of the great social and cultural observers of our times. If you haven't heard of me, it's a testament to my extraordinary modesty. Take my word for it.

It's Sunday afternoon. The garden has long been put to bed. Deer season, when taking a walk in the woods is like going for a vacation in Iraq, is a distant memory. Baseball season is over and has not yet egun. The Red Sox have failed again, but hope springs eternal.

Nothing better to do than to iron my shirts. I put on a rented video of "The Sopranos," HBO's morality tale about the Mob in suburban Jersey. This show may be old news to the rest of America, but it's just trickling into my consciousness. I'm about eight episodes into the first season. The problem is, I don't do television. At least I tell people I don't. But Tony Soprano has captivated me. The only way I can justify my tube addiction is to pull out the ironing board to iron my shirts. That makes me productive.

First point of keen, social observation...I am ironing my own shirts. As a male of the species, a white one anyway, I went through the first fifty years of my life letting others iron my shirts, thinking it my birthright. This, by itself, is worthy of a column, if not a full-length book. The thought of my own Father standing at an ironing board is unimaginable. Did he fight in the Big One only to come home to iron his own shirts?

Aside: maybe this is my penance for side-stepping Vietnam. In college I took my shirts weekly to be professionally laundered. Now, thirty years later, mistrustful of commercial cleaning processes and cheap as hell, I am ironing my shirts, watching Tony Soprano, and contemplating the Big Picture. (Observe that we have already touched on major themes of the changing roles of gender and socio-economic evolution in the latter half of the twentieth century. Self-reliance and non-toxic living have emerged as subplots.)

As Tony breaks peoples' legs, wipes out the competition, and carouses with wild women in the Bada Bing Club, I read the labels on my shirts. I buy my dress shirts from Land's End, so in one sense my shirts all come from Dodgeville, Wisconsin. Upon closer examination, however, my shirts are as international as the Olympics.

The first, a blue pinstripe button-down, comes from Hong Kong. Years ago Hong Kong was the mecca for expensive, custom suits. Now, it's the magnet for China's rural poor to work in what we might describe as sweat shops that provide their workers a small boost up on the global scale of materialism. One person's sweat shop, I've learned, is another's golden opportunity.

The next shirt comes from Mauritius, and I can't even tell you what continent that's on or in. Also, since I have a strict policy against research or fact checking, you're going to have to look it up yourself.

Next up, a blue Oxford, is from Malaysia. This, I can tell you, is a place far away, across the Pacific, probably next to Asia. Undoubtedly, it's hot, swampy, and teeming with people willing to work making shirts for me to buy from Land's End.

And the fourth is from Mexico. Ole! These are worldly shirts that I own. I go up to my closet and find shirts from Bangladesh, Pakistan, Bulgaria, Thailand, Turkey, but nothing "Made in Vermont." These shirts have traveled the globe to reach my ironing board. Something trips my totally beyondered trigger.

This past summer I visited the Ethan Allen homestead in Burlington's Intervale. The docent there gave an interesting presentation on how the early Vermonters made their clothing from the stalks of the flax plant. First, they cleared the land. Then, they planted flax. Next, they harvested the flax. Then, they beat the stalks into a tangled floss; then, they used this nasty-looking comb to straighten the fibers to be spun into yarn. (You can tell that I paid very close attention.)

Even after all this time and effort, you're still a long way from a shirt. The yard must be loomed into bolts of linen cloth that a skilled seamstress can then transform into a shirt or frock. The whole process takes a lot of patience, a lifetime of specialized knowledge, and about a year.

Ay-yi-yi. Why didn't they just pick up the phone and call Land's End? It's toll-free!!

The population of Mexico City is now 27 million, and growing by a gazillion per day. The population of Vermont, by contrast, reached its high point in 1829, around the time when the descendants of Ethan Allen were still flogging their flax into frocks. (By the way, you can still buy a custom tailored linen shirt for about $200.)

Tony Soprano, meanwhile, is kneeling over some helpless guy, pounding him repeatedly with his right fist and screaming, "Give me the #!!&*%$##!! money!! Give me the #!!&*%$##!! money!!"

I don't whether it's good or bad that my shirts come from all over the globe, just as I don't know whether it's good or bad that I could no more transform a bale of flax into a linen shirt than I could whack a stool pigeon (Tony's creeping in). But I can tell you that life in Vermont has changed a lot since 1829. It's a lot easier to iron my shirts while watching "The Sopranos" than to figure out how to get from flax to frock.

I finish ironing and put the board away. Tony is back in a space where baked ziti is more significant than his ##$!!@&*! money. What does it all mean?

The world is changing, and the pace of change is accelerating. We've exported our drudgery to the Malaysias, Mexico Cities, and Hong Kongs of the world, where people are glad to make our shirts. They ship the shirts halfway across the globe, then the delivery truck is boosted by Tony and his friends in a small-scale heist. Meanwhile, most of us couldn't make a shirt if our lives depended on it. We're too busy "livin'."

And meanwhile, I'm the smartest guy in the world. I watched TV for an hour, got my shirts ironed, and collected the material for this column, for which I am being paid a small (actually very significant) fortune. Tony and Ethan would be proud of me.

All Aboard

*This is a great time to get the hell out of Beyonder.
Alas, they've eliminated the overnight roomettes on
the Amtrak service to Vermont.*

They actually knew my name!

I climbed on board the Amtrak Montrealer in Montpelier at
9:15 p.m., bound for New York City (or, as some Vermonters call
it, "The Big Crappie"). The night oozed with romance even as I
waited on the platform. Before long that most plaintive of sounds
drifted up the valley, the whistle of an oncoming train.

Being a seasoned traveler, I followed the crowd and boarded
at the rear of the train. I showed my ticket to the conductress (is
this the gender-correct term?) who said:

"You've got a long walk."

I pushed my way through several passenger cars, the club car,
the lounge car, and the dining car—seven cars in all, until I
approached the sleeping area.

"Mr. Morris?" asked another conductor, a sharply pressed
black man who responded to my nod by grabbing my bag and
saying, "Just follow me."

Having been hustled by New Yorkers smarter than I many
times before in life, I thought this might be the start of yet another humiliating (and costly) ruse. "My name's William," he said,
"Just give me a call if you want anything."

Now I was really getting suspicious. Maybe I shouldn't have
let him take my bag. How'd he know my name, anyway? Maybe
he was in cahoots with my travel agent.

"Here's your roomette. Do you know how our rooms function?"

I felt like saying, "What do you think? I'm from Vermont,"
but I settled for striking a dumb, immobile pose.
"Overherestheclosetandtotheleftisyourcomfortcontrolthefoldin
gsinkshouldberemovedwhen "

Within thirty seconds he had given me a speech that was

every bit as compact as the roomette where I would be sleeping. I didn't understand much, because I was trying to think what the proper tipping etiquette was in this situation. After providing me with a bucket of ice, an after-dinner sweet, and a small portfolio of stationery, William left me to my own devices.

What a masterpiece of design this roomette was! Here was a bedroom, bathroom, and living room all in a space less than half the size of my minivan, yet the overall impression was of space and luxury. Compared to the experience of being wedged between a fat lady and a traveling salesperson thirty thousand feet over Newark, this was style!

And privacy. There was a 2x3' mirror opposite my seat in which I could make disgusting faces while pretending that I was Humphrey Bogart or Inspector Clousseau. And I could moon people with total impunity from my window. Who would know? It was dark, we were passing through the wilds of Vermont. I couldn't let an opportunity like this pass. But I did. Would Bogey have mooned the town of Bellows Falls? No.

I enjoyed my roomette until the clicking and swaying lulled me to sleep. At first I thought one slept in the seat (hey, I've done worse), but I heard William helping another passenger fold down their berth. Suddenly, it fell into place—the rear wall of the compartment was actually a folding Murphy bed.

"This is pretty hot," I said to myself, managing to pull down the bed without folding myself into the wall a la Laurel and Hardy. I even put my shoes into a special, little compartment so that William could shine them during the night. Total decadence!

William awoke me at 6:30 a.m., as requested, and brought me coffee and juice. You've got to be kidding, I told myself. I checked the shoe compartment. There they were, ready for Manhattan. Try asking your stewardess for a shine the next time you fly the friendly skies.

I folded up my bed, got dressed, and enjoyed the passing graffiti of the outskirts of New York City. Yes, there were teeming masses out there, but for the moment I felt infinitely superior. I would arrive, rested and ready to take the island by storm. For the first time in my life, I really wanted to give someone a tip.

Two days later, Manhattan had overwhelmed me, and I was

ready to limp my whipped and tired butt back to the serenity of the north. I arrived at Penn Station two hours early, and the train was two hours late. By the time the Montrealer arrived I had spent so much energy fending off bums and so much money on bad beer that I no longer felt like being a human shill for Amtrak. "If I had flown," I told myself as the train was finally announced, "I'd be climbing into my own beddy-bye, instead of a train that will take nine hours to make a trip that technology makes possible in forty-five minutes."

There's a lesson in this tale. It has something to do with the relative values of time and service in modern society, but I'm too fuzzy headed to express it coherently. If you figure it out, please drop me a line.

City Versus Country

I hate it when I meet someone smarter than me am.

A rube from the northern Appalachian backwater of Beyonder came to the Big Apple to celebrate a noteworthy event in Manhattan's fashionable SoHo district. It promised to be a clash of cultures to be conducted over a civilized ritual known as the cocktail party.

In Beyonder we don't do cocktail parties. We do kegs in backyards. We do horseshoes and volleyball, but we don't do cocktail parties.

(Just to come clean on the hypocrisy front, I am an urban refugee who escaped to the green hills of Vermont from the Boston-Washington megalopolis. I preach the noble simplicity of independent life, but I am truthfully a product of privileged, white upbringing who can balance a wine glass on my hors d'oeuvres plate.)

At this event, I could feel smug and superior. After all, I'm from the country—Vermont!—where the air is clean, and we leave the keys right in the car. We burn wood, a renewable resource, and we are at one with the planet. I do all the right things. I recycle. I go to town meeting. I mend my fences.

I reflected on city life. People in New York live like animals in cages. You can see the breakdown of societal order in the graffiti and the litter. The homeless are everywhere. Some of the panhandlers, by the way, are getting very creative. One of them even asked if he could borrow my Grey Poupon.

There were omnipresent admonitions of the breakdown of societal order. Right in my hotel room were signs commanding: 1. Don't leave valuables in the room, 2. Triple lock the door, 3. If someone knocks on the door, shoot first, ask who it is later, and 4. In case of fire, get the Hell out. This is living?

I resisted the temptation to wear a plaid shirt with a tie, although when asked what I would like to drink, I couldn't resist asking if there was homebrew or hard cider. Might as well give the people their money's worth.

Before long I was conversing with a young woman who had lime green hair and pieces of metal pierced through various parts of her anatomy. She wore a t-shirt that proclaimed, "No Drugs, No Toxins....This woman is a Pure Animal." In Vermont we would probably refer to her as "quite a rigging" or "a real piece of gear."

"How can you be so concerned about non-toxic living," I asked, "when you live in an environment that is trashed?"

"How can you preach the virtues of simple living," the woman countered, "when you live a life of obscene energy consumption?"

"What do you mean?" I protested. Her missile had struck a sensitive area. I fired back with a description of a self-contained, quiet life—heating with wood, tilling a garden, and doing all the right stuff. I cited my employment of compact fluorescents, water-saving showerheads, and numerous components of the energy-efficient life.

"Your problem," she said calmly, "is with the fallacy of the basic concept. How many rooms in your house?"

"Eight."

"I have a three-room walk-up. I have fewer windows than you, fewer light sockets, and no yard. I take up less space. How well insulated is your house?"

"Well, it's a leaky old farmhouse, but I get more of it insulated every year." It was time to turn the tables and go on the offensive: "If your apartment is anything like my hotel, it's hardly a model of energy efficiency."

"My home, as with your hotel, is insulated by other rooms on all sides, including top and bottom. Whatever heat I waste is recovered by my neighbors. How many vehicles do you own?"

"Three, but they're all very efficient," I protested, knowing how this information would be turned on me.

"I own none," said the woman. "I work ten blocks from where I live. I walk or take the subway everywhere. I leave Manhattan only four or five times a year, and then it's by train, or some other form of public transportation. Who's spewing more gunk into the atmosphere? Me? Or you with your three vehicles? Do you have a garden?"

"I sure do." Now, here was an area of clear superiority for the Beyonder lifestyle.

"Then you probably have a rototiller. And a lawn tractor. And a chain saw. In fact, I'll bet you have a workshop full of little Briggs and Stratton internal combustion engines. I buy everything locally, mostly on the block where I live. You'd be amazed at what I can get within a hundred yards of my home—mangos, papaya, asparagus, artichokes."

Alright, alright, alright. I had seen the exotic displays of fruits stacked outside the corner delis. That morning, in fact, I breakfasted on some exotic Asian pear that came from who-knows-where.

"Face it," she said, turning. Her final statement was flipped as casually as a scarf over her shoulder. "If everyone was as gluttonous as you about planetary resources, there wouldn't be room for many of us. There's only one answer for a responsible person—live in the city and leave the country to the animals."

My hors d'oeuvres suddenly looked as unappetizing as the prospect of living in Manhattan. Properly chastened, and hopelessly outflanked, I couldn't wait to head north.

The Eco-Curmudgeon

*I'm just an old eco-curmudgeon, spouting off on
Earth Day. I spend a lot of time railing about the state
of the environment. I can be very self-righteous, and
very boring, as I portray myself as the sole protector of
the planetary resources.*

T.S. Eliot said "April is the cruelest month." Geoffrey
Chaucer said "Whanne that Aprille with his shoures soote"
(which translates loosely to "April weather sucks"). And I say,
"I'm sick of this, this, this ... *stuff.*"

By "stuff" I mean slush, snow, taxes, small talk about sugaring
season, votes on the school budget, mud, sleet, puddles, snow
tires, income taxes, eternal hope for the goddamn Red Sox, dead-
lines, work, Mondays, phone calls, fax machines (go fax yourself!), Nirvana at 98 decibels, Nirvana at 103 decibels, anything
that begins with "eco," midwinter girth, woodstoves, presidential
politics, local politics, Easter bunnies, checks that bounce, wind-
shield wipers that don't work, and—more than anything else—
people who tell me that I've got a bad attitude.

Ah, but this is Spring, time of renewal. I'd be sick of spring,
too, if it was close enough to be sick of. As it is, however, I won't
have to worry about that for another two months, so instead I
have to content myself with being sick of things that remind me of
spring. Such as Earth Day. Aha, you say to yourself. This is just a
big build-up to Stephen's Annual Earth Day Rant.

Heh-heh, you're right.

Don't get me wrong. I think the environment is a very nice
place. I don't want to pollute it, drop acid on it, run Love Canals
through it, or subject it to nuclear meltdown. But I must confess,
I am getting greened to death. Here are a few samples from the
mailbox recently:

A note (printed on recycled paper with soy-based inks)
accompanying an unsolicited plastic gewgaw arrived recently,
informing me that this company no longer uses styrofoam

peanuts. Instead, they use 100% recycled polystyrene, a revolutionary material, not grown on trees, most notable for the fact that
it looks and feels exactly like styrofoam peanuts. The result, from
my personal perspective, was the same. The dogs got into the
trash and before you could say "R-r-rainforest Crunch" there were
white plastic uglies all over the lawn. They will stay there until the
snow is all gone.

Here are a few quotes from the card. "This company
cares...This is an exciting time for us. We look forward to the '90's
as an opportunity to help save the earth....We are always on the
lookout for products that help society." Yeah, like the gewgaw.
The card also provided the intriguing fact that recycling one aluminum can saves enough energy to run a television set for three
hours. Is the point that we're supposed to recycle aluminum, or
watch more TV?

It makes you think. Yes, it makes you think that maybe the
toxins in our water supplies have addled our brains.

A similar card from a different company begins: "Really. We
mean it." You mean what? The card goes on to say that the company loves me, the planet, and that they, too, do not use styrofoam
peanuts which deplete the ozone and are "an absurd and unsightly nuisance." They haven't seen the polystyrene in my front yard.

Another company tells me they plant two trees for every one
cut down to produce their catalog. They do not mention that the
tree cut down was a hundred years old and two hundred feet
high, and the seedlings are the size of matchsticks. Not a fair
trade.

Another postcard presents "an energy policy worth fighting
for." Didn't we just send a half million people halfway around the
world for that? If I remember, that didn't work out so well.

Now, here's something that I can get behind—a solicitation to
adopt a tree in Nicaragua. Only ten bucks! Of course, some of the
money goes for the "attractive certificate" that acknowledges my
contribution. (Just for a point of comparison, see how many
seedlings you can buy locally for $10. I like the rainforest, too, but
my sawbuck will do much more good spent in Vermont.)

My favorite green appeal comes from a mail-order cosmetic
firm whose catalog contains ten separate mentions of the fact that

they are "against animal testing." The company objects to it on the grounds that it is "cruel, irrelevant, and unnecessary." Instead, this company guarantees the safety of its products through "a battery of controlled laboratory tests on human volunteers." Maybe I'm missing the point; won't be the first time.

Environmentalists, not known for their senses of humor, probably resent me poking fun at businesses working to improve the planet and might suggest that I turn my criticism on the vast majority of businesses either causing the problems or doing nothing to solve them. It is a point well taken, but there is a serious message to my madness, as well. There is a fine line between sincere motivation and marketing strategies designed to exploit positive motivations. If the "green bandwagon" becomes overloaded and trivialized by companies mistaking 50 simple things you can do to save the planet with 50 simple things you can do to make a killing off the green movement, then another good idea will bite the dust.

Beeping Watches

This essay was written in 1286. Of course, I'm joking. I wasn't even born in 1286, but this article is so technologically dated that it makes me feel as if I should be stuffed and put on display in a museum with my watch set to beep on the hour.

The scene was quintessentially Vermont. Christmas Eve. Outside, a light snow fell, muffling the silent landscape. Within the Upper Granville church, the community gathered to offer thanks through silent prayer. Echoes of children singing "Silent Night" were the only vestige of sound. The church was redolent with smells—evergreens, kerosene lamps, Mrs. Blanchard's chocolate chip cookies. The scene was not unlike Christmas Eves celebrated in the same place for the last 100 years.

The good reverend had suggested silence as an appropriate medium for sending the message of gratitude. Little did he know that as the prayer was beginning, the clock was striking eight. Well, not exactly. Instead of the evocative resonance of a tolling bell, there was the communal cry of digital watches:

Beep-beep. Doot-doot-doot. Eeek-Eeeeeeek.

Here's the scenario. You have, say, three children. Each of them has a birthday and Christmas every year. In total that's six "gift occasions." For the last four years each child has received a digital watch with built-in beeper on each occasion, mostly from sadistic grandparents who can never think of gift ideas.

Each watch comes with an instruction booklet that comes in four languages (none of them Japanese) with operating instructions incomprehensible to anyone over 20. The kids immediately program every digital feature—the daily alarm, the hourly reminder—that involves a noise. Then, of course, they lose the booklet.

And your home, on the hour, sounds like the nesting area for a thousand bats: Beep-beep, Doot-doot-doot, Eeek-Eeeeeeek.

The electronic sound is impossible to echo-locate, meaning that you can search for hours to find an offending watch. Once found, if you are like me, you are too cheap to throw it out. After all, it keeps great time. If digital watches did not keep great time, then they couldn't go off simultaneously during church services.

Beeping watches draw attention to themselves at the most inopportune times. Many a moment of passionate ardor has been doused by the dreaded sound:

Beep-beep, Doot-doot-doot, Eeek-Eeeeeeek.

My worst digital moment came during a tense face-off I was having with my boss. He had just suggested that I quit, and I counter-proposed that he just fire me. Reaching the moment of truth, we stared across the desk at each other, unflinching, nostrils flaring. The next one to speak would lose.

Beep-beep, Doot-doot-doot, Eeek, Eeeeeeek.

The tension drained from the situation like air from a razor-slashed balloon.

"I'm sorry. Is that me beeping?"

"Oh no, I think it's me. Sorry."

Most humiliating is when the alarm (which you set earlier that morning to remind you to pick up a video on the way home) goes off, and you can't remember how to turn it off. This only occurs when you are in front of a group of people discussing a sensitive subject.

There's this doctor I know. Doctors are entitled to watch videos, right? So he sets his alarm as a reminder. At just the time he expected to be driving home, he happened to be meeting with the hospital board of directors pleading for a million bucks to build a health care facility for the homeless and:

Beep-beep, Doot-doot-doot, Eeek-Eeeeeeek.

He pushed all the buttons, but the little fella kept on squeaking. The alarm is supposed to shut itself off after ten seconds, but someone at the Casio factory must have put in the wrong microchip, because this one squealed for what the man described as "half my adult life."

Any semblance of competence slipped away. "If the guy can't even turn off the alarm on his watch," the board members said to themselves, "what's he gonna do with a million bucks?"

Our doctor friend considered options—sticking his arm in a drawer, yelling "Omigod, I'm due in surgery!," or pretending it was not his watch. Instead, he opted for sawing off the offending arm and throwing it out the window.

Naw-w-w. Not really, but you get the point. Beeping watches. Bleeping beeping watches.

The Funniest Guy in Beyonder

I thought this was a riot, even after one of the people mentioned sent me a threatening letter from his lawyer. After the lawsuit, in which I was require to pay $1.5 million for character defamation, we all had a good laugh over a beer.

Every other week, when this column appears, I wake up on Sunday morning and rush down to the Upper Granville General Store to buy all the newspapers. Then, after a brief exchange of

Vermont humor with the storekeeper ("Your piece in the paper this week?" says he. "Don't know where else it would be," say I. Guess I still don't quite have the hang of it.) I rush home and thrust the Vermont *Sunday Magazine* into my wife's face.

I study her face for telltale signs of mirth as she reads my column. Occasionally there's a chuckle or a murmur of approval. Twice there have been audible guffaws, and last August, I'll never forget it, she issued an unmistakable chortle.

After finishing "The View," she turns to Dave Barry's column, which is relegated to the back pages of this magazine. The next few minutes are among the longest of my life as she snorts, giggles, and titters her way through his column. At the end of her review, I help her up off the floor.

"Well?" I ask glumly.

"His was better," she says. Not that I'm competitive, but since I've begun writing this column, Dave has been better 37 times, while I've triumphed on a mere four occasions.

I know what you're saying. "Why doesn't this guy get a new wife, one with some literary taste or at least the ability to lie?"

I've considered that. But, by my own reckoning, I would have given myself the nod only twice.

Of course, being funny isn't everything, but as the great Vince Lombardi said, it's what you get paid for. My column is filled with searing social commentary, a commodity less in demand than Dave's stock in trade—eel snot and monkey pus. Also, Dave works out of the cultural wasteland of Southern Florida, while I work the fertile hardscrabble of Northern Appalachia.

This brought to mind an interesting question: Who is the funniest guy in Vermont (and I don't need to explain that I include gals in the guy category)? I excluded Dave from consideration, and disqualified myself, for obvious reasons. (A pox on all of you in Beyonder who just thought to yourself, "Yeah, because you're not funny.") Here they are then, the funniest guys in a very funny state:

Bernie Sanders: Give the guy credit, he's taken the dull institution of Congress and turned it into a Laugh Riot. He's a veritable Eddie Murphy, without the foul language, of Capitol Hill. We'll never forget his classic routine where he delivers stirring, anti-Gulf War oration to the empty chambers of the house for the benefit of the television cameras. Bernie, you're a stitch. Nothing like a Vermonter to keep those stodgy pols from taking things too seriously.

Marcellus Parsons: Here's someone whose name gives away the big punch line. Say it out loud. See, you're smiling. His name can't be pronounced without cracking up, and yet, he does it every night, wearing this grim, wooden puss. Number one, you don't believe this is really the guy's name, do you? No way. He's probably a Bob Smith or Ed Billings. And secondly, the guy is setting us up. After years of lulling us into thinking he's a dour, faceless commentator, he'll show up on camera wearing a dress and talking like Tweety Bird. He's fooled some people, but not me. The guy cracks me up.

Red Elmore: Here's a funny man whose entire claim to comedic fame is captured in one line. Everybody now, "Out of towners, call collect." Not since "Take my wife, please," has a line captured the mirthful imagination of the Beyonder populace.

Honorable mention: Tony Adams (ex-sportscaster)—sorry, you qualify only if you're trying to be funny. Bob Kalvados (current sportscaster)—newscasts aren't that funny, but Bambinos' commercials are pretty good. Madeleine Kunin—where's "Straddlin' Madeleine" now that we need her?

Let's not forget the writing team of Mares and Bryan (*Real Vermonters Don't Milk Goats*, et al)—the funniest team since Martin & Lewis or Abbott & Costello. They need a live act, though. Jeff Danziger (cartoonist)—captures the meager humor of the hardscrabble landscape beautifully. He does it well enough to make the rest of us superfluous. Tim Brookes (columnist whose slot is on this same page on alternate weeks)—very funny guy, but sorry Tim, the current score is Dave 4-you 0.

Also making the top twenty is my son, Patrick—you should have seen his "Frosty the Snowman" at the Brookfield School Christmas pageant. And the Voice on the Idlenot Dairy ("Oy-dull-not") commercials—I love those neon-colored cows. Let's not forget the buffoon on the Sleep Quarters commercials, the fat guy who brandishes the pom-poms and says, "Sleep Quarters, Sleep Quarters, We've Got Your Bed, Lose this commercial and shoot me in the head!" Anyone with enough self-confidence to do this on TV deserves recognition.

And finally, the Beyonder award for the funniest guy in Vermont, a guy so witty that he makes our faces wrinkle into smiles just thinking about him....A man who has not rested on his laurels, but who keeps bringing us rapier-sharp, mirthful images, such as the most recent one in which he rides, waving to imaginary crowds, in his chair, shaped like a human hand, down the crowded streets of Montreal, a man who shows us that in this day of high-tech computer graphics you can still make low-tech video—Ladies and gentlemen, the undisputed king of Vermont comedy, the funniest guy in the Green Mountains (drum roll)— Nat Lash.

Delusions of Grandeur

The cruelest month lingers...six weeks, seven weeks. Still April marches on, leaving winter farther behind, but spring no closer. You turn inward.

Soon after graduating from college, I started keeping a modest, spiral-bound notebook entitled "Million Dollar Ideas and How to Save the Planet." At some of the oddest moments—chopping ice dams on the roof, plummeting down a muddy dirt road on a mountain bike, sitting in church on Christmas Eve—something that promises certain and imminent wealth inexplicably enters my brain and eventually my notebook.

Flipping back through past ideas provides insight to the passage of time and the evolution of culture. The original book was started in 1972. Volume II, a handsome cloth-bound birthday present, served me from February 9, 1982, to the Millennium. Volume III is a "somewhat blank book" featuring the artwork of friend, neighbor, and famous artist, Edward Koren.

Some of the ideas are not money-making schemes so much as profound observations on the culture, such as #5 (4/14/72) when I noted, "The most relevant question of these times is whether to gain or lose consciousness." Wow. That is followed with an idea to invent a tool handle with a snap-lock head that accepts a variety of heads. Next to it is a clipping from a Brookstone catalog, added some eighteen years hence, of just such a device.

#54 (2/3/73) is to create a Stone Age Village where the inhabitants have to literally live the period life. Here's an idea that preceded the television show Survivor by almost thirty years, and I didn't earn a nickel.

This is an Olympic year and so was 1976, when I had the thought to have an Industrial Olympics where normal working people could show off their skills, such as driving a forklift or wielding a jackhammer. Surely this could be as interesting and competitive as Olympic horseback riding or sailing.

And speaking of sports, how about the idea of a professional basketball league where no one could be over six feet or a football league where no one could weigh more than two hundred pounds?

The ideas reflect the various passions of my life. For instance, I like beer, so there are ideas for clear beer twenty years before Zima and an all-grain, organic health beer twenty years before Wolavers. I like food, so there are ideas for herbed butters and chocolate whipped cream. I like books, so there are any number of book ideas, even some for food books and beer books.

I also use this book to record fractured clichés. When someone says he wouldn't do something for "all the money in China," it goes in the book. "She's the kind of person who'd give you the hair off her back" made it in as well.

Not all the ideas are brilliant. Some of them are quaintly dated or just plain bad. Did I really think I could make a million dollars by starting a business to convert Super 8mm movies to videotape? What was I thinking (or smoking) when I suggested opening a restaurant based on Eskimo cuisine? Please pass the blubber.

By contrast the idea recorded the day after Thanksgiving in 1987 still has potential—Gobbler Farms, a fast-food restaurant built around serving turkey in its many post-holiday manifestations. Think of it…turkey clubs, open-faced sandwiches with gravy, turkey soups. Why hasn't Burger King or Taco Bell thought of this? Do I have to come up with all the new ideas?

I am not afraid to take on the big issues. By the mid-1980s video cameras were becoming popular, so it was easy for me to foresee the decline and fall of all the great universities as all the best professors delivered their lectures in the comfort of your living room. The last time I went to Burlington, however, UVM was still there.

By the 1990s I had entered my forties. You'd think that I could be normal and just have a regular mid-life crisis, but I bypassed the sports car and continued to seek new paths to fame and fortune. There was my pet rental business for the person who wants only occasional companionship. How about pretzels in the form of peace symbols?

For a while I got on a Spam kick. What can I say? Spam is a very funny luncheon meat. I also keep a list of great names for bands, in case anyone is looking for a gray-haired rhythm guitarist with a one-octave range. What do you think of "Run For Your Coats?" Or "The Band With No Name?" "Don't Drop the Soap?"

Solar-powered Christmas candles. Importing Norwegian kicksleds? I spotted that trend so far before its time that it still hasn't happened.

Here are more book titles: *The Last Hippie in Montpelier*. *Red Meat and Marlboros*. I have no idea what this last book is about, but I'd buy it.

Interspersed amongst the great ideas are a few gratuitous top ten lists and painful observations on what the Red Sox must do to finally win the World Series. There are sketches of the perfect barbecue grill, an ongoing quest. Have you ever tried to empty the ashes from a Weber? I can do better.

At the Millennium I double checked my bank account and started Volume III, undeterred by consistent and repeated failure. What's money, anyway, aside from the provider of all happiness?

Of course, not a single one of the ideas has ever earned me a cent, and the planet, depending on your perspective, remains in peril. I persevere, Vermont's Don Quixote, addicted to my own delusions of grandeur.

These days the ideas come a little less frequently. Maybe I've thought of everything. The latest entry is my original recipe for Steamed Salad. It's a good recipe (no kidding), but not likely to earn much money or save the planet. I now spend more time revisiting old ideas and noting which have become realities.

As I page through, I see jobs changing, society lurching forward, and my kids growing up. I see less youthful arrogance, less unfocused testosterone, and one lesson learned—that you don't have to be a rich man to have a rich life.

Fog for Brains

Nothing makes one an observer of the human species so much as parenthood. I might never have noticed the phenomenon of F.F.B. Syndrome had I not had an 11-year-old child. It's not like you have any-thing else to do.

Nothing makes one an observer of the human species so much as parenthood. I might never have noticed the phenomenon of F.F.B. Syndrome had I not had an 11-year-old son. "F.F.B.," as I'm sure all readers know, is the acronym for the most common of adolescent maladies—Fog For Brains. The symptoms combine narcolepsy (sleeping disease), excessive eating (in particular pizza, dudes), and a tendency to stare into space until prodded by a blunt object such as a 2x4.

A child afflicted with F.F.B. is capable of losing anything smaller than an adult elephant and, conversely, incapable of finding any object not attached to his body. He can tolerate indescribable squalor, but will devote hours to the combing of his hair, anointing the scalp with assorted mousses, gels, and magic potions to get the appropriate sense of casual disarray. The average F.F.B. boy on a special occasion will carry $6.58 of cosmetics on his noggin.

In a scientific breakthrough, I managed to insert an entire video camera inside the skull of an 11 year old to record a typical minute of cranial activity. The picture, as expected, came back completely blank; just a wash gray, thicker than the wet blanket that covered Sherlock Holmes' London. A certain amount of auditory activity was noted, and appears here exactly as recorded:

"Food. Maybe eat. Me. I should. Dinner sometime. Mom's voice, calling me. Mario. Would 8 and 3. Must defeat Rocky Wrench. Jump Mario! Jump. Enter the rocket engine. Rocket. Rocket Roger. Mom's voice. Food eat. Roger Clemens. Baseball card. Topps 1985 rookie card, now up to $20 in Beckett's Monthly. Lawn mowing. Money. Work. Jump, Mario! Throw fireballs. Mom's voice. Dinner. Have we eaten yet? Money. How much? $8.35, not counting the silver dollar from the Tooth Fairy. Large, hard object now striking head. Pain. Voice. Father. Food. Dinner. Now."

Here is a true story. I have observed a Little League team for the past two years. At least 60 percent of the team is afflicted with advanced Fog For Brains. The coach tried a variety of signs to communicate the strategies of the grand of game—a tipped cap meant "steal," a bat gripped by the barrel meant "bunt," etc. None of these worked, so he tried a different tack.

"When I want you to bunt, I'll look you right in the eye and say 'Bunt!'"

The first batter came to the plate; the coach looked right at him and said, "Bunt, Ricky." The kid nodded and touched the brim of his cap (the signal to acknowledge receipt of the sign), maintaining a major league poker face so as not to alert the opposition, then promptly swung away. When he came back to the bench, the coach's blood pressure had risen by 20 points and he had already chewed two Tums. He maintained composure, however:

"Didn't you hear me say bunt, Ricky?"

The kid nodded, but his expression, said "Whaddya think, I'm deaf?"

"Why didn't you bunt?" asked the coach.

The kid reacted as if he had been asked to explain the founding principles behind nuclear crystallography. "I forgot the sign," he answered, implying that the coach was at fault. The kid came to bat a second time. The situation did not call for a bunt, but, what the hell, I think the coach was just curious.

"Bunt, Ricky," he said, cupping his hands so that everyone in the park could hear.

The kid touched the brim of his hat, then swung away. When he came back to the bench, the coach (whose hair had now turned gray and who appeared to have aged 20 years) asked, "Did you catch the bunt sign, Ricky?"

"Yeah, I saw it." Silence.

"Why didn't you bunt?"

"You didn't give me the sign," he said nonchalantly.

Most amazingly, an adolescent can carry on a seemingly intelligent conversation while in Fogland. I find this more amazing than those stories of sleep walkers who get dressed and drive to the 7-11 and back while snoozing. Consider the conversation I had with my son preceding the publication of this article:

"Son, I've written an article about your Fog For Brains, but I didn't want to print it before checking with you."

His initial reaction was the universal F.F.B. response: "Huh?"

"Well, I know kids can be sensitive, so I didn't want to print anything about you and your Fog For Brains, until I cleared it with you."

"No problem, Dad," he said affably, adding with a note of genuine curiosity, "What's the article about?"

The good news is that F.F.B. never lasts more than a decade, and is rarely fatal, although it can result in bedrooms that look like war zones. Parents sometimes confuse symptoms with another adolescent bane—drugs. The biggest difference is that the drug user will occasionally pick up a pair of underwear to convince an adult that things are normal.

This is a danger sign. A healthy adolescent will never pick up a pair of underwear from the floor, except in the rarest circumstances—such as the need for a handkerchief.

Clixed-Up Michés

Now, you are in a truly desperate time. Earth Day is past. You've greened up you roadside, and still you remain ensconced in a seasonal never-never land. It's hilarious. It's demonic.

Some people, especially in Vermont where the winters are long, collect things. I know people who collect rare wines, deer antlers, Blue Willow china, baseball cards, snake skins, campaign buttons, barbed wire, beer cans, coins, stamps, and telephone insulators.

I collect clichés.

Clichés are trite, shopworn, overused phrases, such as, *She is as dumb as a box of rocks.* Readers of my writing are no strangers to clichés. I am to the cliché what Tiger Woods is to the golf club. In my personal collection, however, I eschew the ordinary in favor of those most rare and valuable phractured phrases (hush of silence, ominous organ music in minor chords wells in background), the Clixed-up Miché.

These are the Hope Diamonds, the albino bisons, black pearls, and three-pound truffles of the linguistic world. These freaks of human nature occur when the brain reaches into the language section for a familiar phrase, and somehow comes out with a mongrel piece of verbiage that makes as much sense as weeding the garden in January.

Warning: Clixed-up Michés can cause a reader to scratch his or her head for prolonged periods, muttering, "What's he talking about?" They make you go "Huh?" For full effect, read them aloud, preferably after sniffing glue. Here, without tiptoeing through the eggshells, is my personal stash.

It was bright mid-October day, twenty-two years ago. I asked a co-worker if he was willing to work Sundays. He replied "No, not for all the money in China."

Uh ... waitaminute. Apparently his brain reached into his

cliché folder for *all the money in the world* or *all the tea in China*, and came up with a hybrid that reminds us that China is a Third World country where people work for fourteen cents a day. A while later this same person told me to *put that in my hat and smoke it.* Off the tip of my head I recognized these as vintage Michés, the kind that draw ooo-o-s and aahh-h-hs on Cliché Roadshow.

A friend of mine, a guy who talks from the hip, once described his sister as the *kind of girl who wears her heart on her shoulder.* I pictured her with a bloody, pulsating organ perched parrot-like next to her smiling face. Did this mean that his sister was passionate or some kind of sicko? Why couldn't she just wear her heart on her sleeve like everyone else? A potential blind date was once described to me as "loyal, true blue (cliché), the kind of girl who would *give you the hair right off her back.*" What short-circuit, interpretable only by Freud, caused this?

Body parts are prominent in Clixed-up Michés. Quick … is it *nose to the wheel, shoulder to the grindstone,* or *nose to the grindstone, shoulder to the wheel?* Let's not open that bag of worms. I was at a business meeting once where someone said, "He cut off his face in spite of his nose." To make matters worse, the perpetrator, an otherwise respectable man, repeated his mistake over and over to an ever-growing chorus of snickers. I'd like to have been a peanut on the wall when he realized his mistake.

There are variations on the common theme, such as Misused Quantitative Reference clichés. Example: Minnesota has many lakes. Carter has many Little Liver Pills. It is mildly clever to say something like, "Vermont has more aging hippies than Carter has little liver pills." By contrast, it is annoying beyond belief to say, "She's more beautiful than there are lakes in Minnesota." Or, "My leg hurts more than Carter has little liver pills." People who say things like this really need to *get their house of cards in order.* Just *take a bite out of the bullet* and move on. *It's spilled milk under the dam.*

There is also the Right Idea, Wrong Words cliché. On a Red Sox broadcast I once heard the announcer say *never wake a sleeping dog up* instead of the proper let sleeping dogs lie. Yogi Berra, from whose lips came *90% of this game is half-mental* and *when you come to a fork in the road, take it*, would agree that this is *like déjà vu, all over again.*

What a bunch of crock!

Now we come to the lightning round, the grand finale of the Fourth of July fireworks. Let's *put ourselves in front of the cart*, because *the handwriting is on the wind.* Bust open the collection; we're *going out in a blaze of cliché glory. Clear steam ahead!* Let's shake the hackles of our language pretensions and search *the four corners of the globe* to find more examples of Clixed-up Michés. Let's not *pull any bones*, especially those of us who are *green behind the ears.* Above all, let's be sure we *don't give away the ship.*

In closing I ask, *how can you keep them down on the farm, now that they've seen Barree?* (Whoops, that's a pun, not a cliché.) Hopefully, there's a *tunnel at the end of this rainbow.* This brings us to *the verge of the brink.* It goes to show that, despite our education, despite our pretensions of sophistication, despite our reaching for *le mot juste* (cliché Francais), *you can't change a tiger's spots.*

(For once, I did not make any of this up. A tip of the head to C. Jane Taylor, Emmett Taylor, and Marie Cook who *took the bull by the hands* and contributed Clixed-up Michés that were truly the *frosting on the iceberg.* Without them, this column would have been as *dead as a pancake.*)

Late additions: *"Shit or cut bait"* … *"Fish or get off the pot…."* *"Happy as a clown in shit"* … *"Mad as a spider"* … *"She gave me the dirty eyeball"* …*"It's not my can of worms."*

The Master of Mulch

They don't call me the "Master of Mulch" because I'm good looking. But I am good looking...damn good looking...some would say too good looking. Even a pretty boy. But I digress. Finally you can do something productive with the newspapers and paper bags you've been accumulating all winter. Quick, before the green things grow, it's time to mulch.

People are always asking me, "What is the best newspaper in Vermont?" As a seasoned media pro, it's natural for people to seek my professional insight.

Actually, I'm lying to you. No one has ever asked my opinion about Vermont newspapers. Not once. It is a subject about which I have thought deeply (well, deeply for me). When comparing papers, I disregard the political orientation or the quality of writing, design, layout, and photography. I have one criterion—the paper's suitability for mulching.

Of all Vermont spring rituals—sugaring, opening day of trout season, sliding off the dirt road into a ditch, the first cree-mee, my personal favorite is "the laying of the papers," when I mulch around the perennials in the garden.

I'll explain.

We used to recycle our newspapers at the landfill. Then I took the Master Gardener course offered by the UVM Extension Service, where I learned the merits of mulching, the gardening practice where you control weeds by laying down a layer of light-impenetrable organic material such as sawdust, compost, straw, bark chips, or dead fish (not recommended).

Mulching appeals to me on several levels. Every weed that doesn't grow is a weed that doesn't have to be pulled. Mulching can be done in that cold, wet period before you can plant anything. Mulching improves the soil, and, finally, mulching saves you a trip to the dump.

Because I passed my final exam, I am entitled to the rights

and privileges conferred upon one who successfully satisfies the requirements of an institution of higher learning. Therefore, I insist on being addressed by my title, "Master." Some people think I take my new credentials too seriously, but I'm the same humble guy I've always been, although I have begun referring to myself in the third person. Because my specialty is mulch, my full title is "Master of Mulch," but to my friends, I'm simply "Master."

A generous person, I walk around the neighborhood dispensing free advice such as, "Master thinks you shouldn't have planted that tree there," or "Master says cabbage will never grow in that spot." Recipients are so respectful of my credentials that the response is usually what I interpret as respectful silence.

Mulching is not rocket science. Any moron can design a rocket. While anyone can lay a newspaper on the ground, very few can do it in an efficient, Master of Mulch kinda way. It starts with how the newspapers are stacked for storage over the winter. My partner in life, an otherwise intelligent woman, has had to be completely trained when it comes to newspaper management. She attacks a newspaper like a terrier in a roomful of rats. When she's done snapping, folding, and cutting she leaves the spent newspaper in a haphazard pile, as if it's a piece of trash.

Master doesn't like this, because crumpled newspaper doesn't lay down flat on the ground. The ideal newspapers for mulch have never been read. They lay flat as my hair after I haven't showered for a few days. If you insist on reading newspapers, it should be crisply refolded, sections separated, color inserts removed, and stacked with folds to the left.

Master has explained this patiently to his partner. His partner thinks Master should get a life. His partner has also suggested that Master do things with newspapers that are not physically possible. Master thinks mulching is just too technically demanding for partner.

Laying down the papers provides a great opportunity to review the previous year, although not in chronological order. This spring while mulching the blackberries on a gray April afternoon, these are a few headlines that caught my eye. "Football Player Slugs Gate Agent." I stop to read this story because the slugee is an old friend and neighbor. "New Brewery in Waterbury." Hm-m-m. I'll have to stop there. "Rochester Boys Have Best Season Ever." I have no interest in the Rochester boys basketball team, but I read about them anyway.

Some would call these stories "yesterday's news," but I think of them as nicely composted. Some stories I missed the first time around; some I have forgotten about; some deserve to be forgotten. Collectively, however, they comprise a discombobulated collage of life since the garden was last in bloom. I think it would be a good idea for the television networks to begin composting the evening news.

On we go to the blueberries. "Clavelle and Douglas Reveal Finances." Oh yeah, this was an election year, wasn't it? Not much of a contest. "Slain Rapper's Mother Remembers Son's Success" catches my eye. This is a fairly predictable, borderline heartwarming story. Mom explains that her son really had a heart of gold. His gangsta' persona was not the real him.

The year scrolls by in jumbled order. The Cats beat Syracuse. Symington wins election as speaker of the house, but doesn't announce her candidacy until I reach the raspberries. The Patriots win the Super Bowl. Then, a few sections later, they win the league championship to get into the Super Bowl. A roadside bomb in Iraq. Another roadside bomb in Iraq. The Red Sox reverse the curse. I pull that one out to save. They may not be in first place at the moment, but they are, until October, champions of the world. I, for one, intend to savor every moment of it.

Which brings us back to the question of the best newspaper in the state, mulchingly speaking. The winner is Seven Days. It's a tabloid, with two thick sections that lay flat even in a moderate wind. (Master has learned the hard way that mulching in the wind is a bad idea.) Moreover, Seven Days is free, so if you get caught short, you can just go pick up another armful. And if you want to take a break, you can read those titillating classifieds to see if you recognize someone you know.

Now, if the criteria were literary quality or journalistic integrity, the unquestioned winner would be *Tales and More Tails of Beyonder*. The Master has spoken.

Part V–The Kaboom

Then, things explode. The April showers have become May's weeds. Omigod, there's action on every front. The lawn needs to be mowed. There are seeds to be planted, perennials to be split, trees to be transplanted, not to mention Little League, Babe Ruth, mulch, AY-Y-Y-Y-Y!

You try to recover your property from the winter road crew, who have dropped a three-foot swath of sand onto your grass. You know if you don't turn it into lawn soon, they will turn it into road. They regard your frantic raking with amusement as they grade the road with a new layer of gravel.

The trees are exploding. It's like the invasion at Normandy. Boom, boom, puff, puff, whumph...only no one gets hurt. There are layers of songbirds and peepers. It's a symphony. There's so much to do, and you're glad to be alive. (PS—you don't have any choice.)

Technowlogee

It's all about nature and harmony, and nothing interferes with nature and harmony so much as technology. I knew things were out of whack when I took my cell phone and wireless laptop with me when I went to help my neighbor with his sugarin' operation.

It was one of those Mastercard/Hallmark / Public Radio / Milwaukee Beer moments in life. You know, one of those priceless, it-don't-get-no-better-than-this times. My technological life was in equilibrium. Everything worked. I had a computer that functioned obediently when I turned it on. When I wanted to print something, I hit a few commands, and the printer would whirr into action. I had a little laptop—nothing special—that I could take on trips. I couldn't play DVDs on airplanes or do wireless email, but I could write memos and reports.

Life was sweet.

Then I bought the digital camera. My computer, which is admittedly a few years old, did not have enough available memory to install the software from the camera, so I thought I would make my laptop my camera computer and stripped all the excess software, folders, and programs from it. But now it was useless to take on trips, so I was looking at a new laptop. After I took about eight photos, its memory was overloaded.

So I bought a new laptop, which was so much more powerful than my existing computer that it made sense for it to be the brain of my entire system, except that my keyboard and monitor would not work with the new laptop, and the printer required a driver that was not supported by the newer version of Windows XP (required by Microsoft). So, now I own a useless laptop, computer, monitor, keyboard, and printer, and I'm ready to throw the new laptop through the window.

I am hoisted by my own technological petard. For those of you who don't know what a "petard" is, be comforted by the fact that I don't either.

A few years ago I wrote a column for this very same newspaper called, "Beeping Watches." It was about the cultural turmoil that was caused by the fact that we were, at that time, wearing watches that were smarter than we were. They only cost about $20 and they had these tiny buttons that we could try to push with our pudgy fingers to make the watches do the things that the owners manual—164 pages long, 1" by 2" in dimension, written in four languages, with no index—said the watch was capable of.

About the only thing anyone could successfully get the watch to do was to start beeping at the most inappropriate time imaginable, such as during your presentation to the board, in the middle of your wife's C-section, during the Christmas Eve church service, and explaining the facts of life to your kid. After frantic seconds of pushing all the tiny buttons, you opt instead for hacking off your arm with a kitchen knife and throwing it out the window.

Now, let me take you on a dark journey deep into the catacombs of technology.

In 1984 (appropriately) we were the first family in our little Vermont hamlet to get a VCR. We justified it because there was virtually no television other than a blurry Channel 3, and we thought our children were being culturally deprived (an excuse that enables you to buy a lot of neat toys and to go on some cool trips, too).

We bought our VCR for $1,200, and it was second hand! The person who sold it to us decided that 12-inch video disks were the wave of the future, so who's the fool? Video Vaults, Blockbusters, and Movie Galleries didn't exist yet, so we had to rely on a friend-of-a-friend who lived in Florida to send us tapes. When a new shipment arrived, the entire neighborhood would gather at our house to watch the talking pictures. I didn't matter whether *Dumbo* or *Deep Throat* that was showing. (*Dumbo* was much better, although the kids really enjoyed *Deep Throat*.)

Now, you can go into Circuit City and buy and entire pick-up load of DVD players for $1,200. Of course, when you take them to the landfill to dispose of them, it will cost you twice that. Or, you could sell them at a yard sale for, oh, a buck apiece. Yesterday's technology is about as valuable as that stash of plastic peanuts you've kept from your mail-order shipments.

I could tell you about the time I tried to get a VCR player repaired, but this is supposed to be a humor column.

So, here I am with my dysfunctional, state-of-the-art equipment on the information superhighway. I have my own website. I'm starting a blog. (Who isn't?) I have a drawer full of digital watches that don't work and that I couldn't give away at a yard sale. I have a cell phone that, in my rural location, makes me long for the days of tin cans attached with a string. I wouldn't know a gigabyte if it kicked me in the shins, and every time it's daylight savings I have to spend half a day figuring out how to reset the clocks in my home and car. Of course, there are those that reset themselves automagically and are incorrect after I reset them.

Have I ever told you that I used to walk eight miles to school when I was a kid?

Instant On

This is almost the same article, written during a different technological era. You can tell I'm still a little hung over from Earth Day. I drank too much of that Solar Tea.

I'm an environmental kinda guy, doing my little bit to keep that big ozone hole in the sky from expanding. I live a life of parsimonious energy consumption. I don't drive a gas guzzling car; I heat with wood; I even installed one of those $25 light bulbs so that the earth would be a safer place for my children. I live lightly on the planet.

I'm even one of those New Age guys who has formed a little business that exists by networking electronically around the globe. My business creates no acid rain, no toxic waste, and no revenue (whoops, that's just in there for the sake of the IRS). My only luxury is a dispenser for spring water that comes from the very same town that I live in.

A Beyonder kinda guy, right? Now it's time for true confessions. Despite my pretentions, I've come to realize that I am a complete power glutton, depleting the planet's finite resources just when we need them most.

Remember my bubbler? Turns out the thing is plugged in, bleeding the resources from Yankee Nuclear (which, as a right kinda guy, I oppose) so that I can have instant hot water for my herbal tea.

But the bubbler is just the tip of a fuel gluttony iceberg. The real sickening thud came the other night, as I was leaving my "energy efficient" office. I turned off the compact fluorescent overhead, and was greeted by the normal display of colored lights that tell me that all is well with my office.

Those lights, I suddenly realized, are sucking up electricity twenty-four hours a day. Despite my good intentions, I am hemorrhaging power around the clock. This means that I am burning up fossil fuels (or creating nuclear waste) even as I am at home swilling beer and watching Murphy Brown.

I counted the monitor lights that tell me that my appliances are at the ready, awaiting my DOS command. When I put my workspace to sleep for the night, there are sixteen—count 'em, sixteen—lights.

Here's the breakdown: two on my laser printer, one on my color monitor, three on my computer (one for power, one for "turbo," whatever that means, and another that has no apparent function whatsoever).

Wait a minute, is this a joke? Tell me there's not a computer design nerd out there somewhere laughing up his sleeve. Tee-hee-hee. Let's put a "turbo" light on the box. People will actually think it means something. The next generation of boxes will probably have toggle switches reading "Fire retro rockets." Back to my monitor lights: I've got three, yeah three, monitor lights on my answering machine. It's a two-line phone, and one of the lights is on to tell me that the second line (which isn't even connected) is off. My fax machine has only one light, to tell me that it is plugged in. My copying machine has two lights, plus a very colorful lime green, digital zero to tell me that nothing is being copied at the moment.

The remainder of my lights are for various surge protectors to tell me that they are ever-vigilant, ready to launch into action at a nanosecond's notice.

Of course it goes without saying that I have been advised by my computer gurus to leave my machines "on" at all times to protect them from the nasty surges of electricity unleashed every time you flip the on/off switch. Of course, if you leave the machines "on," you are more vulnerable to the megasurges that can come through the phone lines or power lines that can leave the inside of your machines in smoking ruins. (True story—I once returned a dysfunctional fax to be repaired. The company reported back that they could not honor the warranty because the machine had been hit by lightning. Inside my office?)

So, you need surge protectors to protect your equipment from surges because you leave the machines on all the time to protect them from surges. This circular logic reminds me of an acquaintance who chain-smoked cigarettes in between cups of black coffee.

"Why do you drink so much coffee?" I asked.

"I have to keep drinking coffee because my throat hurts," he replied.

"Why does your throat hurt?"

"Because I smoke so many cigarettes."

"Why do you smoke so many cigarettes?"

"Because I'm jittery from all the coffee."

Oh. Back to my flagrant, irresponsible, planet-destroying energy consumption, as typified by the sixteen monitor lights in my one little office.

I lead an enviable life. I can ride my bicycle to work. I can go cross-country skiing at lunch. I can send files winging to California while I watch Beyonder snowflakes drift down outside my window. But let's face it. We live in an instant-on society. We want to punch a button, and we don't want to wait. As my energy-oozing office is indicative of, however, even the best intentioned of us can be energy hypocrites. We try to consider the impact of our actions on the next seven generations, but in today's society we can barely keep a nuclear family together, let alone think seven generations into the future.

Recycling Made a Slob Outta Me

Spring cleaning takes on an infinite number of shapes and variations. With me the most sure sign that good weather is actually on the way is when I clean my workshop and fill up the truck for the semiannual, ritual trip to the dump (now the "sanitary landfill").

Let me tell you about my workshop.

It's a simple place. The walls are rough sawn, addled with nails and hooks that hold this and that. There is a jukebox that holds all my old 45s and plays them with scratchy reverence. There is a deep sink that is perfect for washing the bottles I use for home brewing.

There are lots of tools, in various states of disrepair and disorganization. Heaven knows, it is not called a "work" shop because any work gets done there. The tools are for caressing, and to make me feel appropriately masculine. I'm always buying new ones at yard sales. Occasionally, when I'm depressed, I even buy something from Sears or Brookstone. I have tools that have not been used in fifteen years and won't be for the next fifteen years.

Such tools can last a lifetime.

If you get the impression that this simple space is a sanctuary for me, an oasis from the turmoil of everyday life, the pressures of the Showdown in the Gulf, an escape from a family that wants more than I can give and a career that somehow never measured up to the potential that everyone thought I had, you're right.

If you get the idea that I like this workshop, you're right. If you think that I lose myself in its nooks and crannies, you're right. If you think that this is the only place in the world where a middle-age guy can act like himself, you're right.

Maybe, then, you can understand why I am distressed that my workshop has become a landfill.

Blame the environmental movement. (I'm probably the only writer in America dumb enough to come out against recycling, but intelligence has never been my long suit.) The truth is, in the quest to save the planet, my family is doing its part by transferring the trash burden from the town landfill to my workshop.

The world used to be so simple. We put trash in a trash can and someone took it away. Don't ask me where. My kids don't believe me when I tell them this. The service was FREE, too. At least we didn't get a monthly bill.

Later, we moved to a community that had an old-fashioned dump. This was a glorious place—fills my eyes with tears just to think of it. Going to the dump was a social occasion to rival the Fourth of July parade. Once every few weeks we'd load up the truck and then everyone in the family would hop in. No one wanted to miss a dump run.

All the neighborhood would be there. The sky was always blue (that's because a smart person only went to the dump on a nice day), dotted with soaring seagulls that lent an aura of a nature preserve to the facility. The politicians and town fathers would be there to greet you and to ask for your vote, even if no election was forthcoming.

This was democracy in action; this was your tax dollars at work; this was America.

A trip to the dump might have cost a buck or so, but it was the best show in town for the money. On top of everything, you were guaranteed to come back with more good stuff than you brought in.

Compare this to a trip now to the "sanitary landfill." You know it's trouble when they stop you on the way in and ask you to fill out a credit application. Then someone comes over to ask if you want the prix fixe or the a la carte menu.

"Wha'?" you say, then not wanting to appear inordinately stoo-pudd, "I'll take the 'fixed prices.'"

"Excellent choice, Monsieur," says the armed guard at the landfill entrance, "That will be a hundred and thirty-two dollars."

Which brings us to the recycling issue. Obviously things are out of control at the sanitary landfill. Why, for a hundred and thirty-two dollars you could get a dentist to get out of bed in the morning. (Just kidding. My dentist wouldn't get out of bed for a hundred and thirty-two lousy dollars.)

So my family decides that rather than to spend the kids' college tuition on trips to the landfill, we will recycle everything. To recycle means, "to separate into separate paper bags." We've got bags for green glass, clear glass, plastic, orange peels, baseball card wrappers, newspapers, mail-order catalogs.

All of the garbage now requires special processing. The bottles need to be sanitized, and the labels removed, meaning that we never have hot water for showers. Newspapers must be cross-tied with a bowline knot, using 22-lb. test, and organic string. The garbage is now separated into so many containers that none of them are ever full, and no one wants to go to the recycling center until all the bags are full. This means that my workshop, my beloved workshop, is always brimming with half-full bags of trash. Is this my reward for being a good planet doobie?

We live in an age when a bomb can be dropped from miles up in the sky by a jet going a thousand miles an hour and guided down the air shaft of a sand-covered bunker. You would think someone could solve the problem of my workshop. This is a war worth fighting, one to which I could surrender my sons with clear conscience.

In fact, I think I will send them out to clean up my workshop right now!

Horsepower Or Horse Manure

What is it about spring that causes the vehicular testosterone of the male of the species to flow so freely? Just when you should be hunkering down in the garden you find yourself obsessed with all things automotive.

Hey kids, what time is it? That's right, little bunkies. It's time for that funny Beyonder guy to get a new car, and you know what that means. When he starts thinking about cars, every one he knows—family, friends, and even loyal readers—is in for some serious boredom.

My thirteen-year-old son is taking an active interest in the process, figuring that in three years he'll be old enough to drive, and the vehicle I buy will be passed along to him. He's taking the practical tack—sober, mature, considerate of all familial interests. That's why he has concluded that the most sensible car I can buy is a Mazda Miata. The Miata is a sleek convertible that, he assures me, is very fuel efficient—the answer to my environmental concerns. Also, by putting down the top, there's no need for air conditioning, and none of those nasty fluorocarbons will be put into the atmosphere. In fact, he says, his voice taking on the quavering timbre of the truly committed, buying a Miata is probably the most important single action that an individual can take to save the planet.

Nice try, son.

I remember trying the same ploy on my father. We actually got as far as taking a Pontiac GTO for a test drive. I stressed the practicality of this model, just as my son tried with the Miata. Even I had to admit, however, that the idea of my mother trying to maneuver this roaring hog around the parking lot of the grocery store was ludicrous.

As time passes I am more amused by the gross folly of a GTO than warmed by the fuzzy memory. This was one of the largest cars Pontiac ever made—eight cylinders, a bajillion horsepower (over 350, I think), and it got about six miles to the gallon.

Gas was cheap, but the voracious appetite of the vehicle kept me constantly impoverished, a small price to pay for the ability to hit one-twenty on the straightaways. After all, isn't freedom of the roads an American birthright? As I grow wise and gray I have developed perspective on my crazed lust for a GTO, and for the mere cost of this newspaper, am willing to share it with you.

The concept of horsepower is essential. My personal "Eureka!" experience occurred several years ago at the Tunbridge World's Fair. I took my, at that time, small son into the barn that housed the work horses. We stood in awe of these gentle behemoths chewing hay. We patted their heavily muscled flanks (as high as we could reach), keeping a respectful distance. We were fascinated by the control that the horse's owners displayed over such towers of power. With sharp "gees and haws," and well-timed hand slaps, they could actually get these giants to do their bidding. It was easy to see why "horsepower" became the standard unit of measurement in matters of work. One horsepower is awesome. Three hundred and fifty we take for granted.

The work horse is more versatile than a GTO, and easier to park, too. This warm-blooded machine pulls a plow, drags wood from the forest, pulls the sled that carries the sap, and takes the family to church on Sundays. For its pay the work horse requires only sufficient quantities of fresh water and grass, renewable resources that do not need to be purchased from the Saddam Husseins of the world. The key word is "sufficient." Depending on the quality of the grassland, up to twenty acres may be required to feed a horse year round. Horses require no waxing, no brake jobs, no STP Oil Treatment. For residue, the animal leaves organic substances that might be put on a garden to enhance growth. In time, a work horse (the right kind, anyway) can reproduce itself. No Pontiac in captivity has ever duplicated this feat.

As I held my son's small hand, I thought about a sixteen year old trying to control a wagon pulled by more than three hundred work horses! The line would stretch beyond the horizon. The reins would be unliftable. How big a barn would be needed? Twenty acres times four hundred—you would need a farm the size of Addison County to feed them. And as for shoveling out the stalls, forgetaboudit!

At the turn of the century, when the horse population of our burgeoning industrial cities was at an all-time high, the waste problem was out of control. Gutters were filled with horsecrap, creating a problem obvious to anyone with eyes and a nose. The internal combustion engine made the waste problem disappear.

Or so it seemed.

Now we are learning that we simply took the refuse from the streets and put it into the air. No problem was solved, but for a while it was made invisible. It has taken us the better part of the century to learn the error of our ways. Our streets are clogged, our air is noxious, our rain is acid. These are high prices to pay to learn that there is no free lunch. But we are making progress.

My father never bought the GTO, and I won't buy the Miata (although I would look great in the silver). It is a consolation, however, to think that in thirty years my grandson will be trying to hoodwink his father into buying the latest solar slickmobile. I hope my son has the wisdom to look him in the eye and to say:

"GET A HORSE!"

The Joy of Gardening

You planted the peas in the April mud. Then you laid the mulch when the ground froze solid again. In this essay I explore the simple pleasures of conjugal gardening.

Here are three things not to do with your wife—wall papering, mixed doubles, and gardening. Don't ask why. Just do as I say. You'll thank me when you celebrate that golden anniversary.

Gardening brings us close to the earth. (Now, there's a brilliant statement; did you pay money for this?) After a long, Beyonder winter Vermonters can't wait to wallow in the muck. Some of us are so enthusiastic about gardening that we plant our crops two or three times, forgetting that there's a danger of hard frost until—oh, say—Fourth of July.

In this cold, soupy mire we perform the ancient ritual of

planting peas amidst a background of chirping birds, mating croakers, and bickering spouses.

The issues are straightforward enough: what to plant, when to plant it, and where. My wife, who goes through most of the year as a reasonable, functioning member of society, becomes a small-minded, opinionated shrew as soon as the first seed packet is torn open.

The first battle concerns mulching. I'm a mulcher; I admit it. It's never interfered with my life or profession. I've never missed work or a column deadline because—as my wife would imply—I've been out late mulching the night before.

My wife, in contrast, is a weeder. She weeds without wearing gloves, saying she can "feel" the weeds better this way, as if weeds are cherished objects to be caressed before death. In my humble opinion whatever ornery ones escape the smothering mulch should be summarily hacked to death with a well-sharpened hoe. Not so, says my wife. Hacking is no more than cosmetic surgery. Without pulling up the roots, one is simply making the garden look prettier. My feeling is that whatever is going on beneath the soil, I don't wanna know about it.

My wife's first foray into the garden wreaks havoc on her nails. This is so predictable. "You better wear gloves," I say. "You'll wreck your nails." Does she listen to me? No-o-o-o. She claims that gloves don't let her "feel" the weeds as well. Gimmeabreak. Who wants to feel weeds?

I get my revenge later, when she complains about the woeful state of her nails. "What did you expect? You should have worn gloves." I don't say "I told you so," or "You ignorant shrew." I don't need to.

A similar situation concerns bugs. Planting time coincides with black fly season, so one of the trade-offs for the privilege of growing green tomatoes is that by the end of the first morning of indentured labor, fly venom courses through the body, making your face look like it's been pummeled by Evander Holyfield. (Formerly, I used to use Mike Tyson's name in these situations, but now that he's in the slammer, I'm switching to someone who's a better role model for young Beyonder readers.)

"I hate black flies!" she screams in a pique of pain and aggravation, pawing at welts with muddy, broken-nailed claws. I've been waiting for this moment:

"You should have slathered on some Skin-So-Soft." "I don't like feeling like a greased pig." Granted, when I'm fully dosed, the rake fairly squirts out of my hand, but I figure those little buggers are sliding off me, too.

But don't think of me as the bad guy. Here's the kind of thing my wife does to intentionally aggravate me. She buys flats of Brussels sprouts seedlings, plants two, and then throws the others away.

"What are you doing?" I cry. "We paid good money for these."

"But two Brussels sprouts plants are all we need. In fact, two is generally two more than we need. You hate Brussels sprouts."

"I know I do, but they grow so well here, and they're our best fall crop."

"Right. They sit here all fall and winter until they are lumpy, slimy stalks that we pull out in the spring."

"I don't care. We bought 'em, we're planting 'em. You're the menu planner around here. You cook 'em; I'll eat 'em."

"Last year, I cooked them; you pushed them aside." See what I mean about this woman's pettiness?

We argue about corn. I like to plant six different varieties in a six-foot-square area. She makes this big deal about cross-pollination, as if I'm a mad scientist trying to mate monkeys and dogs. Any idiot knows that the reason our corn is small and deformed is because she plants the corn too close together. One year, I'm sure, she substituted seeds for those miniature little Chinese corns for the sweet corn seeds. How low can a person go?

If we survive Memorial Day Weekend, an uneasy truce goes into effect. The rule is quite simple—only one of us is allowed into the garden at a time. By the Fourth, the danger is passed, and we can even pick peas together, although if it's a bad crop, there is always the risk of unearthing the freshly healed wounds of the spring. ("You planted them too deep!" "That's because you had to plant them so early that it was the only way I could keep them from freezing!")

By midsummer, however, the garden is on autopilot, meaning

that neither of us care about weeds or slug infestations. Now we can repair the damage of the vernal hostilities by relaxing in the backyard, barbecuing on the grill, sipping an ice-cold beer, and chowing down on those shriveled little ears of deformed corn.

Sports Dad

And now it's time to "Play Ball!" Baseball, we all know, is a year-round pastime, especially for Red Sox fans. In the North Country the fever becomes acute during mid-May, when for the first time temperatures are reliably above freezing.

I remember when I was top dog in this family. People talked about me in terms of potential. Even as I approached the so-called "middle years" there was no mistaking the alpha male in this household. He was the guy who played centerfield in the men's softball league and who flirted with the forty-minute mark in the Fourth of July 10K. He was the man on the windsurfer and mountain bike. He was first and foremost, an athlete.

All that has changed now. This same guy is now an athlete's Dad. His time, energy, and income are devoted to the glorification of his offspring, ages 10 and 12. As you can tell from reading the first paragraph, he's not real happy about it.

Like millions of American males approaching the peak of athletic prime (thank you, Nolan Ryan, for pushing this back a few years), I suddenly find myself reduced to the role of support Dad. I drive the van, buy the equipment, tote the video camera, and maintain a stiff, yet nurturing, upper lip on the sidelines.

A generation ago a man in mid-life crisis went out and bought a little red sports car. I can't do this, because parents of sports-age kids are required to transport up to seven Little Leaguers, soccer players, or wrestlers to various venues across the state in suitable comfort. This means tilt-back seats, air conditioning, and a stereo that can bang out M.C. Hammer at a hundred decibels. You cannot fit seven twelve year olds in an Austin Healy (although I'm sure they would be willing to try).

More importantly, I cannot afford the little red sports car because 40% of my after-tax income is tithed to the sports equipment companies. Some call America the land of the free; I call it the land of the dedicated sports shoe. When I was a kid, we had a dedicated sports shoe called the sneaker. Now, sneakers are hundred-dollar fashion statements with high-tech, space-age componentry that can only be worn en route to a sporting event, where you then put on your dedicated shoes.

To make matters worse, at the growth rate of adolescent feet, the usable life of dedicated sports shoes is roughly seven-eighths of one season. Isn't it amazing what technology can do today? The final indignity comes at least once a season, when your child spaces out and leaves his sneakers or cleats at the field, gym, lake, or pool.

Only one thing makes me angrier than a kid losing a pair of $50 shoes—that is, a kid losing just one shoe. Am I telling it like it is?

I'm not alone in servitude. My wife, Vice President of Food, Flak, and Nourishment, must accommodate eating schedules dictated by games played at odd hours in distant parts of the state, and food whims not seen since the days of Henry the Eighth. "Mom, this sandwich had Miracle Whip on it. Mom, you know how I feel about Miracle Whip. Mom, I can't eat this sandwich, and if I don't eat it will affect my performance, which will affect my relations with my peers, and my entire self-image and IT'S ALL YOUR FAULT BECAUSE YOU PUT MIRACLE WHIP ON MY SANDWICH!!"

Not that the sacrifices are without rewards. I remember a Little League game a few nights ago when my ten year old came to the edge of the dugout and motioned to me in the stands.

"He's calling you! He's calling you!" buzzed the excited parents around me. "You better go," said one father, a touch of sadness in his face. "Once, when my boy called, I was a little slow getting there. He played out his option!" The other parents gasped. I trampled three adults (two of them pregnant women) to see what the little guy wanted, maybe a batting tip or a word of encouragement.

"Yes, yes, my royal son, dost thou call?"

"Yeah, go get me some Gatorade."

"But, but we didn't bring any Gatorade, my liege."

"Go buy some."

"But your majesty, the closest store is twelve miles away!"

"So? While you're at it, get some bubble gum for the team."

He dismissed me with a wave of the hand. I scurried away. If I drove at breakneck speed, maybe I could be back for the final inning.

Maybe in future years, after he's signed one of those multiyear contracts, he'll remember that bottle of Gatorade that gave him the energy boost he needed to get that walk that drove in the winning run, and he'll wonder where he got it, and he'll think of a man, himself once an athlete, and he'll…Nah!

At the end of the game as I was chauffeuring home the herd now devouring $54.60 worth of fast food, I decided to try a new tack. I took them down to a part of town favored by local teenagers who hang out endlessly, sitting on steps, smoking cigarettes, saying "yes," listening to devil rock on boom boxes, and contemplating the next homemade tattoo.

"There!" I said, infusing the scene with as much enthusiasm as I could muster, "Maybe you guys should forget about sports. Doesn't this look like fun?"

Dreams At Bat

*Little League. No two words in the English lan-
guage (except, perhaps, "Ugly American") conjure up
the image of a society gone amok. The phrase brings to
mind overbearing parents, win-at-all-cost coaches, and
children psychologically impaired by the pressures of
competition. But this description applies only to the
Flatlands. Little League in Vermont is a spiritual experience akin to watching a Champlain sunset off
Camel's Hump or tasting the first-run sap on fresh-fall-
en snow. Not only is Little League what Vermont is all
about, it is what baseball is all about.*

Last night the Randolph Red Sox nipped the Randolph
Athletics, 9-8, in a game that spanned the gamut of human emotions. The setting was idyllic—freshly mown grass, a warm sun
setting beyond right field. We wait so long for this. There is winter, then purgatory, then Mud Season, then a little more winter.
The boys start playing ball when patches of dry ground must be
carved from seas of slush, when the crack of the bat shudders
through numb fingers with a stinging curse. When the season is
finally right for baseball, let us not take it for granted.

The Red Sox were last year's league doormats, but a year's
experience has transformed them into a veteran squad where it is
no longer an act of God when a fly ball intersects a mitt. They are
currently in first place. The As are an expansion team, boys playing organized ball for the first time. Six weeks ago they were
learning the difference between first and third base. But that was
light years ago. Now they've learned how to bend the rims of their
caps to look like major leaguers and how to chatter in the infield
without sounding like mega-dweebs.

The Red Sox draw first blood, but it is the As upon whom the
baseball gods smile this night. Fly balls find outstretched gloves, a
raw-boned pitcher discovers that control, not power, keeps you in

the game, and a little third baseman wearing pants two sizes too large cracks a shot over the centerfielder's head. The feckless doormats have become upstarts, and as the Red Sox come up for their final at bat, the As cling to a one-run lead that seems thinner and more tenuous than a spider's thread.

On the sidelines the scene is vintage Vermont, vintage baseball. Neighbors catch up on town events while monitoring progress of the next generation. The dads, too nervous to sit still, walk and pace, dissipating their tension by joking with the coaches and umpires. No one disputes; no one second guesses. The season is too short and the town too small.

Meanwhile, moms sit on the bleachers, shading eyes from the sun, and debate the age-old question: "How do you feed a boy dinner when games run from 4 p.m. to 8:30 p.m.?" One of the Red Sox moms tried the innovative approach of giving her son a submarine sandwich to eat during the game. By the fifth inning the sandwich was still on the bench, having been dropped on the ground twice and nibbled on by every team member except her son. Back to the drawing board.

On the As' side there was a growing aura of disbelief. Supporters who hoped for no more than a good showing were tasting the thrill of victory, but sweeter still, an upset that only weeks before had seemed as likely as August snow.

But it is not to be, not this night for the As. The Red Sox maintain composure. A nineyear old ignites a rally with a single and stolen base. He is brought in by a double to right by a boy earlier mired in an 0-for-season slump. Then, a dribbler is thrown into infinity by an over-adrenalized fielder, and the better team, for now, has won.

For a moment the field is a tableau of exultation and despair. The Red Sox maintain their hold on first place, while the As realize that even the best-played game can extend two batters too long. But the emotions are quickly tempered by sharing. You guys played a great game. We almost had you. Yeah, but you deserved to win.

There is a scurry to pick up the bases and to leave the field in good shape for tomorrow's game, tomorrow's drama. Parents hustle kids to get home quickly. There is still dinner and homework to squeeze in before bedtime.

As the boys leave this field of dreams, their minds are already on the next game, the next triumph. In four years these same kids will be hanging on street corners, cigarettes dangling and hormones raging. They will have forgotten how close the upstart As came to knocking off the Red Sox. But the game will be embedded in their souls for their sons.

Let's end it just a little easier. It is still the top of the inning. The As are three outs from jubilation, but the Red Sox ooze with the confidence that comes only from having been there before. Youth, spring, and baseball in Vermont. Nothing else matters. "If only," you tell yourself, "it could last forever."

And the best part is, it can.

On the Firing Line

The scale of Little League is perfect. That's why it captivates us. The age range is perfect, too, because kids change so much between 9 and 12. This way everyone eventually becomes a star. (Yes, I was one of the parents who was just a little too intense.)

This one falls into the "baseball is a metaphor for life" category.

I don't mean to insult the intelligence of the fine people in my town, but if one were to turn the Camcorder on the crowd at the Little League field while the local stalwarts are playing, you would see and hear some pretty shopworn verbal drool. I'm right there with them, screaming out clichéd inanities after every twitch and pitch.

To the player who has just hit the dirt to avoid being beaned by an errant throw we yell, "GOOD EYE!" To the pitcher who has uncorked a wild throw to the backstop, "JUST MISSED!" To the player who never swings, "WAY TO LOOK THEM OVER!" To the player who swings at even a fluttering piece of paper,

"WAY TO GO AFTER IT!" To the player who has just let a ball go through his legs, we yell the rather Zen-like, "WAY TO BE THERE!"

We're talking intelligent human beings here—professionals, members of the school board, pillars of the community—screaming exhortations like, "WAY TO BREATHE WHILE YOU'RE STANDING IN RIGHT FIELD!" and "GOOD WARM-UP SWING!"

On this particular day the rampant use of clichés was explainable. The occasion was the first game of the All Star tournament to see which American team would eventually go down to defeat at the hands of the Taiwan Nationals. That showdown, however, was light years away. The hometown team's goal was more modest—to win one, count 'em, one tournament game. That would be one more than they had won collectively for the previous five years. You see, the hometown team in this story is from Randolph, Vermont, a town most recently known for the three major fires that have devastated its downtown. The third of the fires took place only days before the first All Star game. The boys, in fact, had been practicing as the wisps of smoke appeared on the horizon off the third base side. Downtown Randolph, for those who never saw it intact, is/was a classic turn-of-the-century railroad town. Its unified three-story brick facade showed conviction on the part of its creators that the investment in structures of substance would be justified by future generations. Although the railroad no longer stops in Randolph (that's another story), this vision has sustained itself well for the past century—until the three separate, but eerily similar, fires. Now, unfortunately, Randolph looks like a smile that has been in a bad accident.

Back to baseball.

The coach tried to keep the boys focused, but with the backdrop of sirens and the buzz of parents bemoaning the latest cruel twist of fate, the effort was futile. Several days hence, as the local All Stars took the field for their first game, the impact of the local disasters was very much on the minds of those in attendance. Could such a small community survive the loss of so many businesses? Who would have the resources, money and energy, to rebuild? Had the town slipped below critical mass? Would it cease to exist? These were the questions, as we waved the tattered fabric that once was the community flag.

The game started poorly for the Randolph nine, much as had the previous dozen All Star contests. Our boys looked small and tentative, the opposition cocky as roosters. After four innings (in a six-inning contest) our boys were down by four and seeming to accept the fate of their predecessors. The parents kept up the chatter, increasingly desperate, a verbal facade of baseball bravery.

Suddenly, in a moment sparked more by frustration than inspiration, one of the parents yelled, "C'MON RANDOLPH, CATCH ON FIRE!"

There was an instant of silence. "Helluva thing for people from this town to be yelling," said one person with a chuckle. He then followed with, "LET'S GO, FIRE UP THOSE BATS." There was widespread laughter. The first batter reached on an error. "BURN UP THAT BASEPATH, BUDDY," came the call. The next two batters walked, then a hit was scorched to the outfield. By the time the smoke cleared, the hometown team had clawed back to within a run.

Hope spread like...well, like wildfire, and the decibel level from the sidelines went a few notches higher to inspire the defense: "C'MON BABY, FIRE HARD," "SMOKE 'EM," "FIRE UP, INFIELD."

And the infield did fire up. Unfortunately, the opposition did not roll over and play dead, but stoked up the heat themselves. The local heroes, however, only fought back harder, and tied the score at the end of regulation play with a perfectly executed steal of home.

"YOU'RE LOOKING HOT, RANDOLPH!"

In the first extra frame the opponents appeared to douse the Randolph fire by taking a two-run lead, but a fresh breeze fanned the smoldering embers in the bottom of the inning, and ignited a full-fledged conflagration.

The first three Randolph batters reached safely ("LIGHT MY FIRE!"). Now, it was a holocaust of flawless baseball execution with a life of its own. Another hit, a walk, another hit...and victory, shared equally by the partisans in the stands and the players on the field.

Fire can be devastation and destruction, but also warmth and light. We're passionate about baseball, because the dramas played on its small diamond stage teach us greater wisdoms of life. On this day a courageous group of eleven- and twelve-year-old boys from a small, battered town in the middle of Beyonder taught me that victory is achieved only when one confronts a situation and decides not to lose.

Fenway by the Numbers

People who know me say I'm cheap. Hey, I say I'm cheap. The numbers at Fenway have not stopped me from being a Red Sox fan, but they've turned my trip to the ballpark from Beantown to Burlington, home of the Vermont Expos. Ticket prices at Fenway now average $75 and select parking can cost up to $100. And still they come.

Baseball fans have a fetish for numbers, whether it's how many hits Boggs needs to climb back to .300 or the number of times Mike Greenwell spits during a pre-game interview. Numbers wile away time in the bleachers during one-sided blowouts. Numbers compare contemporary players with the heroes of yesteryear. Numbers tell you who's coming in to pinch hit for Luis Rivera.

There were enough numbers involved in my family's last outing to Fenway Park that I thought I was going for a degree in economics at MIT rather than a day at the old ball game.

We start with 44, the number of degrees on this April day. As a Vermonter I thought I could deal with cold, but 44 degrees on a gray day in Boston with a cool breeze coming in off the Bay is chillier than I have ever felt in a lift line at Killington. We wore every scrap of cloth we could find in the car and still froze our butts.

The next number is 12, which is the number of dollars it costs to park your car for the game. (The concept of paying money for your car not to move is a novel one for Vermonters, whose cars do not move—for free—every time it hits 30 below.)

We parked, instead, in a secret spot not more than 6 or 7 miles from the park. Granted, we risked a $20 ticket and $80 tow (more numbers), but I'm not such a sucker to pay for parking.

The walk gave me a chance to explain economic principles to the children, such as "supply and demand," which is why a glass-littered chunk of pavement that looks like a perfect setting for a mugging is worth so much at game time.

Then there is the concept of "free enterprise," which explains why several members of the Red Sox earn more than the cumulative state revenues of Vermont. It is fashionable amongst the underpaid writers' set to decry what these inflated salaries have done to the grand old game. Not me. The players would be fools or communists not to take what they can get. The fools are the ones paying the bills.

The next economic principle I explained was the concept of "monopoly," which is the only way to explain why the same watery Coke that costs .60 outside the ballpark costs $1.40 within. Who is this guy Harry M. Stevens, anyway. And how did he get the exclusive rights to the concessions at Fenway? What's he got that I don't got, aside from millions of dollars?

The next number is 15, as in section 15, right behind the first base line. I remember as a boy that superb seats like these were available right until game time. I also remember that the Sox personified quintessential mediocrity. Now, they are contenders, and I know it's only spring, but this year they are going all the way!

The next number is one and a half—the number of hours before game time that the gates are opened. This pre-game period is now my favorite part of the event, because you can observe the grace and ritual of infield practice. You can hear the chatter and patter, the same at Fenway as any Little League field in Vermont.

"OK, good throws, good throws....let's go for two now."

You feel like part of the game when you watch infield practice. For my sons the pre-game time is when you hunt for autographs. My 12 year old (a perfect age for baseball) tied a baseball to a piece of monofilament fishing line and planned to dangle it, complete with pen and sign ("Please sign. Thanks. Jake from Vermont."), over the lip of the dugout. Great plan, but it didn't work.

"No dangling, kid," said an usher, one of those great Boston characters with the map of Ireland on his face. I thought my son's idea was clever enough to warrant exception. The usher's tone implied that there were no new tricks to be tried, so my son joined the entreating hordes, pleading for a signature from anyone wearing a Red Sox warm-up jacket.

So much for the human side of the baseball story. Back to the numbers. It is 160 miles from Vermont to Fenway. The average player now makes $880,000 per year. (Don't even begin to try to relate that to what you do for a living! It's too depressing.) A sausage with peppers and onions outside the park costs $4, but is a great value, because it will stay in your stomach for at least a week, a great souvenir of the ballpark. The Sox haven't won the World Series since 1918. And more than 29,000 other baseball fans were willing to pay the freight to watch the hometown boys take on the Kansas City Royals on this frigid day.

And then there was the final score. Clemens gave up only 3 singles in beating Bret Saberhagen and the Kansas City Royals, 1-0. It was a classic pitcher's duel, the kind that keeps the conversation going in the car all the way back up Interstate 89! Boggs went 0 for 3, but now has worked his way over .300. The car didn't get towed, and we needed the walk to thaw out.

The only part of the day not expressible by a number is the memory. That's because it is priceless.

Babe Ruth and the Turkeys

Just as the scale of Little League is right, for the kids playing Babe Ruth baseball, it's all wrong. But then, there's a lot wrong about just being 13 to 15.

Let me tell you a story about personal growth. Ricky Reyenger, David Lewis—the names don't matter—five of us, all thirteen years old, thought we would make our fortunes by raising turkeys. After all, the chicks were kinda cute. And they only cost a buck apiece. We bought an even dozen. The grain was another five bucks each. Come Thanksgiving, we'd all be rich.

We shook hands. We swore an oath. We built a pen. All that remained was to throw a few handfuls of grain in the pen every day, and to figure out how we would spend our profits.

A few weeks later the fuzzy chicks had transformed to the Turkeys from Hell. They were now full-fledged adolescents— large, raucous, ill tempered, omnivorous, with elongated necks that belonged on camels, not birds. The "lifetime" grain supply had long since been ravished by a gobbling horde that could— daily—defecate twice their collective body weight.

We had made a large error, a dozen large errors. The pen, once comfortable for a dozen chicks, was now woefully inadequate for even one of these monsters. Friendships became frazzled by this revoltin' development, and it was, only in retrospect, a growth experience.

This, of course, is an article about baseball. Baseball is America's national pastime, because it is about Coming of Age and the Big Themes of Life.

What do baseball and turkeys have to do with each other? Both demonstrate the sensitive trials of coming of age. I have two sons. Last year both were in Little League. This year, the older one has moved up to Babe Ruth League, a program for thirteen- to fifteen-year-olds. His brother is still a fuzzy chick, while he has become a gangly, adolescent turkey.

Unlike the foul fowl mentioned earlier, however, I feel great sympathy for this turkey, as well as the other turkeys on his team. A year ago these guys ruled the roost in Little League. They played in an immaculate stadium, lovingly tended by the town fathers. The grass was neat, the lines crisp. In the outfield hung the signs of area sponsors touting wares to the often sizable crowds. They dressed in bright uniforms bleached free of grass stains by diligent Moms. Festive families cheered the small gladiators in between bites of hot dogs from the concession stand.

Little League celebrates the glorious fantasies of childhood, when a twelve year old can have the entire town calling his first name. In Little League a bonehead play of game-breaking dimensions will generate comments like, "Nice try, Son, you'll get 'em next time." While Little League suffers from competitive excess in many places, in Beyonder the apparent excess is one of nurturing. A kid can't take a swing in the on-deck circle without receiving five or six helpful pointers and encouraging exhortations.

Babe Ruth is about harsh realities. You make a bonehead play, and the coach might call you a "Bonehead." Moreover, your teammates will call you something worse.

In Babe Ruth, the proportions are out of whack. The players are too small for the field. The throw between third and first, that Wade Boggs can make with a flip of the wrist, is a fling of a country mile. The catchers bounce the ball to second base; the runners take an eternity to make it down the line. Stolen bases happen in slow motion. Most runs score on passed balls. A batter hits a shot good for extra bases in Little League and it doesn't even make the outfield grass. Even the chatter at the pitcher now comes in low, flat voices that seem alien to the bodies.

Few spectators watch. Concession stand? Yeah, right. There's no immaculate stadium, no nurturing. You crowd the plate, you're likely to get busted inside. This is hardball. Instead of the friendly town field, they haul their butts off to the outer recesses of Beyonder where other bands of young turkeys have been cast loose from flocks.

But you know what? As the weeks go by, and Mud Season turns into full-fledged Vermont summer, these kids begin to look more and more like real ballplayers. No one says much, but the players and coaches can feel it happening.

With humans, to be a "turkey" means to be a geeky, awkward, loser. For boys who play baseball at the Babe Ruth level, despite some validity to the "geeky" and "awkward" charges, they are clearly not losers. The ones on the diamond are the ones who have the courage to transcend pin feathers and to confront the overwhelming size and weapons of the battlefield. They could stare at a Nintendo, hang out at the quick-stop, or listen to Guns 'N Roses, but instead, they play ball. They practice to become tomorrow's champions. Whether or not that ever happens, a lot of growth takes place along the way.

Lose Your Lawn

Finally, we're done with baseball and can delve
into other springtime topics, such as the backyard.

How did we become a nation of manicured, toxic lawns? How did a lowly perennial that imitates a carpet become our dominant ground cover? My personal theory (I make it personal to avoid the rigors of research or fact finding) traces the perfect lawn back to World War II. Our boys returned from the Big One with expectations of peace, prosperity and perfection. This vision included a trophy wife, nestled in a neat suburban home, surrounded by a flawless lawn and a picket fence. Peace reigned, and since the big enemies—Adolph Hitler and Isoroku Yamamoto—had been vanquished, only crabgrass remained.

Grass is an inoffensive perennial that is minimally decorative, inedible, provides no shade and attracts only the "wildlife" that subsists on kegs of beer. It is also overwhelmingly the ground cover of choice in North America. Its virtue is its uniformity. This is the Marine haircut of the plant world.

Since I'm on the soapbox: Why do we grow lawns in regions intended for cactus and Gila monsters? Why are there golf courses in Phoenix? Whose idea of sanity is it to pump fresh water from ancient aquifers so we can make the desert look like the rain forest? And why do we nurture our lawns with water and fertilizers so that we can then attack it with an arsenal of lawn tractors, weed whackers, bazookas and mortars? Our neighborhoods sound like war zones on Sunday afternoons.

We're living the American Dream, internal combustion-style, but we know the dream has to change. We're using up the oil; we're using up the fresh water; and we're putting the waste into the air we breathe. If you want to do something about it, take a look at your own back yard. If it's covered with grass, then you have an opportunity to take dramatic and effective environmental action by joining the revolution to lose your lawn.

I signed on after reading a delightful manifesto by Toby Hemenway called *Gaia's Garden: A Guide to Home-Scale Permaculture*. Permaculture is a system that works with the ecosystem to maintain permanent horticulture by relying on renewable resources. Hemenway shows that by treating Nature as an ally instead of an enemy, you can create a beautiful, productive, ecological garden in your own back yard. Hemenway takes the teachings of permaculture pioneers David Holmgren and Bill Mollison and makes them accessible to the average person living in the average home. The result is deceptively simple, deceptively beguiling, and completely revolutionary. It makes so much sense you'll never look at lawn care or gardening the same way again.

The natural world is neither flat nor rectangular. The natural world is not uniform, but diverse, with plants grouped in complementary ways that fill ecological microniches. In Gaia theory the world is treated as one huge, interconnected and interdependent system. A garden of Gaia is one in which the cultivation mimics the layers of growth you see in a forest. From the roots to the treetops you select plants to play mutually supporting roles in a rich gardening system.

Getting from here to there is not as difficult as you might imagine. You do not have to dig up your yard with a backhoe or pulverize the sod with a rototiller. If you are a patient person, you can just do nothing. In a few years natural processes will be well on their way to restoring biodiversity to your back yard. You can speed the process, however, by following Hemenway's advice.

A key concept is to build soil by adding organic matter. No digging. No power tools. No chemicals. Put down a layer of cardboard or newspaper, then add up to a foot of straw, seaweed, wood shavings, or any combination thereof. Then plant into the mulch, not the soil. Eventually the roots will penetrate the enriched topsoil. By planting perennials, maintenance is minimal.

As with all new and revolutionary ideas, the lose-your-lawn movement will be threatening to some. We've been conditioned to distrust things that don't require motors, medicine, or pasteurization. The companies that profit from the sales of fertilizers, herbicides, and lawn tractors won't embrace the idea of *Gaia's Garden* until they figure out how to make money on them. Millions of marketing dollars have been spent to perpetuate the myth that a weed-free lawn, along with even teeth and 2.1 children, is essential to personal happiness. We dutifully mount our lawn steeds to keep Nature at bay. Then we water like crazy so we can do it again next week.

We are still firmly ensconced in an age when our species removes any impediment to comfort through the addition of more power. Too hot? Too cold? Just add power. Need to go higher? Faster? Step on the accelerator, unleash the power. The size of our lawns, once limited by a human's time, energy, and patience for pushing a mower, has grown in direct relation to the horsepower of our lawn tractors.

Permaculture advocates are challenging the myths by offering delightful and superior alternatives. Your lawn does not have to be an extension of your living room, but rather can bring Mother Nature to the back door. You can design your outdoor space for visual appeal, edible yield or attracting wildlife. The choices are infinite so long as you embrace the one inviolable principle: You must work with, not against, natural processes.

If this revolution is successful, our back yards will be converted into mini-nature preserves offering beauty, harmony, and delicious food. Sunday afternoons will be for relaxing to the soothing sounds of songbirds, not the hue and roar of warfare waged on grasses struggling toward the sun. With organic produce growing in your back yard, your food bills will go down and your health will improve. Moreover, you won't have to drive to the store, and the grocery store won't have to transport your fresh produce from hundreds—sometimes thousands—of miles away, meaning less fossil fuel will be used transporting what's essentially water (the primary component of fruits and vegetables) across the planet. All because you lost your lawn, and replaced it with *Gaia's Garden*.

The revolution is barely a conspiratorial whisper at the moment. However, a new story is emerging that we can embrace, not conquer, nature in our own back yards.

Walk, Don't Run

Still in the Left Coast mode, I joined up with 80,000 others to run the Bay to Breakers race in San Francisco.

The View From Beyonder portrays the contemporary rural experience as lived by the eclectic individuals known as Vermonters. The experience is periodically validated by traveling beyond state boundaries to compare life here with the rest the world. A middle-aged jogger, I have run in all the major local road races—Randolph Fourth of July 10K, Northfield Observances, the West Brookfield Classic....you name it, I've run it. On a recent trip to California, I ran San Francisco's famous Bay to Breakers Race, a description of which will clear up, finally and forever, any confusion between the two states.

In Vermont we put on shorts, t-shirt, and running shoes. Someone says "go" and we run like heck toward the finish line. The first one over wins. Got it?

Here's how they do footraces in California.

First, the city puts out a hundred or so porta johns. (In Vermont we just run behind the bushes.) Then, they play rock music (very loud) while helicopters hover overhead. Finally, 90,000 people gather (roughly the combined populations of Burlington, Montpelier, and Rutland).

Many are dressed for Halloween. Among those I encountered were Minnie Mouse, a Teenage Mutant Ninja Turtle, a Yuppie (jacket, tie, paper mache BMW, and car phone), and a larger-than-

life Kraft Macaroni and Cheese box. There were pussycats, goril-
las, and chickens. There was a line of thirteen joined people
(called a "centipede") in tiger suits wearing big, orange foam rubber claws. There was a human six-pack, a chain gang, and a contingent of men dressed in diapers and baby bonnets.

"I can beat these guys," I said to myself, my visage a portrait
of Yankee grit. Not a whit of competitive spirit was evident from
the crowd. People were laughing, drinking cappuccino from
paper cups, and dancing.

The gun sounded—not a gun, actually, but a DJ urging us to
have a good time. My muscles tensed, ready to begin the grueling
7.5-mile course with its notorious hills. After five minutes, I let
them relax, as I had progressed not a single inch. It took, in fact,
twenty minutes to reach the starting line, an interesting lesson in
crowd logistics.

When we did start moving, it was an inch at a time. Running,
amid such a sea of humanity, was out of the question. I reckoned
my starting position around 75,000th place.

For a half-mile we shuffled, then broke into a leisurely stroll.
By mile two we could actually jog, two steps sideways for each
step forward. The winners of the race had by now crossed the finish line.

I began my move, streaming by others as if they were walking
(which they were—no sense working up a sweat). From the downtown we moved along Hayes St., a favorite residential neighborhood of Hell's Angels. At first I thought the leather-clad, tattooed
subhumans with hunks of metal hanging out of every body orifice
were fellow runners. But today was their day to stare at us.

We flowed into a neighborhood of Victorian homes with the
residents hosting spirited race parties. Music, champagne, and
food were everywhere, along with yelling, whooping, and chanti-
ng.

"This is not the loneliness of the long distance runner," I told
myself. "This is not the agony of da feet. This is too, too...." I
searched for the right word, "too much fun."

How would these people ever build character? How would
they face the frigid slaps of Mud Season after an eternity of winter?

My disdain transformed into a renewed desire to dominate. I found an open seam by a sidewalk and passed another five hundred or so racers. I was making my move.

I passed a team of fraternity guys in togas pushing a beer-drinking corpse on a hospital bed. I passed a human cable car. I passed another four thousand or so people. We reached Hayes St. Hill, a typically steep San Francisco incline. My superior conditioning paid off as I streamed by thousands more. At the top, however, I was met by the sight of an endless ribbon of runners. Looking back, the same ribbon continued as far as the eye could see. I paused to drink it all in. A thousand runners passed me.

Have I mentioned that it was an exquisitely beautiful day?

We entered Golden Gate Park. Already I had passed a man running in a trench coat (and nothing else), a man wearing a hospital johnny (and nothing else), and a woman wearing little more than a string holding a sign reading "no tailgating." There was a guy with a "kick butt" sign on his posterior running with a girl with a "squeeze butt" sign on hers. I ran by a one-man band, a steel drum band, a jazz band, and a rock band.

When we went through an underpass the runners broke into an Arsenio Hall Oo-oo-oo-oo dog-pound chant. When we passed a band playing "Jailhouse Rock," the runners clapped in unison. Aw, what the heck, so did I.

Meanwhile, I streaked forward through air laden with the astringent smell of eucalyptus. I caught up with a chaotic contingent of more than a hundred Hash House Harriers ("A Drinking Club With A Running Problem") blowing bugles and shouting, "On-on! ! !"

The Pacific Ocean came into view. (I have mentioned that it was a beautiful day, haven't I?) I sprinted past a running Velveeta Cheese box as well as a guy wearing a giant crab on his head.

Unofficially, I finished 32,987th. "Did you have a good race?" asked the man in one of the twenty-five or more finishing chutes. He was dressed as Conan the Barbarian, complete with horns and loincloth.

"Let's put it this way, I didn't win," I replied.

"Let's put it this way," he said, the California sun glinting off the gold tips of his horns, "No one cares."

Match-Up with Mellowness

Vermont's Sister State (some might say its evil twin) is Mendocino County, California. It is everything Vermont is not, and then some! I've spent half my professional life shuttling between the two, and I can say definitively, Mendocino is superior in every way—climate, produce, seacoast—but Vermont wins!

We traveled to California this spring and stayed with friends in Mendocino County, a few hours north of San Francisco. Mendocino is approximately the size of Vermont, with only a tenth of the population, so comparisons are inevitable.

Our friends were quite charming, generous to a fault, but I could see through their false hospitality. It's easy to be friendly when you live in a world void of adversity. They live without mosquitoes, black flies, tourists from New York, freezing rain, or washboard. Their gardens grow twelve months a year! They smile benignly, as if lobotomized, because they don't know how to frown. Our facial muscles, by contrast, are in much better shape.

We got along o.k. They showed us the sights, and we made an effort to fit in culturally, eating seventeen varieties of sprouts, soaking in the hot tub, and not flushing the toilet. ("If it's yellow, it's mellow. If it's brown, flush it down.")

We sought cultural bridges. For instance, my wife pointed out that we didn't flush the toilet either, not because of any water shortage, but because we're always afraid that the septic will overflow.

"Heh-heh. We live in an old house," I offered by way of explanation.

"Oh, so do we," replied our hostess with pride. "Ours was built in the 1940's. We don't flush because we're saving the planet."

See what I mean about Californians?

Our house was built in the 1840's, not that the depth of our cultural richness implies superiority (heh-heh-heh). I'm not that petty. Rather, I went out of my way to be complimentary about California.

"Don't you get sick of all this sunshine?" I asked.

"Well, it does get hot in the summer," said our host, obviously rubbing our faces in meteorological excrement. Tell me he didn't know that we lost vegetables to frost in August!

"You should come visit us," I volunteered. "You won't complain about the heat."

They accepted the offer, and suddenly we were faced with the prospect of matching Vermont with the tourist wonderland that is Northern California.

"How, like, will we, you know, kinda entertain them?" asked my thirteen-year-old son, the one with the hormone problem.

"Why, we'll show them the sights," said I.

"But there's like, nuthin' here, 'cept, y'know, trees 'n stuff." I stated that the wonders of Beyonder could match those of any place on earth, especially in the summer. I challenged him to name highlights from our California trip, and I would match each one with something equally spectacular from our backyard.

"The Golden Gate Bridge," came the first challenge. The Floating Bridge in Brookfield, countered I. Here is a true architectural wonder, a wooden bridge that floats, that captures the wonders of the culture. Cross over the Golden Gate on a nice day and there will be a stream of walkers, bikers, and joggers, all wearing Walkpersons (note the Californication of this column). Similarly, at the Floating Bridge there will be a cross-section of real Vermonters soaking up the summer, not a bunch of Japanese tourists clicking away with motorized cameras.

"The Floating Bridge experience is superior," I pointed out, "because you can fish or swim from the bridge. Can you do a swan dive off the Golden Gate? And which bridge would you rather be on during an earthquake?"

The first point was clearly mine. "OK," said my wife, rising to the challenge, "Watching Barry Bonds hit one into McCovey Cove from SBC Park on the Bay."

"You must be joking," I sputtered. "You call that a baseball experience? Compare that to watching any game at all at the ball field in Rochester. It's so green in Rochester that it makes Wrigley

Field look like a parking lot. The views are spectacular, and the fans are so enthusiastic they make the Bleacher Bums look like old spinsters. No ten-buck parking fees, four-dollar hot dogs, or watery beers. The weather's probably better in Rochester, too."

"Alright, alright" (another concession). "Match a hundred thousand people at a free rock concert in Golden Gate Park."

"Easy, South Royalton town band on the green for free every Thursday night."

"OK, any shopping mall."

"Chelsea Flea Market. Gotcha."

"Chinatown." I hesitated. Could this be my downfall? Would the Man from Beyonder be stymied by the exotic colors and infinite variety of the tastes of Chinatown.

"Easy," I said, but I was groping. "Ummm-m, for colorful excitement and tasty diversification what could match the midway at the Tunbridge Fair? Clearly, this is superior to Chinatown." There was a brief silence. Had I triumphed yet again?

"YOU LOSE," they shouted in unison. Well, I was doing pretty well up to this point. I just hope our California friends, not to mention my own children, recognize that this was all a ruse to remind ourselves how great Vermont is. I've done my job; the rest is up to you.

Part VI—The Beginning (of the End)

It's over before it begins. Like youth, love, fireflies, and shooting stars summer is fragile, ephemeral and eternal. The summer solstice begins the High Holy Days that culminate in the strangely warlike Fourth of July. On the streets throughout Beyonder high school bands, Little League champs, old soldiers, and beloved politicians toot, wave, salute, and pose.

We rediscover our animal selves. We strip down as close to naked as possible and cook our food over open flames. Nothing is more liberating than flashlight tag in the tall grass where you can lay down and disappear.

Our minds go blank as we stare off the end of the dock into the mesmerizing lake, but not for long as great thoughts emerge from the ripples. Glub really is all you need.

By Bennington Battle Day, a remembrance of when the great Colonel Bennington single-handedly withstood an alien invasion back in ought three, summer is showing its age. There's gold in them lawns and the green hillsides now show the odd flash of premature red. Too soon the school buses appear, too soon. There's silence in the north. The songbirds have reared their broods and now head south, leaving a territorial silence behind. The joyous shouts of children squirting each other with a hose are no more.

Only the Red Sox slog on, pretending that summer still reigns as the king of Vermont.

The Dumpster Cooks

This was intended as the first of a series of columns that will eventually be compiled into a James Beard Award-winning book and will form the foundation of a wildly popular show on the Food Network. Eventually, I will collect my experiences into a memoir that will become a major motion picture, starring John Goodman as "The Dumpster."

I was a very good little boy. When my Mommy told me to clean my plate, I did. Occasionally, she served something that I just couldn't stomach, and she'd use the "one little bite" gambit, saying, "How do you know you don't like it, unless you try it?" I would agree to the "one little bite" only to have her respond with a heaping shovelful.

But, for the most part, I was glad to leave the plate clean.

Life ensued. There were fewer and fewer food items that I refused to eat. I even started liking pea soup and squash. These days I always clean my plate...always, even without my Mother around to admonish or praise. It's my thing. I eat what I'm served.

This was not a problem until I began living with a woman who was raised by nuns. (Not literally, I'm invoking what is called "artistic license," meaning I can lie in print). Nuns, like Moms, tell you to clean your plate. And like me, my partner likes to please, so she always leaves her plate clean. Unlike me, to her the end (a clean plate) justifies the means (scraping her unwanted food onto my plate). After she finishes scraping, she grinds her heel into my stomach by growling:

"D-U-M-P-S-T-E-R!!"

The utterance is enough to dissolve her into mirthful tittles. I, meanwhile, stare helplessly into a small mountain of barely warm, greasy Chinese food that can no longer be recognized for its component parts. It's now moo-goo-chow-glop. Dutifully, like a WW I soldier at the trenches, I slog onward until it's gone.

But here's an unexpected turn of fate. Not only does the

Dumpster eat, the Dumpster cooks, and in his own twisted way, he cooks good. I have developed a set of rules, practices, techniques, and philosophies known collectively as The Dumpster Method. Master these nine inviolable principles and you will be able to cook and eat just like the Dumpster:

1. Use it or lose it. The only sin greater than throwing away edible food is forgetting to return the video to the video store, thereby incurring the dreaded late fee. The trick is to transform the food into something yummy before it grows that technicolor mold.

2. Always use full packages. Leftovers = good. Half-filled pasta boxes on the shelf = bad.

3. Measure with your mouth. Only wussies on the Food Channel measure ingredients with calibrated spoons or cups.

4. When in doubt, put it on the grill.

5. The only unforgivable mistake is overcooking.

6. Eat your other mistakes, and loudly proclaim how good they taste. You will be surprised how many people will believe you.

7. Never use more than a single pot.

8. Garlic is good, more garlic is better.

9. Anything edible can go into a burrito.

Any questions? Now (a little pause here, as I am about to utter the trademark Dumpster phrase that the studio audience loves to say along), WHAT'S IN THE REFRIGERATOR?

You open up the refrigerator, and you see...nothing. At least you think you see nothing. That's the difference between you and The Dumpster who sees an impending feast. What's this? A small jar of capers. What's this? An onion and a few dried carrots. What's this? Say no more; time to start cooking.

Boil water for pasta. Le Methode Dumpster (pronounced "Doom-stair") requires that the properly stocked kitchen always have pasta, burrito skins, black peppercorns, olive oil, garlic, and

Parmesan cheese. Everything else is optional.

Add a full box of pasta (remember rule #2) to the pot and stir with a wooden spoon. While the pasta cooks, chop the onion and grate the carrots. When you think the pasta has about a minute left to cook add the onion and carrot. Drain everything into a colander.

Return the pot to the stove (now set to low) and add some olive oil. For those who want a more precise definition of "some" it means "not too little and not too much." I always start with a little and add a little more. It's much easier that trying to wipe excess oil off individual pieces of penne.

When the oil is hot add some chopped garlic (in this case "some" means twice as much as any sane person would use). The garlic is cooked when it turns translucent and the kitchen smells like the back alleys of Naples. Add the contents of the colander to the pot and stir until everything is evenly coated. Quick, rinse the colander with hot water so that you don't have to wash it.

Add the capers. If you really want to be creative, use up the last of those raisins in the glass jar. And what the heck, throw in a few chopped walnuts. Give the dish an exotic sounding name (Penne Palermo), and serve with Parmesan and ground pepper.

Total cost, next to nothing, only one pot to clean, and people will actually think you know what you are doing. Next, if enthusiasm warrants (meaning, if my editor actually lets me do another cooking column), join The Dumpster as he prepares Mexican Hot Dogs on the grill. Just remember, it all begins with WHAT'S IN THE REFRIGERATOR?

Dumpster Dogs

The Dumpster cooking concept has yet to take hold, but it's only a matter of time until the Food Channel comes calling. Soon, America will be shouting, "What's in the refrigerator?"

Hey, kids, what time is it? It's summertime and summertime is Dumpster time. For those of your who missed the previous install-ment of "The Dumpster Cooks," The Dumpster is the nickname I have earned for my ability (bordering on compulsion) to finish everything on my plate, no matter how putrid, greasy, malodor-ous, or massive. Repulsive as it sounds, I have developed a method of cooking that reflects the philosophy, techniques, and refined palate of the aforementioned Dumpster.

Today, The Dumpster does dogs. (Yes, I know, usually dogs do dumpsters, but this is my essay.)

There's no time like the summer for hot dogs. But at too many summer occasions, the hot dogs are charred little cylinders of salt, sawdust, and fat served in a limp, white roll with a squiggle of yel-low bile. Those days are over. Welcome to the wide world of Dumpster Dogs.

It starts with the dog itself. A hot dog is not a hot dog. For those of you who have taken the time to read the list of ingredi-ents and nutritional charts on the hot dogs at the local market, you should get a life. Let me save you time and aggravation. All hot dogs are lousy for you. If you want healthy, eat celery. If you crave an artery-clogging experience, nothing satisfies like a dog. You won't be disappointed.

All dogs are not equal. At the bottom of my list are Fenway Franks, whose claim to fame is that they are "just like the ones you get at the ballpark." This means "not very good and over-priced." These days going to Fenway is such an upscale experi-ence that the food courts resemble the open buffet on a cruise ship. They don't serve Fenway Franks any more, but you can get a decent Portobello Panini that you can wash down with a crisp Sauvignon Blanc.

My dog of choice is all-beef, kosher knockwurst, but the Dumpster treatment works equally well on chicken sausage, kielbasa, sweet Italian sausage, hot Italian sausage, bratwurst, and anything in between.

Now comes the time we've been waiting for, when we stop the intellectualizing and start the salivary juices flowing. This moment is always marked by The Dumpster's trademark war cry, "WHAT'S IN THE REFRIGERATOR?"

The first stage is to make the secret Dumpster Sauce. Go to the refrigerator and take out every condiment that has not been used in the last two months and that does not have a festival of mold on the surface. Put them all in a bowl. That's right, put them all in a bowl. No measuring spoons, no recipes. This means the sweet pepper relish, the Key Lime mustard that someone put in your Christmas stocking, the last of the Grey Poupon, Nellie-from-up-the-road's green tomato relish. This is your chance to clean your refrigerator of wayward condiments that have been clogging up the works since last summer's barbecue.

The Dumpster isn't kidding. Put them all in a bowl and stir. What will emerge is a tangy, purplish goop with lumps. Mm-m-m.

Next, take a good-sized Vidalia onion and chop it fine. Don't use a yellow storage onion. You want the best! You are now ready to go to the grill.

Over a well-established bed of hardwood charcoal coals (please, no briquettes, no gas, and no charcoal lighter), slowly grill your chosen tubular morsel. When cooked, move it to the side. Onto a flour tortilla (I like the burrito-size), spread your secret Dumpster sauce and add a generous layer of onion. Place the tortilla on the grill, put the dog on the tortilla. Fold or roll the tortilla, depending on the relative size of the dog to tortilla and your skill with barbecue tools, and serve. The tortilla will take only a few seconds to heat. Don't burn it.

Variations on the Dumpster Dog are the Chihuahua (using up your leftover salsas or, even better, fresh salsas from the garden; The Dumpster also fancies himself to be a connoisseur—or is it "common sewer"?—of salsas) and the Goomba (sautéed peppers and onions substituting for the raw Vidalia). Remember to put your remaining secret sauce back in a jar in the fridge. You will need it again before the summer's through.

Those of you whose idea of cooking involves measuring spoons, recipes, and multiple cooking utensils are probably quite horrified at the prospect of Dumpster Dogs, but come on over to my backyard. When that secret sauce is dribbling down your chin and those arteries to your aorta are just about fully closed, you'll appreciate what The Dumpster means when he says, "It don't get no better than this."

Long Live the Swim Hole

"Sacred" and "secret" are the only appropriate words for Vermont swimming holes. There aren't that many days when you absolutely, positively have to cool off, but when one comes, you better know where to go.

Summer is almost over. (This is a safe statement in Vermont where summer is "almost over" anytime after May.)

Hopefully, everyone has had occasion to enjoy that most delicious of state pleasures, the secret swimming hole.

Someday, someone (undoubtedly a greedy flatlander-type) will write the forbidden book, A Guide to Vermont Swimming Holes. This person will find himself incurring a wrath so violent that the Ayatollah's treatment of Salman Rushdie will seem timid by comparison. After all, the Ayatollah merely threatened to kill the author of The Satanic Verses. I would personally drag the varmint who reveals the location of secret swimming holes the entire length of Route 100 behind a manure spreader. Then, I would turn him over to the next state resident.

Sandy beaches, crashing waves, girls in bikinis, Quebecers in bikinis... forgetaboudit! These are components of the summer experience on Cape Cod or the coast of Maine, but not Vermont. The requirements for a proper Vermont swimming hole are majestic only in their simplicity:

1. The swimming hole must be reachable only on foot or, in a few permissible cases, by four-wheel-drive vehicle. (For this rea-

son alone the swimming hole next to the Warren Store is eliminated. Who wants to skinny dip in full view of New Jerseyites eating pasta salad?)

2. The water must be moving, yet clear enough to permit the sighting of underwater creatures such as brook trout or leeches.

3. The temperature of the water cannot exceed 55 degrees. The water need not be deep. Some of the best holes permit immersion only with ungainly contortion. Don't worry about it. Swimming holes are not called "swimming holes" because you swim in them.

Swimming holes are precious because our need for them is so rare. Thus, the loss of one assumes the dimension of tragedy. One of the more traumatic moments in my life came on a sweltering August day when I went to a hitherto secret swimming hole only to encounter what appeared to be an explosion of multicolored nylon, aerodynamic foam helmets and Perrier bottles. It was, for the swimming hole aficionado, the worst nightmare: My secret swimming hole had been discovered by a bicycle tour!

It would have been bad enough had they discovered the secret on their own, but they were guided by little maps put out by a treacherous tour operator, a Benedict Arnold who had no appreciation for which of the state's assets can rightly be peddled and which others we keep for ourselves. Foliage we peddle. Lake Champlain, we peddle. Killington, we peddle. Holsteins, we peddle. The Tunbridge World's Fair, we keep for ourselves. Swimming holes, we keep for ourselves.

Got it?

On discovering the bikers I felt violated, soiled and abused. And there was no one to help. The state needs the equivalent of a rape crisis center for victims of swimming hole abuse. It should be staffed by sympathetic, caring counselors who speak in carefully modulated tones and who understand the trauma of swimming hole loss. Perhaps I am being too personal, but I confess, to this day I cannot go back to that once favorite swimming hole for fear that my solitude and bliss will be shattered by sudden appearance of a herd of Flatlanders in lycra, riding 10-speeds with little fluorescent flags on the back.

Rather than dwell on the loss of one precious hole, though, let us revel in the fact that there are still holes aplenty, tiny sanctuaries from the rarest of Northern phenomena—excessive heat. It's summertime, and may each of you find relief from the sultry August afternoons, but God help anyone of you decides to write a book on the subject.

H_2O 'N' U

A personal aside to all my Flatlander friends who have ponds: This column does not refer to you. Your pond is both an engineering masterpiece as well as a stellar example of environmental design. You are to be commended for your tastefulness and vision, not to mention how much you have enhanced the value of your property, you shrewd son of a gun, you.

Earlier, I spotlighted the most fragile and precious of our natural resources, the secret swimming hole. This, the second in a two-part series, concerns a different aqueous body that is sprouting faster than teenage acne and is cratering the landscape in just as unsightly a manner—the pond, otherwise known as the scum hole.

The blight of ponds has been brought upon us by that ubiquitous incarnation of evil, the Flatlander, an omnipresent vermin who buys a piece of Paradise, and then, oblivious to the fact that if God had meant Vermont to have a lot of lakes he would have called it Minnesota, gouges out a gaping hole that fills with water; then, if the water does not disappear, covers with algae.

Why Flatlanders feel so compelled to construct ponds is unknown. Some attribute it to nostalgia for the suburban inground pool. Others say a pond is the closest reincarnation of the Jersey shore possible in the Green Mountains. Psychologists call the phenomenon the "thwarted mud puddle syndrome."

People construct elaborate rationales to justify this "mud-puddling." They describe their pond as a trout farm or a secure source of water in the event of a house fire or a means of giving Duane, the backhoe operator, much-needed work.

Under no circumstances, however, does the pond owner mention "recreation" as a motivation.

Once the pit is half finished, however, the proud owners (trout farmers that they are) immediately purchase a small fortune of inflatable flotation devices. In fact, they purchase so many inflatable gewgaws that they now have to buy a portable air compressor from Sears. The acquisition lust accelerates through kayaks, canoes, row boats, paddleboats, and in extreme cases, windsurfers. The net result is an "ecosystem" surrounded by enough Taiwanese-made inflatable alligators and dinosaurs that it resembles a staging area for the Macys Thanksgiving Parade.

Not content to end the materialistic frenzy, the pond owner now tries to inflict the pond on you by inviting you to a "pond party" where you stand in frigid water, sinking up to your knees in muck while talking about your favorite subjects—flow rates, drainage patterns, and hydroscopic soil characteristics.

My favorite Vermont pond story concerns a proud, pond-owning neighbor whose Morgan horse stooped to take a sip from the new resource. (Did I mention livestock watering as a pond-building rationale?) A snapping turtle who resided in the pond resented the intrusion and clamped onto the equine snout, thereby causing great pain and tremendous chaos. All efforts to remove the obstinate reptile merely resulted in more pain. The lady of the house finally had to call her husband at work to shoot the thing. As I heard it, the entire community dined on turtle stew.

This humorous story was related to me while sipping a gin and tonic at a pond party. Once the punch line was concluded, the host asked if I would be interested in a dip. With visions of a 50-pound snapping turtle dangling from my nose, I politely declined.

The love affair with the pond continues for the first few summers, or until the finite limitation of man's ability to plan and control nature becomes apparent. Either the pond overflows in April or it dries up in August, or it becomes a Mecca for a host of unwanted watery pests, like salamanders and tadpoles. The good news is that in pond making man's interference with nature is transitory, a grown-up's mud puddle. Twenty years after the first scrape of the bulldozer, you'll never know there was a pond.

So, with apologies in advance to the fire fighters, trout farmers, backhoe operators, Sears employees, gewgaw vendors, snapping turtles, Flatlanders, Real Vermonters, psychologists, residents of Taiwan and Morgan horses of Vermont...happy splashing!

Don't Make Waves

This is it! The heart of Beyonder. Up here we wave. Down there, they don't.

One of the nice things about Beyonder is that people wave to each other. When you think about it, this is behavior without precedent in the animal kingdom.

"Look, look! There's a member of our species!"

Of course, we do it because we're stimulus-deprived, but isn't it odd that the same Vermonters who will not speak to a neighbor until he has lived in the state for two generations will wave to any idiot who happens by in a motor vehicle, even a Flatlander with Jersey plates?

Initially, visiting Flatlanders look away from waving Vermonters, thinking they are about to be hit up for spare change. Then they adopt the practice with a vengeance, sticking their hands in the face of every man, woman, child, dog, and tree they pass.

The Flatlander wave, however, is without panache, an enthusiastic but graceless shaking of the proffered palm that misses the point. Anyone living north of Putney has developed a personal wave that is as much a part of an individual's identity as a fingerprint. Here are a few classics from my neck of Beyonder:

The two fingered tradesman salute (I'm sorry, I just can't write "tradesperson"). This jaunty greeting, favored by the working-class hero who has at least six months of work lined up, is flicked off the top of the pick-up's steering wheel with casual, confident ease. (In some remote areas of the Northeast Kingdom, the index and middle finger are reportedly brought to the brow.)

Guess what I did last night? This is the wave following a night of overindulgence (or if you have the flu). The steering wheel is gripped with both hands, and the wave is executed by lifting the index finger of the right hand approximately three quarters of an inch into the air, just enough to be barely perceptible. No eye contact required.

"Hi, didn't I meet you at the PTA?" This is the wave exchanged by transplants to the North Country who recognize each other's Volvos or Caravans. The wave is brief, vigorous, and overly enthusiastic. "Perky" is the word that comes to mind. If you encounter this wave while you are in a "Guess what I did last night?" frame of mind you might have to stifle a retch.

The alien contempt. This is the wave that native Vermonters use to return the "Hi, didn't I meet you..." from transplanted Flatlanders. It is a simple, unenthusiastic motion, usually delivered backhanded. Vermonters don't express emotions demonstrably, but this one, translated to words, would clearly say, "Go back where you came from."

The "I'm the busiest person in the world" wave. Watch for this one from anyone who drives a Saab (which, we all remember, stands for "something almost always broken"). It is always delivered without eye contact, because the driver wants you to think that he, she, or it has fifty thousand more important things to do than waving at you. This is surprising, because as far as you know, this person spends his, her, or its time driving aimlessly, looking for people to wave to.

"You remember me from high school." This greeting is unique among North Country greetings in that it does not involve the hands. Instead, it is done by screwing the face into a contortion that you haven't seen since Jimmy Ruggillio made the same face behind the back of the assistant principal when you were in ninth grade. You thought it was a riot at the time. Now you wonder why this person, who isn't even Jimmy, and is over fifty years old, is making the same face.

The old Vermontah. This is one of those genetically defined characteristics that I have as much luck in mimicking as I do Michael Jackson's moonwalk. You approach the old Vermontah (who may in fact be young, old, male, female, or otherwise) wondering whether or not a wave will be forthcoming. If you wave first, they will immediately counter with "the alien contempt." If you don't wave, they will hit you with "the old Vermontah," a casual lifting of the hand that carries with it the message:

"What's the matter with you, you uptight refugee from the huddled masses? Don't you realize that this is the country, and up here folks are folks. We keep our distance, but we're all in this together, and we damn sure have to acknowledge it by this simple gesture of humanity. So get with the program!"

You (admittedly, a transplant) approach with trepidation. You prepare for a modified version of the "busiest person" salute, but chicken out at the last moment, convinced that the old Vermontah is preoccupied and unaware of your presence. You accelerate only to be caught at the final moment by a brief head feint, then the laconic wave.

It's too late to respond. You're already past, and you realize that you've been outfoxed again. Sometimes it takes two generations to get it right.

Those Darn New Yorkers

We are fair and open-minded people in Vermont. We think that all humans have dignity. We draw the line, however, when it comes to people across the lake or river. You can't be too mean or vicious to a New Yorker or New Hampshirite.

Those darn New Yorkers, we should poison gas 'em.

Omigod, omigod. Someone at the state tourist division is running for pen and paper right now, full of economic indignation. Don't I know how many millions are contributed to the state's coffers by denizens of the Flatlands who gawk at our dying leaves and slide down our hillsides with boards on their feet? Haven't I seen the ads on TV that tell me I better count my blessings and make nice to tourists?

Look, I've got nothing against fleecing Flatlanders. Some of my best friends feed families off scraps of Flatlander bounty, but before you send an indignant missive let's hear the other side of the story—how is a Vermonter treated when he ventures onto the New Yorker's turf?

It was a lovely day and my spirits were high as I drove into Manhattan on the Henry Hudson Expressway. "Start spreading the news," I crooned softly to myself, oblivious to the obscene gestures proffered by every third passing car. This was my kind of town.

My spirits remained undaunted even after spending SEVEN-TEEN DOLLARS TO PARK MY CAR FOR SIXTY-FIVE MIN-UTES. For my second appointment, I decided to risk a meter, making sure to read every word of the posted regulations. I was willing to get a ticket, but I did not want to get towed.

I ended the appointment using the excuse that the meter had run out.

"Where are you parked?" asked my host.

"Seventh Avenue," I replied.

"Well, you'd better run," he said, "because they tow everyone at four o'clock."

"But," I protested, "I read the signs. They said nothing about towing."

"Well," he shrugged in that helpful, New Yorker way (I even detected a hint of a smile), "everyone knows they tow from Seventh Avenue at four o'clock, no matter what the signs say."

His definition of "everyone" did not include dumb rubes from Vermont.

The tow truck operator, in the process of hoisting my car, was similarly friendly. Not only would he not put the car down, but he refused to give me a ride to the impound area or even to tell me where it was. This is the scene that never makes it into the "I Love New York" commercials.

After walking 19 blocks to the heavily armed garrison where impounded autos are kept, I found myself in the company of hundreds of other miscreants whose fair and equitable punishment for not feeding the meter a quarter was an enormous fine, thousands of dollars of gratuitous damage to their vehicles, and an interminable wait while state workers took leisurely dinner breaks.

I should add that it was 95 degrees outside, hot enough to fry an egg on the sidewalk, if not my forehead.

People were emancipated eventually by a state drone calling names from a barred window. I watched fellow scofflaws come and go, while I remained ignored. Like everyone, I was hot, tired, and angry, and late for my next appointment. Like everyone, I was anticipating reunion with my car the way a sailor anticipates shore leave after five months at sea.

There was one individual, however, who did not share a desire to end the nightmarish experience, judging from the repeated calls for "Mr. Donor," who did not make an appearance.

I went from impatient to furious. Finally, having had enough, I stormed the window.

"Everyone's going before me!" I exploded. "What's going on here?"

"Name?"

"Morris. Stephen Morris."

"We do not have any paperwork for Mr. Morris."

"Yes, you do! I can see it right there!" I gestured emphatically to the familiar green and white license, indignation mixed with state pride. "Oh, no," returned the clerk. "This paperwork is for Mr. Donor of Vermont." To understand the irony of this situation, pull out your driver's license and read it. This virtuoso display of bureaucratic incompetence humbled me. I managed a whimper/sputter. For a nanosecond, I considered correcting the error, then thought better of it. If the State of New York wanted me to be "Organ Donor," I would oblige. Anything to get back my car. "I'm Mr. Donor," I said, thereby unleashing a torrent of abuse from the clerk for having ignored the calls.

Remember this story the next time the weather turns greasy over the Killington Gap. If you see a land yacht with New York plates (and no snow tires) stuck in a ditch, and if you get out to help, whereupon the driver yells at you because there is no sign saying that snow-covered roads are slippery, remember that New Yorkers—not Arabs, not the Chinese, not Russians—were the enemy against whom Ethan Allen defended Vermont.

Those Lovable Lampreys

This is like "Those Darn New Yorkers," uninvited guests who stay too long. Come to think of it, they are both invasive species.

I don't know whether to believe this story, but my uncle grew up in the Boston area and is a very honest guy. He says that when he was a boy, lobsters were so cheap and plentiful that people used them as fertilizer. Not the shells, but the whole crustacean. They were a poor man's food, something to be consumed in the last few days of the month when the budget had to be stretched.

This, of course was in the days before Lobster Thermidor selling for fifty bucks a pop at the Ritz.

What happened is that lobsters got themselves a good press agent who groomed them, taught them how to interview, and repositioned them at the upper end of the marketplace. As a result, when people see lobster they salivate and reach for their wallets. There's even a chain of restaurants called The Red Lobster. This fame and prosperity has been accomplished despite the fact that lobsters are so ugly they look like escapees from Stephen Spielberg's special effects department. They are inconvenient to eat, requiring special implements and a bib, and they contain vile green stuff that has the consistency of mashed brain.

My point is, someone did a good job of, as they say in the marketing biz, turning lemon into lemonade. All we need to do, to turn Vermont from a Northern Appalachia into a hot bed of prosperity, is to get the same public relations firm that did the lobster makeover to do the same thing with the lamprey eel.

The poor lamprey, maligned in bait shops from St. Albans to Bridport, has an image problem worse than Teddy Kennedy's, and yet this squirmy little devil is a pitchman's dream. Instead of damning the poor creature by blasting him into oblivion with chemical weapons from the arsenal of Saddam Hussein, let's make nice to the little bugger and kill him with kindness. Greed will succeed where pesticides fail.

Let's admit the lamprey has an image problem. Last year in the Burlington Triathalon, one of the swimmers actually emerged from the lake with a lamprey affixed to his perfect body. It looked like one of those emaciated lake trout that are always being waved in our faces on the eleven o'clock news. The lamprey, in the minds of most Vermonters, is vermin, genetically defective scum that despoils our precious natural resources while contributing nothing to the quality of life in the Northland.

This is precisely the kind of thinking that we need to stamp out. We've got to start thinking of this slithery bloodsucker as our little buddy.

We will need the help of the state, beginning with the designation of the lamprey as the official state fish. We could even create a cute mascot called Elmo the Eel or Larry Lamprey. His smiling visage (we could make a big deal out of his unique smile) could grace state highways with a big "Welcome to Vermont" exhibit of Yankee hospitality.

Instead of portraying the lamprey as ravenous snakes, let's think of them as Baby Champs, miniature versions of the state's loveable, mythical sea serpent. Champ sightings have been discouragingly sparse in recent years and the explosion in the lamprey population could be used as evidence of his presence. Little lampreys could be sold to children for home aquariums to bring the legend to life. (Just don't put any other fish in the tank, and for god sakes, don't flush the adult eels down the toilet or we might end up with real Champ-sized creatures.)

The lamprey's reputation as a gourmet delicacy could be improved. If The Red Lobster can be the name of a successful family eatery, what's wrong with The Slippery Sucker? Burlington's fancy eateries could feature exquisite dishes of Lamprey Piccatta and Eel Bolognaise, while lakeside stands could take advantage of the eel's long, slender shape and sell 'em boiled in buns (Eel Dogs) or dipped in batter and fried (Corn Eels).

We could start rumors that lampreys are aphrodisiacs and develop the Japanese market. These are the same people who treasure rhino horn and sea urchins. Lampreys could become the sushi of choice from San Francisco to Tokyo.

The hunters could do their part. All we'd have to do is refer to the male of the species as a "buck" or a "bull" and flannel-shirted warriors would show up in droves for the pleasure of an annual eel slaughter.

The pelts could be used to make wallets, attaché cases, belts, and even ladies' coats that, in turn, could be sold via mail order in The New Yorker. Not even the animal rights people could object to lampreyskin garments and accessories.

By touting the lamprey's virtues we will make the slippery suckers so desirable that catching, skinning, and eating them will become a major source of revenue in Vermont. The eels will become as valuable as morel mushrooms or wild ginseng. Before long, guaranteed, we will have an endangered species on our hands.

Now, as for Asian Milfoil ...

The Moments of Summer

It goes by so fast, a series of moments connected by a thread of fear. Before long the fun will be over. We'll return to a world of daily chores, long nights, and enslavement to the woodstove. Even with a green-house effect there will be plenty of cold, followed by plenty of mud.

Damn.

I wish summer could last forever. Maybe just another month or so. If it hasn't already happened, you'll be at a barbecue and notice that someone is wearing a down vest. Someone will report that there was snow at Killington (probably the Killington public relations department), and you will know that the long slide out of summer's opulence has begun.

What's your favorite summer moment? Here are my nominees, rated in order of preference:

#1 Ducking (not dunking, ducking). Even on the hottest day

when you know that you want the soothing relief of immersion in cold water, there is hesitation before plunging into Vermont's cool waters. The heart pounds and you hold your breath. The momentary shock (is it pain?) is soon replaced by the relief of body heat leeching into the water.

#2 The First Firefly. They came early this year, doubtless due to the warm, dry June. By the Fourth they were as spectacular as the fireworks, although their light show is enhanced by the sounds of a summer night.

#3 The Taste of Barbecued Spam. Nothing captures the spirit of summer so much as the sizzle of Spam on the grill. When that first salty fat matter hey! I'm kidding. Get a life. Spam?

#4 The First Red Tomato of the Summer. It's warm from the sun when you pick it. True aficionados will bring the salt shaker out into the garden. Sweet corn ranks a very close runner-up.

#5 Fourth of July. This is cheating, really. There are so many moments that make up this holiday that sensory overload rules! Just a few—the grand finale, the grandeur of the parade, the clink of horseshoes, the psccht-t-t-t of the keg. Here is an entire summer concentrated into a single day.

#6 The Clap of Thunder. Vermont is not vintage thunderstorm country. We are spared the violent majesty of nature, but no one is immune from the naked fear provoked by the bolt and flash of a summer storm.

#7 Cree-mee. With apologies to Ben & Jerry's, lemonade, strawberry shortcake, and cold watermelon, when you totally give yourself over to indulgence, cree-mee is the way to go. And no flavor will do but vanilla. Bland, yes. Fattening, sure. Personality-less, I suppose. But cree-mee is Vermont, and it hits the spot on a hot Sunday afternoon when you need a treat.

#8 The Potluck. When the gardens are in full bloom, and you're invited to a potluck gathering there is a breathtaking moment as you survey the table of neatly prepared summer salads that is worth holding in memory. The still life distills the hours of loving preparation into a moment of anticipated pleasure, that is fulfilled in the heaping plate. Afterwards, the table looks as if a bomb has hit it, and you are holding your gut so that it does not fall to the floor.

#9 The Flash of the Brookie. All you hear is the stream. The bait is presented. Nothing. Again. Nothing. Again. And then there is a flash that you know will be followed by the small, energetic tugs of a brook trout seeking freedom. Lasting only a nanosecond, the thrill even surpasses that of a shooting star.

#10 The Red Sox. At least once a summer there is a day when the home team plays good ball and you tell yourself, "This is the year. We're going all the way." For this year's team, that moment came in spring training, and it's been downhill ever since. Still, it's only August, and if they can run off ten or twelve straight before September, who are you kidding?

My apologies to the town band in the gazebo, one measure into "Stars and Stripes Forever," marshmallows, the smell and roar of Thunder Road, meteor showers, the smell of fresh mint, and the moment the drive-in movie actually starts. These are all great building blocks of a season that never overstays its welcome.

The moments of summer. Add them together and you might not get much more than a minute. Take them away and we will never make it through the next winter.

Memories of Mercedes

The vehicular testosterone of The Kaboom holds strong into summer. We do stupid things. We make bad decisions. We buy new cars.

Part One—Things Are Good

A Mercedes Man. Admit it. It conjures up certain images. A propertied man, perhaps a little gray around the temples. Imposing and yet elegant. Someone who swaddles himself in performance and the precision of German engineering. Moneyed, yet tastefully so. Understated because he can be. A Mercedes Man.

These are the memory synapses that flashed when I drove past the farmhouse on Camp Brook Road, en route from Rochester to Randolph on a sunny day in May. It was the kind of day that makes Vermonters finally feel secure in the fact that they have broken the stern spine of winter. The leaves pop, the juices flow, and the male of the species contemplates his vehicular status.

Camp Brook Road is not generally a place to go car shopping, especially for a Mercedes, but Vermont is a place where magic happens. I had been passively car shopping for a third family vehicle, one designated for the two teenage members of the family. The criteria were simple enough—safe, reliable, in good running condition, and cost NOT TO EXCEED $3,000. Thus far we had considered, and rejected, a Chevrolet Celebrity wagon with lots of rust, a majestic 1972 Lincoln Continental coupe that stretched halfway from Randolph to East Barre, and a slew of Japanese gazukimobiles with a zillion miles on their respective odometers.

Never, in our wildest dreams had we considered a Mercedes. Yet, suddenly here was one, a stately machine the color of aged burgundy, dappled by sunlight, its hood ornament glinting proudly for all to see. And it had a "For Sale" sign on it! Although I barely caught it out of the corner of my eye, for a male in a car-heightened state, it was long enough to fall in love.

In the next nanosecond my mind processed information as follows. A Mercedes? Naw. Don't be ridiculous. Besides, this one looks too good, and good means expensive. Still, who knows? And it doesn't cost to look. A Mercedes? Nah. But it is good looking. No, I'm running late. I can't be frittering around looking at cars, BUT it would save time to just cross it off the list now instead of making a separate trip back.

I braked, fatefully, made the U-turn, and went back.

This was a stunning car—a 1975 280-C two-door coupe, a deep wine color reminiscent of Chateau Lafite-Rothschild at over a hundred bucks a bottle. It had a bright red accent stripe, with a hood ornament that reeked of old money, and the Mercedes logo emblazoned on all four hubcaps. It was one of the best-looking vehicles I had ever seen. The body was close to perfect, with only few tiny rust spots. The owner came out and yakked about the engine and mechanical condition. Only 42,000 miles on the odometer, which the owner admitted didn't work. There were even remnants of a decal for the Mercedes Club of America. "Please," I said to myself, "say the magic words." It didn't take the seller long. I think it was his third sentence.

"And it RUNS GOOD," he said.

"Runs good." Could there be two sweeter words in the English language? Not when it's a sunny day in May, and you have discovered the car of your dreams in the outposts of Camp Brook Road, halfway between Bethel and Rochester.

I countered with my own sweet words, at least for the other guy:

"How much you asking?"

When he replied $3,500, I tried to contain my surprise. A price of three times that amount would not have surprised me, but one that was within a scant $500 of our target price was unbelievable, too good to be true. And what's five hundred bucks these days, with the stock market near an all-time high?

The car was inspected, registered, and ready to roll.

I played it cool, and said that I would need to show it to my son, Patrick, who was nearing the end of his junior year in high school. Although young and relatively inexperienced in the vehicular ways of the world, when I told him about my discovery later that evening, he immediately grasped the significance. He would have the only Mercedes in the high school parking lot.

As we prepared to set off for a test drive, my wife (who is not a member of the male species, and therefore woefully incapable in matters of this sort) tried to insert a note of rationality. Shouldn't we have the car checked out by a competent mechanic? Isn't a car like this likely to be very expensive to maintain? Is it a gas hog? What's its maintenance history? And shouldn't we a least see if the seller will accept less?

I patiently pointed out her inexperience in these matters. A mechanic would charge $150 just to find something wrong with the car, and who couldn't find SOMETHING wrong with a car built in 1975? The car was already six years old when its driver-to-be was born. But hey, we're not looking for perfection here. And the guy already told me it RUNS GOOD. We're just looking for reliable transportation, and Mercedes are renown for their longevity. And safety! Let's not forget the all-important safety factor. Sure the price is a few bucks more than we intended to spend, but THIS....IS...A...MERCEDES. A car of this vintage will maintain its value and undoubtedly be worth more in two or three years. And did I mention the guy told me it RUNS GOOD?

For once my teenager and I (the other son was still at college) were entirely in sync. The car, he agreed, was a classic, and therefore a sound investment, worth it for the value of the hood ornament alone. A short test drive later convinced us further of the merits of our decision. Sure, it was funky to drive, but hey, what do you expect of a car that was made when Gerald Ford was president?

We decided not to dicker to price, because horse trading is beneath the dignity of a Mercedes owner. If we needed to be concerned about a few hundred bucks, then we shouldn't be buying a Mercedes.

Part 2—Things Get Bad

The seller insisted that we pay him cash, which seemed odd, but, frankly, he wasn't a Mercedes kinda guy. He was probably selling the car, because he couldn't handle the prestige.

The first premonition that maybe, just maybe, this was not the greatest idea came about ten minutes after our packet of cash was exchanged for the key. My son was driving, and I was following in the family van when a giant cloud of blue smoke emerged from the exhaust. I choked my way through it. Probably just a few errant drops of oil, I reasoned.

For the next week or so we strutted the car around to the friends and neighbors, so that they could see firsthand the vehicular acquisition that had catapulted us to new social standing. We tried not to let our core values be changed by our new status. We shouldn't abandon our friends, I explained to my son, just because they didn't own Mercedes.

A second glitch occurred two weeks into the honeymoon. We were sitting with a group of friends on the front porch when the Mercedes, carrying my son and his girlfriend, made a majestic entrance into the driveway. The entrance was punctuated with a resounding "pop" followed by the hiss of steam, and the acrid smell of anti-freeze boiling as the contents of the radiator spilled over the engine and down onto the driveway. No big deal, I said, probably just a broken hose. It looks worse than it really is.

The girlfriend, however, had a different view. "I don't ever want to ride in that piece of junk again!" she declared, adding that she was humiliated whenever the car belched one its blue clouds. Clearly, she was not a Mercedes lady.

The broken hose, in fact, was no big deal. What was a big deal, however, was the fact that my son now had to choose in his love life between his car and girlfriend. An even bigger deal was the fact that the mechanic who fixed the hose, Chip of Chip's Auto Body Shop in Randolph, informed us that the floor beneath the driver's side was rotted out and that there was no way the car would ever pass inspection again unless fixed.

Was this anything he could fix, I asked? He made one of hose faces where you put your teeth together and inhale sharply. He gave me the names of a few people who specialized in sheet metal work. The smug, I-told-you-so look on my wife's face didn't help matters, but hey, I told her, this is only July and the inspection is good until December.

As the summer limped by, however, the frailties of the car became more apparent. The clouds of blue smoke became more frequent and more noxious. The heater appeared to be permanently stuck in the "on" position. Horsehair stuffing from the leather seats fell onto the backseat floor where it combined with incoming water from the leaky floorboards, making a sticky, brown goo. I never calculated the gas mileage, but it was surely in the single digits (high-test, no less), and the oil consumption was nearly the same.

Increasingly, my son avoided the car like the plague except on those occasions when he and a bunch of male friends would go for a toxic joy ride. They discovered that the cloud of blue smoke was particularly impressive after descending a steep hill. Somehow, what was humiliating to the girlfriend became a barrel of laughs when the car was filled with his bonehead friends. My lectures about how a vintage car needed regular maintenance fell on deaf ears. Worst of all, summer turned to fall. And what happens in Vermont each fall?

IT GETS COLD!

Never too proud to admit a mistake, especially when the reality of it is squatting in the driveway every day, I put "For Sale" signs on the car, and hoped to find other Mercedes Wannabes whose quest for status would supercede their common sense. To my chagrin I discovered that everyone in town was smarter than I was. Perhaps the clouds of blue smoke were not the best advertising.

We took the Mercedes to a body shop to assess the floor situation. It took six weeks for a one-word analysis: "Hopeless."

"You mean I'm the owner of a $3,500 lawn ornament?" I blustered. Needing sympathy and guidance, I received, instead, two wisecracks:

"You paid $3,500 for that rust bucket?" said the mechanic.

"You think you're keeping that car on the lawn?" said my wife.

In desperation I returned to the original seller. "Ridiculous," was his one-word assessment of the body shop's one-word assessment. Obviously the man just didn't understand Mercedes.

By now December had arrived. The inspection deadline had come and gone, and the weather deadline had passed for the time when the Mercedes made any sense at all as a Vermont mode of transportation. We struck a deal with the seller to store the car for the winter and to help us sell it in the spring.

The long, cold Vermont winter gave me an opportunity to clearly assess the situation.

I was a Mercedes Man, but I wuz screwed. And I wuz an idiot.

To review, I had paid $3,500 for a vehicle that was currently uninspectable and, according to the body shop guy, would cost more to fix than it was worth. My son, for whom the vehicle had been ostensibly purchased, never wanted to see the car again. My wife had been proven to be married to a moron, and to add insult to injury, the car was now in the possession of the same guy who took advantage of me in the first place.

I avoided thinking about the Mercedes for most of the winter. I had made $3,500 mistakes before, but this was different. This was a car. I had never made a vehicular mistake, if you understand the nuance. Guys don't make car mistakes. It's not allowed. I mean, I bought two Chevrolet Vegas, and hadn't admitted to a mistake. This issue struck right to the heart of the species. To make matters worse, a Mercedes Man was required to handle the situation with a certain European panache. And my panache was in a deep, frozen ditch.

Spring came, and the Mercedes remained in storage. I checked periodically with the guy selling it, but there wasn't a lot of activity. The car now was officially an albatross around my neck. Supposedly there was an Internet site featuring the car, but I wasn't able to find it. I searched in vain for an encouraging word. None came. By July the peak of car rutting fever had passed, and my bad situation would soon get worse.

I decided to take the car to the antique car auction run by the Thomas Hirchak Company of Morrisville held in Stowe each August. The fee was $100, no sale was guaranteed, and I would have to figure a way to transport the now unregistered vehicle, but my options were running out. I drafted my son to the venture reasoning that he should share in any automotive humiliation. Hadn't I bought the car for him? If nothing else, he now understood the term "bad karma."

I completed the paperwork for the auction, sent in my check, and arranged to take the day off from work. Sellers are permitted to place a "reserve" bid on their car, a minimum amount below which it can't be sold, but I decided against it. This car was going to be gone, even if only for $1.

The story could proceed to a logical close, but the God of Vehicular Vanity and Retribution decided that I had not been sufficiently punished. Forty-eight hours before the auction I received a call from someone from Springfield, Vermont, who had seen the car on the Internet and who had to have it. It almost seemed like more trouble than it was worth, but I agreed to meet him and show him the car. He turned out to be a recent high school graduate (just like my son) who was joining the Navy, and who thought it would be nice to own a classic car.

One side of me said, "This uninspectable maintenance glutton would be the worst financial mistake of your young life."

The other side said, "It sure is a great looking car, but it is a (dramatic pause) Mercedes, and it RUNS GOOD."

After twenty-four hours of frantic deliberation the young man decided not to buy the car. I would like to think that this is because I had been so completely honest and upfront about the car's limitations. The more likely explanation is that the lad's father had exercised a combination of common sense and tough love and said, "A '75 Mercedes? Are you out of your mind?"

With a heavy heart and a sense of foreboding, I went to pick up the trailer to take the car to the auction. It was 95 degrees out. The clerks at the trailer rental place were surly and incompetent, not so incompetent, however, that they failed to point out that the half-trailer I had reserved would not work with an automatic shift car and that the full-size car hauler required was too heavy for my Caravan to pull.

"Nonsense," I protested anemically, reaching for a well of testosterone that just wasn't there. We went so far as to hook up the car hauler, which dwarfed the van, causing my testosterone to leak out onto the parking lot. I slunk home, a vehicularly defeated man, resigned to the continued ownership of a Mercedes that served only as a monument to vanity and incompetence. I would have this Mercedes yoke around my neck for the foreseeable future or the rest of my life, whichever came first.

I called the auction company to tell them I wouldn't be there. To my surprise the person on the other end of the phone seemed genuinely disappointed. "Too bad," he said, "We've had a bunch of inquiries on your vehicle."

A bunch of inquiries?" This meant that someone wanted to buy my German-engineered piece of shit. "Well, maybe I can make it. I'll think of something." I called the most reliable mechanic I know, Chip of Chip's, and laid it on the line. "Can you get a 1975 Mercedes from Camp Brook Road to Stowe tomorrow morning by ten o'clock?" He moaned about being too busy, but when I explained that my masculine pride was on the line, he took pity and agreed. The towing charge would be $136, he cautioned.

By 10 a.m. the next morning my son Patrick (the original co-guilty party) and I reconnoitered with Chip at the auction site off Route 100 a few miles south of Stowe Village. As he drove off, he asked, "Now, you won't be needing a tow back, will you?"

"Of course, not," we chortled back, full of transparent bravado. We were brimming with macho confidence. This car would sell. It had to sell. If it didn't we would be out $100 auction registration, two $136 tow charges, a day of lost work, and we'd still own the #@%!!**&% Mercedes!

There was a prediction of rain showers, and you could tell that this was an event that would be a lot less fun in a downpour. An enormous farm field was converted into an antique auto super mall. After registering we moved our car into slot #21, right next to a 1975 Jaguar XKE in mint condition. Its owner polished nonstop, holding an aerosol bottle in one hand, a chamois cloth in the other. Patrick and I looked at the bird shit on our car, and suddenly felt like residents of a Third World country. A Mercedes has never looked so dowdy.

We bought a bottle of spring water and used my handkerchief to smear around the bird shit in a futile attempt to match our neighbor's cosmetology. We overheard someone asking the Jaguar owner how much he expected to get for his car.

"Well, these are going for anywhere from $32 to $70,000," he said, his voice smug with confidence. I suddenly hated this guy with a passion I hadn't known since the Yankees beat the Red Sox in the 1978 playoff game. This guy was instantly my personal Bucky Bleeping Dent (the hero of that game for the Bronx

Bombers). He turned over the Jag's engine, and it roared into a rich 20-valve symphony.

Meanwhile, we prayed that no one would ask us to start up our Mercedes for fear that we would envelope the entire Stowe auction field in a cloud of blue, noxious smoke.

There actually were people interested in our car. The most enthusiastic was a middle-aged Mom with two kids from Portland, Maine, who developed a crush on our car. We answered her questions honestly and enthusiastically (well, fairly honestly). Neither of us told her that rather than being the most distinguished car at the local country club or PTA meeting this would be her one-way ticket to vehicular hell. We knew that this car would be as problematic for her as it had for us. We never told her it RUNS GOOD. That's only for guys.

People pried us for information. Had we, for instance, put a "reserve" bid on our car, meaning a price below which we wouldn't sell it? We hadn't. The car could be had for a bid of $1. Bidders like this, because means they can pick up incredible bargains. It makes sellers very nervous, and injects a note of high drama into the proceedings. The most frequently asked question, oddly enough, was, "Does the air conditioning work?" It did, we answered, neglecting to mention that this was a moot point since the heater was constantly on, too. We pointed out the rusting floorboards to everyone and repeated our mantra:

"RUNS GOOD. RUNS GOOD. RUNS GOOD."

After a viewing period from 11 a.m. to 1 p.m. the auction began. A full house was packed into a huge tent. The auctioneer was on an elevated podium as the cars were paraded in front of him. The rain was holding off, and our spirits were high as the auction began. In lots of five the cars left the viewing area and drove into the tent to meet their fate.

Ten cars later, however, our spirits were lower than a mud puddle. Nothing was selling, or if something sold it was for a pittance. We watched in horror as a beautiful 1970 Cadillac de Ville in immaculate condition was offered initially for $8,000 and eventually brought $1,100. Most vehicles did not even reach the reserve amount. This wasn't looking good. Before long, it was our turn.

We followed the Jaguar toward the auction tent. A carnival atmosphere surrounded us as we proceeded. A gaggle of onlookers surrounded us, throwing out last-minute questions:

"Do you have a reserve?"

"How does it run?" ("Runs good," of course. We NO longer spoke in capital letters.)

"Does the air conditioner work?"

"You willing to dicker if it doesn't sell?"

I reminded Patrick, who was driving, not to stop the car on an incline, lest we treat the crowd to a display of the Mercedes' blue cloud-making ability. Was it possible that our foray into the rarified world of Mercedes ownership would have one last cruel twist in store?

Now, the Jag was inside. The bidding started at $60,000, then quickly dropped to $30,000, then finally to $15,000 to "get it started." Finally there was a bid. The price quickly rose to $20,000, but stalled at $21,000, a mere pittance for a car that was the class of the show, and that the owner valued at up to $70,000. Auctions make honest people of us all. The owner of the Jaguar stopped the auctioneer by getting out of the car. The auctioneer gave him the floor. He announced that he had a reserve of $32,000 on the car, but that he really had to have "at least $27,000" to let it go. He didn't get it, and the car left the tent, unsold. Its luster looked a bit dulled and its puffed-up owner suddenly looked shriveled behind his steering wheel.

Now it was our turn. What humiliation awaited us? No bids at all? Selling the car for $100? Handing the key over to the nice lady from Portland? We had already determined that anything under $1,000 would be a humiliating defeat. Over $2,000 would be a victory.

We crept forward to the dais. I could hear the auctioneer reading the descriptive copy I had submitted. "The best-looking car in town...Imposing, yet elegant." What a crock!

The bidding started at $4,000. If our car followed the pattern of others, this would be halved, then dropped to $500 to "get it started."

The price dropped to $2,000. Then, amazingly we heard the auctioneer say, "We have two, do I hear twenty one hundred?"

One of the auctioneer assistants poked his head into the driver's side window.

"You must be pretty pleased with that," he said.

"Happy enough to kiss you on the lips," I thought, but just smiled and nodded. Inside I was doing my Roberto Begnini imitation, "Imma so happy. I lovva you all," I wanted to scream.

The bidding finally stalled at $2,550. When we heard the punctuation exclamation of "Sold!" Patrick gave the audience a thumbs-up, and we drove out of the auction tent, giving each other high-fives and whoops of delight.

But who had bought the car, we wondered? Did the unsuspecting lady now own our problem car from Hell? I went to the auction office to complete the sale. This was the easy part. I signed a mileage statement, and the title, and was told to leave the key in the car.

"That's all?" I asked, incredulous that the ordeal of Mercedes ownership had come to such a quick and painless end.

The clerk told me, "That's all. You should get a check by next Thursday."

"Can you tell me who bought it?"

"A Mercedes specialist from Waterbury. He buys older cars and fixes them up."

Relief. A pro now owned the car, someone who knew what he was getting into. No guilt at selling the car to someone's Mom.

The trip home was jubilant. When we arrived home we recounted several bogus and disastrous accounts of our adventure before revealing the happy outcome. Sure, the experience had cost us over a thousand bucks, but it was a small price to pay for Mercedes ownership for a year. We had the transportation and prestige, plus my son had received some valuable lessons in life. From a vehicular perspective, he had experienced a rite of passage. I realized that he had learned his lesson well when he commented on the low prices some of the cars at the auction had commanded.

"Let's go again next year," he said. "We could buy a really nice car for $2,550." Attsa my boy, I thought, smiling as I looked out at the empty, Mercedes-less driveway.

The Drive-In

I'm not sure how the Randall Drive-In hangs on, but it does, and it's great. America doesn't know what it's missing!

Want a summer ritual steeped in Americana? Go to a drive-in movie. Want to give it a uniquely Vermont twist? Go to the Randall Drive-In, midway between Bethel and Randolph on Route 12. The Randall is midway between the 1950s and Brigadoon. Before the show (usually a double feature) you will want to eat dinner at Onion Flats, practically across the street and another of a dying breed—the seasonal canteen featuring fried foods and cree-mees, owned and operated by real people, not a conglomerate. Your belly packed and the evening taking on that soft quality of dusk, it's time to waddle off to the show.

You have packed appropriately, the car loaded with blankets, snacks (although the thought of food at the moment is repulsive), bug spray, pillows, and lots of kids. This drive-in is neither for theatrical experience nor steamy passion; it's for getting very close to summer nights.

The last time I went to the Randall, the fare for an adult was $4.50—not too bad. But the good news was that kids under 12 were free—a late-summer thank-you from the owners. Moreover, each child received a toy as a further token of appreciation. I felt that maybe I should be giving a gift to the lady at the ticket counter.

Inside the theater, the atmosphere is more festival than drive-in. The first thing you notice is that, rather than a paved tarmac, the Randall is all grass, more golf course than drive-in. If this is not the most laid back, well-groomed drive-in Vermont, then I'm a native Vermonter.

The patrons of the Randall don't just park, they sprawl. Our family's technique is to back into the space, throw open the tailgate, and watch from the flat bed of the station wagon. Others are seated in lawn chairs in the backs of pick-ups. Some favor the kids-on-the-the-car-roof technique. Some even eschew the vehicle entirely, opting for lounge chairs covered with sleeping bags.

This inventive approach to comfort is surely what the creator of the drive-in had in mind, rather than the six-screen extravaganza with the constant exhortations to visit the caferama with its arrays of sumptuous, foil-wrapped garbage. I can't comment on the cuisine of the Randall (the memory of Onion Flats was too close), other than to say that they serve food that they prepare themselves and that the prices are reasonable.

The minutes before show time, always longer than you anticipate, are the best. Rather than having an isolated and forlorn playground for kids, here the playgrounds are the grassy strips between rows. Moms spray kids with bug juice, while Dads glance at watches, thinking ahead to when the kids will have to be carried into bed at the end of the night.

Everyone sees someone he knows; that's a requirement at the Randall.

The show begins. The opening cartoon is a bit faded, but the visual image improves as darkness descends. Bats swoop through the projector beam, picking off the mosquitoes in a show of strength that beats the insects into submission for the balance of the night. It's time to start the feature.

Although most of the features are first-run flicks, this is not the environment for the serious film buff. The last time we went, the people next to us tied their dog to the bumper. Unfortunately, the dog was directly in a strategic path leading to the snack bar and yelped whenever he was stepped on, a noise not conducive to serious film viewing. This is, of course, not a problem at the Randall, which shows few, if any, serious films.

Did I really see No Holds Barred with Hulk Hogan at the Randall? Should I admit this in public? I also admit to having seen Spaced Invaders, perhaps the stupidest piece of celluloid ever foisted on the American public. Actually, I slept through it, another advantage of the drive-in, especially in these days of reclining seats, Hey, it was fun.

I don't know the people who run the Randall, but I hope they have fun doing whatever they do on weekend nights in the summer. When the cold sets in, the memory of being united with a summer night is cruelly distant. Only the carryover from vivid summer experiences, such as those provided by the Randall, keeps us pressing on.

Burner or Toaster?

A divided world can coexist peacefully around a campfire. What the world needs now is more marsh-mallows. (And who says I am not a deep thinker?)

The world is divided into two types of people. That's right. For all the infinite variation of the human species, there is a line of separation as precise as the equator, and just as encompassing. The line cuts across race, nationality, creed, sex, religion, age, and political preference. Even the differentiation between Chucks and Flatlanders is not as distinct as this.

I'm talking marshmallows, of course. You are either a Burner or a Toaster, and never the twain shall meet. Your style is embla-zoned on your personality as definitively as your genetic make-up. You are a Burner or a Toaster, and that's that.

It's summertime and therefore campfire time. Across this great nation people from six to sixty will be sharpening green boughs and impaling onto them white, puffy confections of sugar, corn syrup, starch, and gelatin, coated with powdered sugar. True, marshmallows have such little nutritional merit that they make creemees look like health food, but, heck, it's summer, and marsh-mallows make us feel young.

First, a few technical tips. Marshmallows are best over a hard-wood fire kindled without petroleum-based starters. Cooking over charcoal briquets is a poor, distant second. Do not even consider a gas grill. Microwave marshmallows? Never!

The choice of cooking utensil should be governed by aesthetic considerations. The thin, green bough is best. The metal skewer is bad, but the bent coat hanger is worst.

Let the fire blaze, then settle to the point where the flames lap languidly at the night. Tell a ghost story or sing a familiar song. Commune with the gods of summer. Try to catch a shooting star. Then pull out the 'mallows, preferably Campfire brand, two layers of six plump lovelies, nestled in the blue and white box wrapped in wax paper.

(Please excuse an excursion into Old Fogeysville, but I'm informed by shoppers more knowledgeable than myself that wax-paper boxes of Campfire Marshmallows have gone the way of silver quarters and wooden baseball bats. The plastic bag of Kraft Sweet 'N Gummies lacks style and practicality. There was something precious about having your own box of marshmallows to share with a special friend.)

Roasting marshmallows is a primal experience, one that provides a window to a person's soul. This small key unlocks secrets from deep in the psyche, and peels away the layered facades. It is now time to declare yourself: Burner or Toaster?

Toasters are fastidious about their lives. By profession they are accountants, lawyers, insurance salespeople, and cash-register operators. The goal is always the same—a perfect, golden brown marshmallow, homogenized, pasteurized, and totally without character—a Bo Derek of the stick.

Toasters do not impale their marshmallows on their sticks so much as they "arrange" them. Once the perfectly centered marshmallow has been prepared, the Toaster then holds it approximately four feet away from the fire, rotating it (clockwise in the Northern hemisphere, counterclockwise in the South) at the precise speed of four revolutions per minute, adjusted for ambient temperature and altitude, of course. Every thirty seconds the marshmallow is visually examined for flaws. If one is found, the Toaster is likely to discard the original and to start all over again.

These are people without souls.

Burners, by contrast, will sometimes put two or three marshmallows on a stick at once. The stick is then thrust into the flames, often acquiring a measure of ash along the way, and held motionless until the marshmallows take on the distinctive orange/yellow glow of an orb of napalm.

The accomplished Burner will twist and contort his stick so that incineration takes place evenly and completely. Then he will thrust the stick into his mouth, risking impalement and burns, and pull off the charred layer, leaving a gooey blob on the end of his stick, which, likely as not, he will thrust back into the fire for a second roasting.

The Toaster, by contrast, will remove the marshmallow by

hand. In extreme cases, Toasters will put the marshmallow on a plate, so as to better handle it with knife and fork. Usually, by the time a Toaster has finished his first marshmallow, the Burner has devoured eighteen or twenty.

Burners, by trade, are artists, entrepreneurs, scientists, batting champions, rock and roll stars, and community leaders. They are the movers and shakers, the passionate arms of forward progress. They move the course of humankind forward while the Toasters are still seeking the perfect tan on their marshmallows.

Burner or toaster? There is no middle ground; no place to hide. This evening, after dinner, let's go cut ourselves some sticks and continue the debate.

Cruise Control

This is one bit of technology that I have mastered.

Interstate 89. A peaceful summer evening. Midweek, no traffic. No crazy Canadians heading for Old Orchard Beach. It's just me and the road. Oh yes, and the car. It's not even a fancy car. Four years old. American made. Got all the whistles and bells, though. Comfortable enough.

Well, not quite enough. Needs a little fine tuning.

As I swing from the access ramp to the main highway, I accelerate to cruising speed (in Vermont, 69.5 miles per hour). I snap on the cruise control and take off my shoes. I will now adjust myself into another world, a world of slothfulness and decadence, a world known as the comfort zone.

First, I set the odometer. Since I will be writing a column about this little slice of life, I will be writing off the mileage. Twenty-seven point five cents per mile. Thanks, Uncle Sam. Heh-heh-heh.

Now, for the temperature. When I was young and foolish my comfort zone was between 50 and 85 degrees. As long as my feet didn't freeze or I could stick my arm out the window, I could survive. As an old, but foolish, guy my comfort zone has narrowed to between 72 and 72.5 degrees, and not only does the temperature have to be right, but so does the air flow. When I am driving barefoot (because the cruise control is on), I prefer a floor-to-ceiling, front-to-rear flush of fresh air that fully aerates my tootsies. But then, don't we all?

On this particular day the comfort zone can be reached without air conditioning, which I am loathe to use because of its deleterious impact on the planet's ozone layer. My environmental conscience has its tolerance limit of two degrees plus or minus. That's when the little guy with the forked tail appears on my shoulder and says, "What, are you nuts? No one's going to see you depleting the ozone. This is your car, your castle."

Next, it's time to think about my butt. I remember when I first bought this car. The salesman said that power seats would pay for themselves at resale time. The same for power windows. That's good news, because these suckers have cost me about two grand in repair bills, and frankly I can use the dough.

The seats adjust up and down, front and back, side to side, left to right, inside and out. There are over 1,500 possible positions, yet I can never find the perfect one.

When I get finished with my butt, I spend a half hour playing with the power side mirrors with built-in heaters which, unfortunately, are not adjustable.

Once I am settled in, with the neck rest adjusted so that I can see all three mirrors by just moving my eyes, it's time for—you guessed it—TUNES!

You know when you have made it in life when you can afford a music system that is twice as smart as you are. Mine is so complicated that even my nine year old can't figure it out. There is a setting for type of tape—metallic or Dolby or retrograde or molybdenum. I owned this car for two years before I learned that these designations did not refer to the music on the tape.

Finally, there is the piece de resistance, the graphic equalizer. All of my friends own graphic equalizers, and not one of them know what the device does, or how to operate it. Every once in a while they slide the levers up and down to make sure that the thing-that-they-don't-know-what-it-does still does it. In my case, it's a moot point, as all my cassettes are missing from their boxes anyway. (This is another of life's mysteries. How can there be so many cassette tape boxes and so few tapes? Oh well, that's another column.)

This is status, the completely adjustable life. As I cruise on down Interstate 89, the only thing that could make me happier would be a bank of toggle switches...and maybe a rheostat or two...and some of those digital gauges. They do not need to be hooked up to anything, just so long as they permit diddling.

My adjustment is now complete. I even adjust my attitude with one of those non-alcoholic beers in the foil-necked bottles that costs A DOLLAR SEVENTY-FIVE!

Comfortable and cruisin'. Too bad I passed my exit twenty minutes ago. Might as well see where this here road ends.

Glub Is All You Need

This essay is funny if you sing it. I thought it up while driving on cruise control.

It has not been unknown for me to share million-dollar ideas with readers of this column. That's the kinda guy I am. This idea is different. This one's mine, all mine.

I was cruising in my pick-up. It was a nice day, bright, warm and sunny. The window was open, and my elbow was angled out rakishly to the road. Birds were singing—you get the picture.

I was singing, too, one of the most familiar Beatles anthems:

"All you need is love, yah-ta-da-ta-dah."

Then, for reasons known only to the deepest recesses of my psyche, I began substituting the sound "Glub" for the word "love."

"All you need is Glub, yah-ta-da-ta-dah."

If Glub is all you need, I wondered, then what is it? A miracle salve, I concluded, combining the best of Bag Balm, Ben Gay, and Neets Foot Oil. Suddenly, it all came together. This is just what America needs—a miracle salve to cure all ills.

Realizing that I was sitting on a commercial gold mine, I mentally reviewed the business precautions I would take (trademarks, sales marks, copyrights, etc.). I would have Glub packaged in bright, colorful tins that complemented the electric green of the product itself. We would go national on commercials with me (who else?) being Mr. Glub. The commercial would show a blotchy-faced teenager, the voice-over saying, "When your complexion's a little spotty..."

Cut to me, Mr. Glub, "All you need is Glub." And the horns go, "Yah-ta-da-ta-dah."

The announcer says, "And your baseball glove's a little stiff." Then me:

"All you need is Glub. Yah-ta-da-ta-dah."

And so on. Glub can be applied to the vinyl seats on a car, your aching elbow, sunburn, rust spots, pantyhose with runs...well, why stop here? If it's really a miracle salve, just apply Glub to your portfolio to increase its value. Smear it on your mother-in-law who won't shut up and the dog who goes to the bathroom on the carpet. What do you say, Mr. Glub?

"Glub is all you need."

By this time I have progressed about five miles up the road (Route 12, in case anyone wants to put up a commemorative plaque). It is still a nice day, and the casual observer might not guess that history is being made in the cab of my pick-up.

I'm moving on to the merchandising prospects of Glub. The tins, of course, would contain a punch-out slot so they could be reused as banks. In a matter of time "Glub banks" would replace "piggy banks" as the generic designation. These tins, needless to say, are destined to become very hot on the collectibles market.

The Glub name will then be cleverly licensed for lunch boxes, T-shirts, and a Saturday morning cartoon show featuring the Glubsters, likable but amorphous little tykes who thwart evil by smearing their enemies with the ever-present, omnipotent ointment.

All you need is Glub, right?

Wait a minute. I'm thinking too small. Why not have edible Glub? Ben & Jerry are successful selling sweet goo. Why not Glub? Let's start with a Glub candy; I see modern day Ju-Jubes called Glub Nubs. There's a theme song. It goes:

"What the world needs now, is Glub, Sweet Glub."

I wheeled into the driveway, anxious to share with the rest of the family our soon-to-be found fortune. I gathered everyone together, speaking slowly and carefully, lest the words and thoughts come so fast as to be overwhelming.

I told them I had come up with an idea that would make us rich while altering the course of Western civilization. The concept was so simple, however, that the brilliance might not be apparent at first. Perhaps it could be best communicated by singing the jingle that first gave it life:

"All you need is Glub," I sang.

And I knew I was destined for fame and fortune when they returned, in unison:

"Yah-ta-da-to-dah."

Still Champions

And then one year, they did us proud.

Summer is so precious here in the North Country. We cling like rejected lovers to those last moments of buttery sunshine. We glory in the bounty of the summer's harvest. We wallow in the rituals of the Tunbridge Fair, the Milk Bowl, and the final strand of summer—the World Series.

Vermont holds a special status in the Red Sox Nation. We are a divided state—chucks and flatlanders, Yankee fans and Red Sox faithful. Is it coincidence that the state's most famous baseball son, Carlton Fisk (born in Bellows Falls) insists on calling New Hampshire "home?"

Red Sox fans in the Green Mountains are like junkies. They can recognize each other by the desperate look in the eyes. A nod speaks a thousand words. Covert meetings are arranged. Soulful itches are scratched.

"What did you think of last night?"

"What could Shilling have been thinking? An 0-2 pitch across the plate? He had at least two pitches to waste."

"It's a macho thing. The splitter's been his out pitch all season."

"That's fine, but does he have to throw it over the plate? Get him to chase it."

"Pedro was the same way. I thought it was a Latino thing."

"What could he have been thinking?"

The conversations take place in aisles at the grocery story, while filling up at the quick stop, or between pick-ups, facing opposite ways, stopped in the middle of a dirt road. My own Red Sox needle swapper is a neighbor who will be identified only as "Donahue." He moved to Vermont from the Boston area many years ago, and he has the proverbial map of Ireland on his face and Southie twang to his voice that marks him as a Red Sox lifer. I don't see him a lot, but when I do, the ritual is always the same, fifteen minutes or so of detailed Sox analysis followed by a perfunctory inquiry about the state of the family, or maybe the weather. It's been this way for, oh, the past twenty years.

I was driving by Donahue's house last October. He was in his garage, throwing around junk and looking generally disgusted. This I could understand, as the previous night the Red Sox had lost their third straight to the Yankees in the playoffs. More humiliatingly, the score had been 19 to 8.

I rolled down the window and said something along the lines of "Whaddya think?"

"I'm disgusted," said Donahue, "I won't even watch the game tonight. I finally figured out that being a Red Sox fan is like being a battered wife. They'll just keep getting beat us up until we stand up to them and 'That's it, I'm not putting up with this any more!' And that's where I'm at. I'm breaking the cycle of abuse. I don't care what happens tonight. I'm done!"

I was too shocked to reply. Donahue "done" being a Red Sox fan? That was like saying "I'm done breathing?" You can shave the hair off your head; you can change your appearance; you can change where you live or your political beliefs, but you can't change your DNA, and that is where the heart of the Red Sox fan resides. That's why my father lived and died with the Sox (mostly died) and that's why my sons wear the blue, red, and white.

I was deeply disturbed by Donahue's declaration. I understood and shared his pain. But to give up? It was Bill Buckner, not the Buddha, who taught me about humility in life. It was Bucky (insert swear) Dent who defined "vale of tears." How can you dismiss a lifelong quest, a crusade by saying "I'm done."

That night was Game 4. Because I live deep within the bowels of Beyonder, far from the reach of cable, broadband, and even WDEV, the only way for me to follow the progress of the Sox is by repeatedly dialing up my Internet provider and logging onto After my fifteenth or so call, with the Sox trailing and Mariano Rivera in the bullpen, I said to no one, "Donahue's right. I'm not going to take this abuse any more. I quit. I'm done." And I went to bed, having turned my back on the Red Sox.

Old habits die hard, and I admit that the next morning the first thing I did was dial in to Boston.com to check the final score, only to learn that the Sox had staged a miracle comeback, one that continued through the next three games against the Yanks, and then four straight over the Redbirds of St. Louis. Something had broken The Curse, and while some credit the clutch hitting of Ortiz, Damon, and Ramirez or the gutsy pitching of Schilling, Martinez, and Lowe, I know that it was really two courageous guys in Vermont who stood up to the bully and said "We're not going to take it any more." Through our rejection we discovered the path to victory.

Of course, Donahue and I were quick to climb back onto the band wagon, especially when the Yankees were vanquished. These days every time we see each other now we close by reminding ourselves that we are still, at least until the end of October, Champions of the World.

Epilogue–The Ritual

Everyplace in Vermont has its end-of-season, end-of-year ritual. They vary by style and setting, but they feature the native cuisine (potluck), and they are marked by an exuberance tinged with the sadness of passage. Off in the surrounding hillsides the first slashes of color have started to appear, signaling the end of the beginning in Beyonder.

The Gilead Pig Roast

The fourth Saturday in August is when Bennett Law and Tom Bivens host the Gilead Pig Roast. It's a Beyonder harvest festival, needing only the Tunbridge World Fair to provide the exclamation point before winter. It is also the quintessential expression of the local cuisine with dishes ranging from Nellie's green tomato relish to Mary's caramelized onions. Yum!

The sign goes up just after the flag is taken down for the Fourth of July. "Gilead Road Pigroast, August 28."

No one much cares that "pigroast" should be two words. And, to be technical, it's Gilead Brook Road, but no one is being technical. This is Vermont and the end of summer. The sign is mounted on the side of Bennett Law's barn. Across the road is his neat yellow clapboard cape. As with many Vermont farmsteads, his property extends on both sides of the road. Because his is the second house on the road, the other 70 or so households will have plenty of chances to be reminded of the big event as they pass onto their Route 12 lifeline to the rest of the world. There's no excuse for not knowing when the pig roast is taking place. All comers are welcome, especially newcomers.

Gilead Brook Road is a "tweener." It links a linear community that lies nestled on the banks of Gilead Brook between Randolph and Bethel. The community starts in the green hollows that are the nether regions of Rochester, then tumbles down paralleling the brook and finally intersecting the paved road (Route 12) at the picturesque Old Christ Church just before the paved road crosses the green iron bridge. The kids go to school in Bethel, but the post office is in Randolph. It is not near to much of anything, but it is within reach of everything, which is part of the area's charm.

Unlike most other Vermont communities, which are formed around a town center, the village green in "the Gilead" (as the locals call it) is the road itself. For the first mile it is newly paved, then it reverts to dirt. Leyland E. Wood in his 1975 book *Two*

Vermont Hollows: A History of Gilead and Little Hollows]
describes the watershed as a "beautiful sparkling clear stream. It
is a hustling, tumbling brook rushing along between rocks and
boulders to the junction with the Third Branch below the high
bridge at the Old Church." The brook is almost always within
view of the road, its flow and gurgle attesting to the recent mete-
orology. At the moment it bears witness to a summer devoid of
rain. From its springtime roar to its placid trickle by the time of
the Pig Roast, the brook is a visual cue to the obsession that uni-
fies the residents of Vermont—the weather.

This is a road that fully displays Vermont's seasonal wonders.
During sugaring season, the roadside maples are tapped, and
sweet steam billows from at least three sugarhouses of various
scale. It's a road of mandatory waving. You can drive in anonymi-
ty once you reach Route 12, but while you're in the Gilead, you're
in a different world where your membership is your distinctive,
individual wave.

The residents are linked by their river of gravel, and common
memories, but little else. As a group they are as remarkable for
their breadth and diversity. They vary by age (0-90+), ethnic background (Yankee, Thai, Czech), and profession (dairy farmer, event
planner, film producer). It's a world that juxtaposes summer residents driving Volvos with old hippies in vans and hardscrabble
natives in pick-ups. Over time the distinctions blur. Musicians and
tradespeople are stirred into a melting pot, then stretched out
along the road, each with a private, and respected, domain. It's a
Beyonder part of the world.

At one time the residents of Gilead earned their livings by
pyrolyzing elm trees, making the black salts and pearlash (deriva-
tives of wood ash) that were shipped off to the cities to be used in
the manufacturing process of lye and soap. Wood ashes were the
closest anyone had to negotiable currency. There was no cash. The
residents grew hops, boiled sap, or raised potatoes to be ferment-
ed into alcohol. Everyone's challenges were the same—to eke out
a living and to keep from freezing. Now, you're as likely to find a
local resident milking the Internet as milking a cow. Even though
this is bedrock Vermont, consultants may outnumber dairy farmers.

Gilead derives its name from the tree called Balm-of-Gilead, once plentiful, but now scarce. Summertime is the most precious season here, as throughout Vermont. The fragile, transitory nature of the summer is underscored by the presence of two seasonal businesses near the intersection of Gilead Brook Road and Route 12. Did we say Gilead is not near anything? Onion Flats, a drive-in and cree-mee stand, officially marks the end of winter when it opens in April, even if there is snow still on the ground. Similarly, just north of Onion Flats, the Randall Drive-In Movie Theater marks the arrival of "when the livin' is easy" in late May. The Randall, with its friendly tarmac of grass, offers a cinematic experience of all-encompassing sensuality that will never be approximated by a Cineplex 12. Combine an Onion Flats dinner and a movie at the Randall to create a consummate summertime treat.

By late August, however, the full blush of summer is turning crisp and fragile. Telltale flashes of color pop out like flashbulbs on the hills. The morning mist hangs along the stream until almost noon. And the talk turns to back-to-school shopping and the Tunbridge Fair. Not surprisingly, at this most forgiving time of the year, the residents of Gilead gather to celebrate their community.

Bennett Law

Bennett Law is a boyish 40 year old, who takes pride in telling you that he is still "carded" at the local market when he buys a bottle of wine. He spent the first half of life in Massachusetts, but was enthralled by pictures of Lake Champlain and came to the Green Mountain State to attend the University of Vermont. After graduate study in Actuarial Sciences at the University of Nebraska, he returned to the state of his dreams. He joined National Life in Montpelier, and now is a professional manager in their law department.

It is as a social activist and host of the annual Gilead Pig Roast, however, where his passion lies. He is careful not to assume ownership. "It's a neighborhood event," he points out, "that just happens to take place at my house."

He bought the house on Gilead Brook Road because it was rural, yet within reach of his thoroughly civilized job. He liked the fact that his property extended to both sides of the road, just like so many of the farms of yesteryear. He takes comfort in the knowledge that the entire Gilead community passes through his property nearly every day.

The classic "Bennett sighting" for residents is early in the morning or just at dusk when he's en route to or from Montpelier, wearing a white shirt and tie, but with wingtips replaced by rubber boots for slopping the pigs. Farmer from the knees down and professional manager from there up, he presents a totally beyondered image to the uninformed passerby.

The first Pig Roast, ten years ago, was not planned. Bennett bought piglets on the advice of a friend. In the true Flatlander way, he began to raise them without so much as a thought to what he would do with the finished product. He began to understand the gist of his folly at potluck suppers when people asked him whether or not he would be slaughtering the pigs himself. The realization settled in like the morning fog over Gilead Brook. You don't raise pigs for no reason, and you don't keep pigs over the winter unless they are in the freezer. Pigs, in other words, ain't pets.

He sensed that his neighbors would have more respect for him if he took personal responsibility for the animal he had purchased, then nurtured. He also sensed that the neighbors thought that the chances of him actually following through on the deed were slim to none. There was nothing in his suburban background to prepare him to slaughter farm animals, causing him to lapse into some deep soul searching. In the end, he resolved to slaughter the pig himself.

Well, not entirely by himself. Carl Russell, a neighbor, offered to help. Bennett learned that to slaughter a pig, you draw an imaginary line from the base of its ear to the corner of its opposite eye. Do the other side, so that you have an "x" that marks the spot in the pig's forehead where he is to be shot. Properly administered, the pig will drop immediately, whereupon the partner is to insert a knife and quickly sever the three main arteries in the throat. When it goes right, the process takes but a few seconds and causes no suffering for the animal. When it goes wrong, the suffering is great for the animal and even worse for the people.

Bennett's first kill was surgical in its precision. Carl dropped the pig with a shot and Bennett cut the arteries with a quick slice. Kermit Labounty, into whose meat locker the carcass was transported, flattered both men when he commented on how clean a kill this was. He could not have paid the men a higher compliment. In the years since, Bennett and Carl switch off between the knife and gun. In the process they have developed a bond that transcends their different backgrounds and lifestyles. Russell, a forester by trade, has been moved to describe the animal sacrifice in verse (see below).

Not all slaughters go well. You don't want to know about these.

The morning of his first slaughter, Bennett was chagrined to awake and see pick-up trucks lining the road. "The neighbors didn't think a Flatlander boy like me would really go follow through with it," says Law. "But the funniest thing was, by the time it came time to actually do the deed, every last one of the gawkers disappeared."

Russell, a man who holds strong principles about raising and slaughtering his own food, was impressed with his partner's forthrightness. "I've slaughtered for other folks who think they're helping, but who are really there lending moral support. Bennett shows real respect for the animals he's raised. He gets right there into the carcass with both hands."

The idea of a community party came as a natural extension. You need a reward after suffering the rigors of raising a pig, then the agony of slaughtering it. What could make it more worthwhile than a party?

Excerpted from *Respect* by Carl B. Russell, self-published, 4/93

> From your period of toil,
> The winds, the water, and soil,
> Are embodied within you.
>
> We are not taking this life,
> Or energy, from you.
> It will always be yours.

We merely use it now,
To feed our bodies
And to fuel our minds, to manifest our dreams,
And to empower our values,
To perpetuate the care of this land, and your kin who
follow.

Through you we touch this soil, to the very heart,
and spirit of the Earth.
You help us to be part of the system,
Allowing us to become products of our own work.

The Rhythm of the Roast (seasonal)

The Pig Roast really begins in January, just after the holidays, when people return to the business of living their lives. Bennett reviews the successes and failures of the past year and makes the appropriate adjustments. In April, just after the disappearance of the last patch of snow, he drives to Williamstown to visit the man from whom he customarily buys the piglets. Inflation has been kind to the purchasers of young porkers. Ten years ago he paid $45 for his initial pig roast piglet. These days the price is $50-60.

The pigs reach adolescence by the Fourth of July, and the sign goes up. Word of mouth will do the rest. One of the great delights of the Pig Roast is to see which former residents of the road will turn up. For several years neighbors drove up to Barre where longtime Gilead native Anita Paquette was in a nursing home. Her fondest wish was to see the road and the neighbors again, and the Pig Roast provided the perfect occasion.

"Everyone looks forward to the Pig Roast as an end of summer event when we can get to know new neighbors and reacquaint ourselves with old friends," says Barbara Wright, whose husband Jake is the unofficial foreman of the tent and picnic table brigade. "It makes Gilead a close-knit community."

The Rhythm of the Roast (the day of)

Bennett Law's Red Salad

"As a single man, I'd often be invited to potlucks and told to bring chips or a beverage. If I persisted and asked to make something, I'd be told to bring a green salad. The red salad is my revolt, a statement that men can contribute to potlucks, too. It was an instant hit, and now has become my signature dish, even though it couldn't be simpler."

4 tomatoes, chopped

2 cucumbers, peeled, sliced in half the long way, then cut into 1/4" chips

1 onion (red, of course), peeled, sliced thickly, then chopped

2 sweet peppers (one red, one yellow), cored, sliced, then cut into 1" strips

1 can pitted ripe olives, drained

1 jar green olives stuffed with pimento, drained

Combine everything into a bowl. Cover with plastic wrap and refrigerate for a few hours. Stir before serving. Requires no dressing.

The pig is slaughtered on Thursday and hung in a meat locker until Saturday. Friday is the logistics day. Bennett puts up the tent, then scours the neighborhood for picnic tables to borrow. He also starts baking in earnest. It may be a potluck supper, but Bennett is its biggest contributor, baking a large sheet cake and at least two pies for dessert. The most common question he is asked is, "What should I bring?" to which he replies, "Whatever you bring, we'll eat. If everyone brings brownies, we'll eat brownies. If everyone brings tabouleh, we'll eat tabouleh." He knows that the Universal Law of Vermont Potlucks will insure that come Saturday, the table will be spread with a perfectly balanced feast.

On the day of the roast he picks up the pig, and wraps it in chicken wire. After an abortive first-year attempt on a rotating spit, he has devised his own method of cooking. He constructs what he describes as a "giant Dutch oven." A sheep-watering trough is placed inside a horse-watering trough. At 10 a.m. a charcoal fire is lit in the larger trough. After an hour, the trussed pig, dressed out at 115 to 140 pounds, is lowered into the smaller trough. It will take 120 pounds of charcoal and six hours to cook the pig. The beauty of this method is that the double trough functions like a convective oven, and there is no need to turn the meat. When the cooking is complete, it is a simple matter of hooking shovel handles into the chicken wire and hoisting out the pig intact.

This year's pig is "Buster." He's an "only child," as his partner died early in the spring. Bennett characterizes him as docile and sociable. He follows in the traditions of Daisy, Violet (who liked having her stomach rubbed), Oliver, Wendell, and other standard bearers of the Pig Roast. Bennett has learned to avoid choosing a name that is shared by anyone on the road.

As the pigs grow and become more rambunctious, it's inevitable that one will escape from the pen. The first time it happens, it's mildly amusing, and the neighborhood responds willingly to the round-up effort. Thereafter, however, runaways become tedious pains in the butt, and poor reflections on their owners.

Some of the pigs are "bolters," and tales of their exploits are part of Pig Roast lore. There was the pig that ravaged an absent neighbor's yard, and volunteers scurried to repair the damage before the homeowners returned to witness the pig's destructive feats. And there was the pig that made it all the way out to Route 12. "That pig was leaving town," remembers neighbor Edie Russell, whose tidy brick home greets the person who turns onto Gilead Brook Road. "He knew what was coming!" That chase was so wild it made headlines in the local newspaper. There are the stories that are retold late in the evening when the bonfire is lit. The bellies are full, the community is together, and the memories are set free.

The pure culinary excellence of the event should not be overlooked. Potlucks bring forth the best of everyone's skills. "We have the best cooks in Vermont on the Gilead," boasts neighbor Edie Reynolds, a remark not likely to go unchallenged.

The glitches have become fewer over the years. Bennett used to become annoyed when at the peak of the roasting and carving activities, potluck contributors would tug on his sleeve asking for serving spoons, the supply of which had long since been depleted. His sister came up with solution that is remarkable for both its simplicity and ingenuity. She gave Bennett the present of forty serving spoons. Far from the finest flatware, for one day a year, who cares? The sleeve-tuggers are no more.

Ten years of Pig Roasts have made Bennett infinitely wiser in managing the logistics of the roast. No longer are the last few days mad dashes to handle the details. He has learned to spread the preparation (and the expense) over the entire summer season. Like an old farmer who has learned that slow but steady wins the race, he paces himself by doling out the tasks gradually. As a result he finds himself freer every year to enjoy the company.

Bennett's Pig Roast Rule #1
" Have plenty of extra serving spoons, because everyone will be asking for them at just the wrong time."

Bennett's Pig Roast Rule #2
"Don't answer the phone on the day of the roast. People are calling to tell you things you don't need to know (such as they've decided to bring pesto salad instead of coleslaw.)"

Bennett's Pig Roast Rule #3
"If people ask what to bring, suggest lobsters or a raw oyster bar. They'll bring brownies and you can never have too many brownies."

Bennett's Pig Roast Rule #4
"Be ready a full week in advance. The day of the roast you'll have your hands full entertaining people who want to help."

Bennett's Pig Roast Rule #5
"If you have 200 people for lunch, 40 of them will stay for dinner. Be prepared."

Bennett's Pig Roast Rule #6
"Don't even attempt an event like this without Jake Wright. All the neighbors are great, but Jake always seems to be there at just the right time."

The Gilead has been a community since the late 1700s. The

population, which reached a high of over 300 in the mid-1800s, fell to less than half that by the 1970s. The constantly changing economic base has evolved through wood ash, potatoes, lumber, sheep, and cows. More remarkable are the constants—the seasons, the brook, the hills, the road, and the community. Especially the community.

"Bennett raises those oinkers," says Edie Reynolds, "but we all feed them apples and veggies from the garden."

Bennett hopes that the young people will benefit most from having an event that happens in the same time and same place every year. This will become an anchor for them wherever they go and whatever they do in life. Carl Russell points out that there are parties everywhere, but the Gilead Pig Roast is unique in its environmental aspects. "Those pigs breathe our same air and drink our same water," he says. "They're as much a part of the community as any of us."

The highlight is the bonfire that takes place after the bellies are full, the dishes have been gathered, and the pressure of putting on a pig roast for 200+ is over. For the first time in weeks Bennett is able to relax and to watch the parade of humanity that comprises the different aspects of his personal life. There are neighbors, past and present; coworkers from National Life; old friends; new friends; and the families of Gilead Road.

A few years ago Bennett Law revealed to his neighbors, and to the world, that he was gay. The gay pride flag was hoisted over the yellow cape across Gilead Brook Road from the barn with the sign inviting everyone to the Pig Roast. For many, this most certainly presented a new cultural challenge. The Pig Roast, however, never missed a beat. Rather than becoming a divisive issue, the net effect has been to incorporate a new group within the larger Gilead community. If anyone objected to this new dimension, they have been respectful enough of the Vermont traditions of privacy and individuality to not let their feelings interfere with the community's annual event.

Diversity is as much a local tradition as cold winters. Leyland E. Wood in his book Two Vermont Hollows described the residents of Gilead of a hundred years ago: "They were radical, positive, and austere in their views, opinions, and religious doctrines, but they had one view in common: to better themselves, support their growing families, and be their own man on their own land. They had nothing but themselves, the animals, and the trees to contend with. There, liberty was not a dream and idea to die for, it was a state to be successfully lived in and an effort to survive. They believed not only in equal rights for everyone but in equality for all, before God. And their fellow men and were quite willing if necessary to support their beliefs in personal encounter or take up arms in war to support their views."

Several years ago the town of Bethel held a parade at their annual Fall Forward Festival in which the various communities were asked to display floats. The residents of Gilead chose the Pig Roast as the symbol of their neighborhood identity. Although Bennett Law was not the architect of the float, his neighbors' decision made him very proud.

Diversity and independence have defined the character of Vermont just as the twisting brook and steep hills define the Gilead. People like it that way and have since the first settlers arrived. Some things change and some things don't. One thing that hasn't changed is the strength of the community. For this tiny Vermont hollow the annual Pig Roast renews the ties that bind each August. This is an event that leaves a pleasant taste in the mouth all year long.

The Public Press

We are The Public Press.
You are The Public Press.

Corporate media conglomerates continue to consume independents. While ownership consolidates, new book titles, specialized cable channels, and new websites proliferate. Amidst a din of commercial noise the bandwidth and coherence of available information is narrowing. Thoughtful authors find it more difficult to find publishers for sustained, original, and independent ideas at a time when technology is making it easier than ever to disseminate information.

The casualty is free speech.

The Public Press was founded in 2004 to protect freedom of speech "word-by-word." It is a grassroots organization, beholden only to its readers, its authors, and its partners.

The goals of The Public Press are printed opposite:

For more information, and to get a free subscription to the newsletter, The Page, visit: **ThePublicPress.com.**

Empower authors.

The Public Press puts the fewest possible filters or impediments between the creator and audience. The Public does not control the publishing process in the same way that a commercial publisher does. As a result there are stylistic and quality variations from title to title. The resulting books are like hearth-baked bread or handcrafted beer compared to more uniform, but less distinctive, products of commercial counterparts.

Treat authors as partners.

The Public Press is destined to become an author co-operative, where the authors are business partners with the publisher, not licensees paid a small percentage royalty on the sales of books. The Public Press offers an alternative to the traditional author/publisher model.

Leave the lightest possible footprint.

Book publishing, historically, has been a notoriously inefficient industry from the standpoint of resource consumption. A book can travel across the country only to be returned, unsold, to its original point of shipment. The Public Press strives for economies of scale-small scale. New technologies have made available writing and editing tools, print on demand options, improved communications, and new sales outlets that make it possible for publishing to be a model of resource efficiency.

Shout from the highest tree.

The Public Press is comprised of a community of individuals who share certain values (such as an appreciation for independent thought and freedom of speech) but who may not share geography or demography. The success of The Public Press is entirely dependent on our ability to reach these people and to convince them to involve others. As opposed to our namesake counterparts, National Public Radio and Public Television, The Public Press receives no government funding.

Also from **Stephen Morris** & The Public Press:

The other books in his brilliant four-part Beyondered Trilogy:
available NOW!

...and his critically acclaimed new novel:

Arthur Gordon doesn't get it. After a string of successful films his latest opus is reviled as sexist and politically incorrect. Emotionally wounded, he retreats to the sanctity of a summer cottage where carefree recollections buffer him from his self-inflicted firestorm. Only after running headlong into the realities of changing times does he decide that redemption will be his only if he can catch a big fish on a little feather.

About the Author

Stephen Morris writes about salt water, green mountains, wild turkeys, cluster flies, rock and roll, and Spam (the semi-edible kind). His novels include *Beyond Yonder, King of Vermont,* and *Stripah Love,* and the eagerly awaited *Darwin and the Tuneel of Love.* He lives in the part of Central Vermont that is next to nothing but close to everything, called Beyonder.

Order books and eBooks online at **ThePublicPress.com**

www.ingramcontent.com/pod-product-compliance
Lightning Source LLC
Chambersburg PA
CBHW020803250626
47155CB00003B/1182